COVENANT

Rashid Darden

Old Gold Soul   Washington, DC

Old Gold Soul
810 Kennedy Street NW
Suite 305
Washington, DC 20011

www.oldgoldsoul.com

www.facebook.com/rashiddarden

Covenant is a work of fiction. Any references to real people, events, establishments, organizations, or locales are intended only to give the fiction a sense of reality and authenticity. Other names, characters, and incidents are either the product of the author's imagination or are used fictitiously.

First Edition

Cover Design by Neil Wade

ISBN 0-9765986-3-9

For

Kelli Auletta
Keith Fort
and
Lisa Rose Middleton

Acknowledgements

God.

Carolyn Darden-Stutely. Darryl Stutely. Roslyn Williams. Sharon Chapman. Kenneth Whitehurst. Kenneth Alston.

Liz Burr, Johnnie Kornegay, Robert Denson, Rod McCollum, malik m.l. williams, Antar Wright.

Erika Johnson, Erin Meadors, Kristin Hinckle, Dana Luciano, K. Elaine Banks, Ina Broadnax.

Frederick Smith, Alphonso Morgan, Brent Dorian Carpenter, Lori Lincoln, Kimberly Noelle, Keith Boykin.

Delphinia Brown, Shari Hunt, Adejimi Shopade, Tomas Bracero, Storme Gray, Pape, Dwayne Smith, Jonathan Beverly, Jaimi Brown, Issam Khoury.

The Faculty and Staff at Jessie LaSalle Elementary School.

The Georgetown University Black House, the Mu Alpha and Zeta Phi Chapters of Alpha Phi Omega, the Georgetown University Step Team, Takoma Station, BLAGOSAH, DC Black Pride, In the Life Atlanta, Red Chair Restaurant, Xi Omega and Sigma Zeta Omega Chapters of Alpha Kappa Alpha Sorority, Federal City Alumnae Chapter of Delta Sigma Theta Sorority, the Gentlemen's Book Club, and Sisters Interested in Reading. The Duke University LGBT Center, Black Student Alliance, Mary Lou Williams Black Culture Center, and Multicultural Center.

Neil Wade. I love you.

COVENANT

September 1

I woke up in bed next to a glassy-eyed stranger, not knowing who he was, but feeling oddly at ease with him.

"What the fuck?" I said softly. My eyes adjusted to the harsh rays of sunlight piercing my blinds until I was able to focus on the furry stranger in my bed. His eyes, genuinely made of glass, stared back at me, smiling – elated that he had been placed in my care.

"A damn teddy bear," I grumbled, grinning on the inside. He wore a "Somebody at Potomac University Loves Me" shirt over his light brown fur. He wasn't a large bear by any means, but large enough to be noticeable to the visitors of my room.

He did it again.

The last thing I remembered from the night before was talking to him, he who had stopped by unexpectedly just to say hello. I was already in bed when he came. Heavy rapping at the door made me believe that one of my roommates had forgotten their key.

I swung the door open, surprised to see him standing there.

"Adrian," he said, sizing me up in a deliberate floor-to-ceiling gesture with his head.

"Hey," I said, feeling naked in my white sleeveless t-shirt, which clung tightly to my slender torso while my blue basketball shorts slung low on my hips, revealing the white FTL band of my boxer briefs.

"Can I come in?" he asked, peering around the door and trying to take a glance at my living room.

"Um," I said, uncertain whether he was intent on breaking the pact before the school year had even begun.

"Dude, just for a minute," he said. "You know I'm not going to go back on my promise. I just…I just had to see you before we… we…"

"Okay," I interrupted. "You can stay for a while."

I tried to hide my smile from him, so I quickly walked toward the kitchenette. "You want something to drink?"

"Naw," he said, closing the door behind him. He sat down on the old brown couch and let his old, tattered gym bag fall to the floor at his feet while I got myself a glass of water. I sat in the gray cushioned chair across from him and slowly sipped my drink.

"You seem uncomfortable," he said.

"Naw…just nervous, I guess."

"Nervous?" he said, leaning forward on the couch, as close to me as he could without sliding off. "I just saw you like two weeks ago, dawg."

"You know how we can get," I said. "We're just chillin' one minute, then the next minute…well, you know."

"Yeah," he said. "I know. By the way, nice shorts."

I immediately sat Indian style in the chair, trying to hide my slender brown legs underneath me.

"You don't get it," he said, laughing.

"What's so funny?" I asked with a nervous smile.

"Those are my shorts," he said. I looked down again. Sure enough, the shorts weren't mine.

I looked at him, seeing a smile wider than the main Quad. It was infectious. Finally, the ice had been broken and I could smile in his presence again.

He was back in my life, if only for a few moments on the night before classes. We both stood up and hugged in the middle of my living room.

"I missed you," he whispered, lips brushing lightly against my ear.

"I missed you, too," I said to him, through his chest.

"You were sleeping, weren't you?" he asked. He backed away slightly, looking down to my eyes while holding on to my arms.

"Almost," I said. "I was just lying in bed when you came over. I have a lot to do tomorrow."

"Come on, then," he said, letting his hands slide down my arms. "Go back to sleep."

"Dude, you know I can't just fall back to sleep now."

"Yeah you can. Which one is yours?" he asked, taking my hand and leading me down the short set of stairs to the bedrooms and bathroom, beyond the darkened hallway.

"The middle," I said. He had brought his gym bag downstairs with him as though he planned on spending the night.

We entered my dark room, lit only by the glow of my computer screen. He sat down at my desk and started checking his email on my Dell. I got under the sheets and laid face up so I could see him.

"You ready for class tomorrow?" he asked me.

"Yeah," I said. "Are you?"

"Yeah, I guess so. I hope I like all of them."

"You will," I said. He turned to face me in the darkness and smiled one last time before I fell asleep.

He must have hidden the teddy bear in his gym bag and put it next to me in bed before he let himself out of my apartment. He still loved me. His swagger, his smile, his voice, his deeds – they all called out to me, but I couldn't answer. Not then, not yet. There was much work to be done before he and I would be ready to move forward.

***

When I woke up in the morning, I named the bear Miles and put him on my desk. Actually, I named him Miles because I rested him on top of my Miles Davis CDs. My apartment, located deep in Hurley Village, was already bustling with activity.

Calen was one of my favorite frat brothers and now my housemate. We were initiated together and had experienced many trials and tribulations to make it to that point. When we were at our darkest hour as a pledge class, Calen was one of the few who showed that he was in my corner regardless of the circumstances. From the outside looking in, we made for a rather odd pair. I was of average height, just shy of five feet, ten inches. Calen, on the other hand was six and a half feet tall, 250 pounds easy. He had a beautiful caramel complexion and a baby face, even though nothing else about him was juvenile.

His laughter emanating from the kitchen reminded me that we were to wear our fraternity shirts. It was a tradition in our chapter that we dressed in paraphernalia on certain days, like the first day of class or Homecoming. My burgundy shirt with old gold letters was already hung neatly in my closet, and khaki shorts were placed on the back of my chair. After I took a shower and dressed I was ready to face my rambunctious housemates.

"Yo, what up Adrian?" my burly frat brother hailed from the kitchen table. "B-Chi!"

"Chi Phi!" I responded. Calen loved saying the fraternity call whenever he had the chance. He was definitely a super-neo. "What's up, fellas?"

Calen's two teammates, Brad and Orlando were relaxing in the living room, watching SportsCenter on ESPN. They returned my greeting and went back to SportsCenter.

"Nice shirt," Calen said playfully, while eating his cereal. "I got me one just like it."

"Thanks," I said sarcastically. "Matter of fact, you seem to be wearing it right now."

We laughed, and I grabbed a bagel from the pantry. It was about 9:30am by the green numbers on the microwave's clock, and there was much to be done today.

"You got a 10:15 class, yo?" Calen asked.

"Naw...I gotta go to the bank in the student center, though. That joint opens at ten."

"Word?" Calen asked. "You know I had an 8:50 already, right?"

"What?" I asked incredulously, pausing while spreading cream cheese on my bagel. "I know you didn't have no 8:50 on the first day... ain't you back kinda early?"

"Naw, they just gave us the syllabus and we was out. Now I ain't got shit to do until 12 or so."

"Messed up," I said, biting into my bagel. "Yo, you know first chapter meeting is in two weeks, right?"

"Yeah...not this Sunday, but the next one. Dude, you think Jamal is going to be active this year?"

Get the fuck off the line, Adrian! His voice rang in my ears as clear as the night he screamed at me to stop pledging his beloved Beta. He hit me -- numerous times -- but I stuck it out. I lost Savion. I sweat blood and tears to get these letters across my chest, but Jamal…I could feel my stomach wrapping around his fist once again. I felt nauseated.

"Adrian? Dude, what's wrong?" my line brother asked.

"Jamal…" I said distantly. "I don't know. I haven't seen him around yet."

"Adrian, you know, I'm sorry," Calen said. "I thought you had squashed that beef from last year. I won't mention…I mean, don't worry. Just forget about it."

I slowly came back to my kitchen and away from the chaos of that infamous night.

"It's okay," I lied. "I'm not worried about it." The truth was that I just didn't feel like dealing with it. Brother Jamal hated my guts and it showed every single day since the night he tried to make me depledge Beta. He hated me because he discovered my secret, my only obstacle to Beta: my boyfriend.

When learning that I was gay wasn't enough to make me drop, Jamal and Brother Craig tried to beat the resolve out of me. I almost didn't make it. I was ready to stop everything and just walk away from what I had invested so many weeks and months of my life into. I died that night. But like Lazarus, I rose again and finished what I started. At least, that's why my pledge Dean named me "Lazarus" – the name embroidered on the back of my t-shirt.

Somebody tapped lightly on our door, and I raced to answer it, glad that something would distract me from the thought of Jamal. I peeped through the blinds and saw my favorite female in the world.

"Hey, boo!" Nina shouted, waking up any other sleeping soul in our entire apartment complex.

"Hey, chica!" I responded, a huge grin crossing my face.

"Your sexy ass roommates up in here?" she asked, huge afro puff bouncing behind her head as she spoke. Her deep brown skin radiated in the morning sunlight. She wore a floral print dress, a festive little number to celebrate the first day of class.

"Yeah, we here," Calen said from behind me. "What's up, girl?" Calen and Nina hugged with much familiarity.

"Hey boys!" she said over Calen's shoulder to Brad and Orlando.

"Hi, Nina." the boys said. They were easily transfixed by her beauty and her confidence. If Nina could do nothing else well, she could silence a room. Men loved her; women were painfully indifferent.

"You ready?" she asked. I picked up my book bag from just inside the doorway.

"Yup," I said. "Let's go."

"Wait, Frat," Calen said, grabbing my shoulder. I turned around and Calen shook my hand. Pulling each other close, we gave each other the secret handshake of the fraternity.

"Have a good day, Frat," he said sincerely.

"Thanks, Frat," I said, grinning slightly. Calen was a good man. He was the polar opposite of Jamal and I loved him for it.

Nina and I walked through Hurley Village toward our student center on this magnificent September day. Late summer at Potomac University was always a beautiful time of year. The campus was clean, the trees were green, and everybody was happy. Even me.

"I am loving those letters, boy!" Nina said. I smiled.

"I'm glad to be wearing them, girl." I sighed. Nina knew just how bad I wanted to be a Beta and what I sacrificed to get those three letters.

"You know, it's not too late for you to be…I dunno, an AKA?" I suggested playfully.

"Adrian, don't you start with me again," Nina said, softly grabbing my sleeve. "I don't want no parts of these Greek hussies on this campus."

"Ha!" I said. "No you didn't call them hussies."

"Yup. You know I don't like being around too many women. They talk too much."

"You a woman, too, honey."

"Oh, I know, sweetie. But ummm…you really don't wanna see me cut a bitch for putting her hands on me, do you?"

"Naw, I guess I don't. They'd be fucking with the wrong broad if they put their hands on Nina Bradley."

"You damn right. Now, are we depositing or withdrawing from this here bank?" We crossed the glass doors into the student center.

"Depositing," I said. "The father figure sent me a check the other day."

"Well…that's good. Right?"

"Yeah," I said. "It's damn good. A nigga is out of your life for a decade, and they start finding inventive ways to make it up to you."

"Damn," she said, partly because of my comment, but mostly because the line to the bank was so long. I grabbed a deposit slip and began to fill it out while we waited.

"Adrian, look look look," Nina said.

"What?" I asked. "Where am I looking?"

"Second girl in line with the sandals on."

"Okay…what about her?"

"Look…at her nasty ass feet."

I looked at the girl from her short denim skirt to her light brown legs, and finally her ashy feet. I stifled laughter.

"That broad look like she been playing soccer in a flour pit, Adrian!"

"Hush!" I said quietly. "You already got me laughin' at this chick in my letters, please don't let her turn around and see us clowning her."

"But she shouldn'ta come out the house without putting some Vaseline on them dogs! I mean, Adrian, come on now."

Tears were streaming from my face by now, but at least I wasn't laughing out loud.

"I mean, maybe," I stopped and giggled. "Maybe she just got out of bed?"

Nina was now convulsing with stifled laughter herself. "But look at all her makeup, man! How she gonna put on her face but not her feet!"

And with Nina's final quip we were gone, laughing so hard that the people in front of and behind us in line were trying to figure out what was going on. Meanwhile, homegirl in the front of the line was oblivious to our inside joke. Nina and I leaned on each other and exhaled a spontaneous "whoo" that signified the end of our episode. Just as that happened, I felt a familiar, strong hand on my shoulder. Nina saw the hand, looked behind me, and smiled. I turned around.

"Hey," he said softly.

"Hey," I said, smiling.

"Oh my god!" a shrill female voice said from behind him. "How are you doing! I am so glad I saw you! Give me a hug, Mr. Beta Man!"

I deflated on the inside, but kept my smile on my face as I hugged her. She was Taina Banks, a beautiful, friendly girl who served with me on the board of the NAACP the previous year. She was now the Vice President.

He…was Isaiah Aiken. Her boyfriend, and my…friend, as of the previous summer, when we were roommates.

"I am just so proud of you, Adrian!" Taina continued. "I remember you were looking tore up when you were on line for Beta, but I will never forget the night of your probate show. Who knew you could sang like that, boy!"

We all laughed. Taina and Nina were cordial to one another, but each had dominating personalities, so it would be interesting to see who might "win" the conversation.

"Hey, girl!" Taina then said to Nina. "Girl, that dress is soooo cute! Oh my God!"

"Thanks, girl!" Nina said. "And you are working those jeans!"

"Okay!" Taina said. "You know I got these right down on Wisconsin Avenue before summertime, right?"

"From the Gap?" Nina asked.

"Naw, girl, from Express!" Nina and Taina's girl talk was legendary. Nina loved to camp it up around ultra-feminine women like Taina. It was almost like watching a man in drag. She wasn't entirely comfortable around girly girls, but she would also not be outdone by any personality more gregarious than her own. As the ladies chatted, I focused on them. I was afraid to look at him…Isaiah.

"Did you see it?" he asked in a low tone, sure that neither Nina nor his girlfriend could hear.

"Yeah," I replied. "You really shouldn't…"

"I know," he said. "I know."

He playfully punched me on the shoulder, lightly at first, then a little harder. I inched forward in the line, and then turned around to face him. He was still the most attractive man on campus, and probably one of the most attractive men I had ever met. He was light-skinned, light-eyed, and had high cheekbones. His voice was incredibly deep. He didn't look like the typical college basketball player, other than his height and broad shoulders. He was almost too "pretty" – a word that was often attributed to preppy, well kept black dudes who wore khakis and button-down shirts. But that was not Isaiah. His striking, runway worthy features were masked by oversized t-shirts, baggy jeans, and boots. And ironically, this basketball player preferred wearing football jerseys off the court. It was Isaiah's shorts that I wore to sleep the night before.

"Don't," I said, moving my eyes toward Nina and Taina, who were still talking.

"All that," he whispered "ain't shit. That's all about to be dead. You know where my heart is."

"You can't do this," I whispered sharply. "Remember your promise."

He frowned. I stepped backward from him.

"So, you coming back to NAACP this year?" Taina asked abruptly.

"Of course!" I exclaimed. "You know that's where my roots are."

"Well why you ain't wanna be on the board this year?" she asked earnestly.

"Girl, you know I'ma be at those meetings. I just wanted to give somebody else a chance. And have some time to be a Beta, you know?"

"Yeah, I guess," she smiled. "Well, me and Isaiah saw you two in here and just wanted to say hi! I am so glad you got to be his roommate this summer! He has not been able to stop talking about you!"

"Oh really?" I asked. Isaiah looked away as Taina continued to smile and nod.

"Yup!" she said. "It's like you his new role model!"

We all had a good laugh at that one, but only Isaiah and I knew the danger involved. I couldn't believe he was talking about me to her.

If he was going to square things away with Taina, he needed to do it. Just don't involve me in it.

"Well, we're off! Toodles!" Taina said.

"Toodles, girlfriend!" Nina chirped. As they walked away, Taina slid her hand into Isaiah's.

"I hate that bitch," Nina said. I burst out laughing.

"Why?" I asked. "She ain't did nothing to you!"

"She's just so fuckin' girly. I mean, damn. Tone that shit down."

We laughed some more. Although I knew she noticed – and Nina noticed everything – she didn't mention the uneasy tension between me and Isaiah.

When I finally got to the teller window, I deposited my check. Five thousand dollars, paid to the order of Adrian Collins, from Adam Collins. My dad.

Some things change.

After classes had ended for the day, I was the first one to meet at the designated spot on the front lawn, which was as emerald green as it was on the day my line brother and prophytes graduated. My chapter, Sigma Chapter, was slated to congregate at the end of the first day of classes, just to see one another, and perhaps take care of some fraternal business. When we met like this, it was always a big production. Sigma Chapter was chartered on two campuses, Potomac University and Rock Creek College, both elite, predominately white schools in DC. Although Beta was a prominent fraternity, it was still rare to get enough interest to sustain a chapter at one school unless it was a black college or large state school. We enjoyed our unique structure as a metropolitan chapter, always having a whole other campus to visit when we wanted to.

I put my book bag on the ground in front of me and saw Calen walking down across the lawn with our chapter president, Aaron Todd, who was wearing a slightly more faded burgundy fraternity shirt than ours. Aaron had pledged the year before us, and was a decent guy. He was a handsome, dark brown skinned young man who wore dark, square glasses, sort of like Malcolm X. He wasn't the nicest brother to pledge to, but he was all about business when it came to Beta. Next to Calen, Aaron looked like a kid. Next to Calen, everyone looked like a kid.

"Beeeeeeeee-Chi!" I shouted across the lawn.

"Chiiiiiiiiiiii-Phi!" my brothers responded. It did feel good to do that call. It was just one thing set us apart from any other fraternity, as well as non-Greeks. We earned to right to shout out from the hilltops that we were Betas.

My line brother Ed ran up quickly behind them, having heard our call. He, too, was dressed like the rest of us in our burgundy shirts. Ed was a husky man, funny at times and very down to earth. He was a good guy, and I was glad he was my line brother.

My heart felt warmer and warmer with every brother that joined the fold. This is what it was all about. I shook the hand of each of my brothers with the handshake that only we knew.

We made small talk and caught up for a few minutes. Soon, behind us, we heard another rousing fraternity call. We turned around and responded. Our brothers from Rock Creek College had arrived at the front gates of the school.

Including Jamal.

My heart began to race, just a little. I pretended it was the excitement of seeing my other four frat brothers from Rock Creek: my line brother Ciprian, the quintessential southern gentleman; my line brother Peter, nicknamed "The Martyr" because he was so giving of himself at all times; my line brother Mohammed, an international student and hilarious Algerian dude; and Tommy Hayes, our past chapter president and new Dean of Pledges. If nothing else, Tommy was a fair man – something we needed in our chapter now more than ever. Jamal lingered at the back of the group, quiet and avoiding eye contact with me.

The entire chapter was all together. The Rock Creek boys merged with the Potomac boys until we were all one joyful mass of burgundy and gold. I gripped my line brothers first, then my elder brothers. I saved Jamal for last.

Among the din of the brothers saluting each other, I spoke to Jamal.

"Hey, Frat," I said, trying to break the ice between us.

He looked at me, then my outstretched hand, and walked past me.

I can't say that I was crushed…just disappointed. Again.

"What is a Beta?" Aaron suddenly shouted above the noise. We all knew what to do.

"A Beta is what an Alpha ain't
What a Que wanna be
What a Kappa cain't
What the Ah-kuhs like
What the Deltas love
What all the ladies can't get enough of!
B-Chi, B-Chi
B-Chi, B-Chi, B-Chiii!"

As we repeated the chant, the nine brothers in the chapter placed all our book bags on the ground and made a circle. This was what we did. We fellowshipped. We sang songs from our pledging days. We were Brothers, with a capital B.

"Adrian, start that joint from the probate!" Calen shouted from across the circle. I smiled widely, noticing Jamal rolling his eyes.

"Yeah! Yeah!" the remainder of the brothers exclaimed. It was agreed. I would lead the next song. I cleared my throat and began a favorite Beta song that sounded like an old spiritual.

"I want me a son
So I can teach him the way
Of my B-E-T-A
And hear his daddy say…"

"All of my love, my peace and happiness, I'm gonna give to Beta," the brothers joined in.

"My son, my son,
let me teach you the way
Of B-E-T-A
Listen to daddy say:
All of my love…"

It was one of our favorites. Simple, not really unique to Beta, but we put our own spin on it, as we did with everything in our fraternity. Through it all, Jamal was just one asshole who would never accept me for who I was. I had a whole chapter of Brothers who were at my side, singing and chanting right along with me, even as Potomac students stopped and watched with awe as we fellowshipped. A bunch of black men stopping to sing in the middle of school property wasn't a common occurrence, so Potomac's students didn't mind gawking at us.

Isaiah was one of those who stopped to stare. He had the same sheepish grin on his face that he always had around me. I didn't acknowledge him at first, pretending to be too wrapped up in our songs to notice. He knew me too well, though. There was no way I could see him and not want to stare back. He was keenly aware of the longing that was a lead weight in my gut – a longing that began the previous summer and threatened to topple our lives if we did not honor our pact.

May 29

I walked through the empty chairs that littered the main quad at Potomac University, late on the evening of my ex-boyfriend's graduation. At nine in the morning the graduating seniors processed into the quad with hoods draped on their arms and faces shining brighter than any star in the heavens. By eleven, they were Potomac alumni. By nine in the evening, Savion was on the road back to New York, to begin his career as a staff writer for some upstart hip-hop publication. Somehow, in the back of my mind, maybe I always knew that he was too good for me, that no matter when he left, he would be leaving me for good.

It was now well after midnight and I was alone. Graduation also saw me bidding farewell to men in my life as important to me as Savion. They were my three Brothers of the Sigma Chapter of Beta Chi Phi Fraternity, Incorporated. Micah was my "front," the man who stood directly in front of me when we were lined up for our pledging sessions. He was the only senior on our pledge line, and after patiently waiting for Beta for years, he was finally initiated. My Dean of Pledges, Steven, also graduated, as did his line brother Craig. Though they were like night and day, each of them taught me about myself and brotherhood.

Looking back, I realized that Beta was not what tore me and Savion apart. I did that very well on my own. I wanted Beta so badly that I alienated the man that I loved most in this world. But more than that, I nearly lost who I really was. I was never "out there" with my sexuality, but since I was convinced that the Betas were not ready for a gay Brother, I did all I could to hide that from them. Needless to say, I was discovered. Even though some of the big brothers had tried to force me off the line, my line brothers rallied around me and allowed me to be who I truly was. And that was Adrian Collins, period. The only person seeing me as the "gay pledge" was me. Once I was able to let go the fear of how I was being perceived, I truly became a Beta.

But at that second, I was still alone. My fraternity brothers had scattered to the four winds for the summer, except for a handful, including Micah, who lived in northern Virginia. That was alright by me, for we all needed a break from one another for a little while. Pledging was a very intense time of living in close proximity with one another. Some days, I even missed waking up and seeing Calen snoring or Peter doing push-ups. But most of the time, I didn't. This summer was mine alone; to take a class or two, work for the Anthropology department, and to just relax for a change. Nina, my closest friend, was still in DC for the summer as well, but like the rest of us, she had her own pursuits to worry about.

I sat down in the empty rows and watched graduates continue to leave the campus with their bags and boxes in tow. Even though I had only completed two years of college at that point, I felt just as much on the edge of the rest of my life as they were. My emotional growth was tremendous in those two years, and I wondered where my life would take me next.

I had already moved into my dorm room for the summer. I did not know who my roommate would be, but I knew that I would definitely have one here in Buckley Hall, a large gothic building on the front quadrangle of the school. The rooms were much nicer than the dormitory I had moved from -- more space and a bathroom that was shared with an adjoining room.

Having been up since the early morning for the graduation, and attending the receptions and parties for my friends, I was ready to at least lie down, even if I wouldn't be sleeping right away. I found that I was in bed an awful lot those days, not really sleeping, but staring at the inside of my eyelids while my life played and replayed itself over and over again. My mind kept working on overdrive, as though I were still pledging, even though the ordeal was over and my free time was mine alone.

I entered the old building through the basement and decided to walk up the four flights of stairs to my room. On the fourth floor, my door was propped open by a large cardboard box. My roommate, whoever he was, was in the middle of moving in. I slowly walked toward the door so that I could see him first.

He bent over at his waist, facing away from the door, removing clothing from a suitcase and placing it in the bottom dresser drawer.

I stood in silence, taking in his entire body from his black basketball shoes to his close cropped hair. He rose, stretching his arms out over his head, finally resting his hands on his sides. Who was he? He was obviously African American. I could tell that much by his light brown skin, exposed by baggy basketball shorts and a crisp, white, short sleeved shirt. His calves and forearms were slender, but muscular. Even through his shirt, I could tell that his wide shoulders topped off a strong back, leading in an inverted triangle to a small waist. I thought to myself that he had to be a basketball player, for his entire body looked like it was made for sport. And that ass…

I tapped lightly on the door and said hello. The body turned around and smiled.

I silently called out to God for here was his greatest creation. In one millisecond, my mind processed six feet, nine inches, and 215 pounds of perfection. This face, with its perfectly white teeth, full lips, high cheekbones, and hazel eyes, seemed to fill the room with its beauty.

"Yo! What's up, Beta man?" he said, snapping me out of my trance.

"What's up, Isaiah?" I responded with a smile. "So, you're living here?"

"Yeah, dawg," he said. "I'm here for the summer. Class, summer league, all that. You gonna be here, too?"

"Yeah, man," I said. "Wait, you're in this room?"

"Yup," he said. "It looks like my roommate already moved in some time today."

"I know," I said. "I'm your roommate."

"Say word!" he exclaimed. He dropped the clothes that he had in his hand and stepped over his boxes to approach me. "You're living here this summer?"

"Yeah," I said. "Moved in this morning."

"Hells yeah!" he shouted, shaking my hand and pulling me into a bear hug.

This was too much. Isaiah Aiken was the same year as I was at Potomac; we were both Juniors now that we had finished two years. He wasn't exactly a drinking buddy of mine, but I had to come to know the man through a few classes here and some parties there. Primarily Isaiah was an athlete, so I didn't see him much, unless I was watching Potomac play their Big East games on television.

I had always watched him from afar, though, and thought what it might be like to get with him. Truthfully, I had dreams about most men at Potomac, but Isaiah was a cut above the rest -- simply one of the finest men on campus. And here I was, still trapped in his bear hug, and about to spend the entire summer as his roommate.

"Wow, man, I can't believe it," he continued. "I thought they were gonna send in one of the rookies to live here, but I see that's not the case. You know, I'm glad it's you moving in and not one of those knuckleheads on the team. I mean, they're my dogs and all, but I've been living with them ever since I started here, and well, I'm glad to be living with somebody who ain't on the team. You ever live with an athlete before?"

Whoa. Was Isaiah always this talkative?

"Naw," I said. "Both my roommates were random white boys, they weren't athletes."

"Ah, okay, well that's tight," he said. "Yo, I see you got your stereo here. You mind if I turn it on?"

"No problem, knock yourself out."

"Cool, cool. Yo, you got any go-go?"

"Do I!" I exclaimed. I reached into the bottom of my desk drawer and pulled out all of my CD's, and gave one to Isaiah to pop into the player. His huge hand carefully cradled the disk and slid it into the machine. Soon, the room bounced with the sound of DC's indigenous music. Isaiah smiled and bopped his head to the rhythm.

"You like go-go?" I asked.

"Hell, yeah!" Isaiah said over the music. "We don't have nothing like it back in Baltimore. That percussion, man! Shit, forget about it. This music got me through my first year at Potomac."

"That's tight," I said. "It usually be like me, Nina, and the rest of the DC heads feeling go-go."

"People just don't know what they missing," he said.

"I know that's right," I said. I looked at the clock on my desk and saw that it was about two in the morning, but Isaiah was wired.

Noticing that I had glanced at the clock, Isaiah asked me if I wanted to go to sleep.

"I mean, I can just finish unpacking in the morning," he added.

"No, don't worry about it. I think I'ma take a shower before I go to bed anyway."

"Alright then," Isaiah said.

I took my shoes and socks off while Isaiah continued to unpack and bop away at the music. While his back was turned, I dropped my jeans to the floor and stood in my boxer shorts and t-shirt. I kicked everything under my bed to keep it out of my way and I walked into the bathroom, closing the door behind me.

The shower on full blast quickly filled the bathroom with steam, just how I liked it. The mirror fogged over and I wiped a patch of it so that I could see myself – a man who was too thin due to weeks of pledging and man drama. My musculature was still defined, but I was resigned to the fact that I'd never seem as big as my big brothers were. My skin was brown. Nobody could mistake me for light-skinned, as my new roommate was. I was lucky to have avoided teenaged blemishes for most of my life, so my complexion was very clear. Not even a razor bump.

I took off my shirt and boxer shorts and threw them lightly to the floor, now standing completely in the nude except for my Beta Chi Phi lavaliere. I wiped the mirror again and looked briefly at my body. I wasn't that bad. I reassured myself that somebody out there wanted me, maybe not Savion, but somebody.

I stepped into the hot shower and pulled the translucent curtain behind me. I closed my eyes and tried to forget about the day's activities, as well as the events of the past weeks. He was gone now. I would not be seeing him again any time soon. I needed to get over him.

My eyes began to well up with tears as they had many times since we parted ways. I faced an entire summer virtually alone. I didn't even feel that I had a home, since my mother and I were barely even speaking. It was just me, working and thinking the whole summer.

I heard the door click from being opened.

"It's me, dawg," Isaiah said. "I'm just putting some shit away under the sink."

"Fine with me," I said, silently wishing that Isaiah would also go away, even though he was easy on the eyes. I did not feel like entertaining him all the way to August as though this was summer camp.

Isaiah quickly left the bathroom again and closed the door. I spent about ten more minutes under the stream, and then I was done. I left the bathroom with the towel tied around my waist. Isaiah was on the phone now, laying on his bed with his eyes open. As I dried off and got ready for bed, I couldn't help but hear his conversation.

"…yeah…yeah…but I'm saying, you know my schedule is tight. I gave you all the dates you could come down. But I mean, you knew I had to be down here for summer league. So what's the problem? Man, whatever…"

He must have been talking to Taina, his girlfriend since Freshman year. Unless he was dipping out on her, I had no idea who else he'd be talking to so late at night. I found some clean boxers and slipped them on under my towel.

"Whatever," he continued, rolling his eyes. "I mean, I know you're doing your thing, but you knew what I'd be doing since last summer. So stop trippin'. You need to be the one making time to come down here, since you know I can't leave. Man fuck it, I'm going to bed. Peace."

Isaiah clicked off his cell phone and plugged it back into its charger.

"You aight?" I asked while slipping on a clean "Potomac" t-shirt over my head.

"Yeah, man, it's cool. Taina trippin', as usual."

"Oh, word?" I asked.

"Yeah. She knows that I'm at Potomac to play ball and go to class. And as long as I'm here, that's what I got to do. No vacations. Coach ain't having that."

"So what's the problem?" I asked.

"Taina. She isn't making any type of plans to come down here to see me this summer. At all."

"Well, where she live?" I asked as I slipped under the sheets.

"Upstate New York. But it's all good. I need some time away from her, I guess."

"Sure. You been with her since Freshman year, right?"

"Right," he said. "Yo, you want me to turn this light out?"

"Um…yeah."

"Aight," he said. He stood up, walked across the room, and turned out the light. Though the room was dark, there was enough light coming through the windows to allow me to see Isaiah walk back to his bed. Facing his side of the room, he pulled his shirt up over his head and dropped his shorts to his feet. In only his boxers, I saw nearly every muscle of his body work in tandem to carry him first to the window to draw the blinds, and then to his bed, to lie down. He didn't see me staring at him because my eyes were only half open.

I used to do that to Savion. Pretend I was sleeping just so I could watch him walk around the room naked in the middle of the night.

"You sleep, dawg?" he asked after a few minutes.

"Naw, man," I said through my pillow.

"Yo…I'm not always an easy person to live with. But if you feel like I'm doing something to piss you off, just let me know, aight?"

"No doubt. That goes double for me. I think this is gonna be a cool summer, man."

If you would just shut the fuck up and let me sleep.

September 8

"Nina, do you think I'm not approachable?" I asked my friend above the din of the notorious Potomac University dining hall.

"Approachable?" she repeated. "I mean, yeah, you're approachable."

I looked around the cafeteria. It was after seven in the evening, the time we called "Happy Hour." You just weren't cool if you didn't have dinner with all the other black people on campus. You didn't have to sit together, but you definitely had to be in the caf from seven to eight to see how everyone was doing, get the news of the day, and yes, get that extra slice of beef or extra piece of chicken from the ladies behind the main entrée counter. Freshmen were still cliquey, the upperclassmen were still on the prowl, and nobody was quite stressed out yet.

"Why do you ask? I know you don't care about all these folks," she said, waving her one free hand in the air, holding her fork steady with the other.

"I mean…I guess I do care. In a way. Like, last year, I had so many cool people to look up to. Steven…Micah…other dudes, too. And girls. Like, how do I live up to what they did here?"

"Adrian," Nina said, putting down her fork. "You know, Micah and Steven and Savion were all really awesome people. But you gotta realize, everybody is different. These new freshmen aren't going to see you and think 'wow, that's the next Micah.' They are gonna be like wow, that's Adrian Collins. And then they're gonna ask people about you, and they're gonna hear how you were on the NAACP and pledged Beta and did more things in one year than most people do in four. You're definitely of the same caliber as your own heroes."

I blushed.

"Are you approachable?" she continued. "Sure, I think you are. You're one of the friendliest guys on campus. But who knows what people think when they see you. Hell, they might be intimidated because you're Greek, or because you're handsome, or because you're an upperclassman now."

"I'm afraid, Nina," I said. "I mean, I'm not concerned about what people think of me. After all the bullshit that happened, I don't care that anybody knows that I'm gay. Hell, some people will hate me, some people will like me, I'm prepared for whatever comes. I just – I just hope that being me doesn't scare people away from getting to know me."

"But I don't see how being you now is any different from a year ago," Nina said.

"Like…I'm out now, I guess."

"Out the closet?" Nina asked softly.

"Yeah, I guess you could say that."

"So like…when did this happen?" Nina asked.

"This summer. Living with Isaiah. Connecting with my dad again."

"Your dad knows?!" Nina asked, surprised at the notion.

"Oh hell no," I quickly said. "It's not just him. I want to be a better person all around."

"Wow. I'm kinda blown, Adrian," Nina said, sipping on her pink lemonade. "I always thought that you would just keep your life under wraps."

"Nah," I said. "I think I was on my way to coming out while I was with Savion. But Beta kinda fucked that all up. Well…I fucked it up, really. I think if I hadn't pledged, me and Savion…well, let's just say I would have been out by now"

"Yeah. I don't doubt that."

"Nina, it's all so crazy, though! Like, I want to just be open and free now. Do all the things I was too afraid to do before. Go out without caring who sees me. Approach dudes on campus. Shit like that. But…I ain't got no gay friends!"

Nina laughed.

"I'm serious!" I continued, poking a French fry in the air for emphasis. "I'm around all these fucking straight dudes in my frat, in my house, in class, on the street. And hell, forget about finding a gay black dude on this campus."

"Yeah," Nina said. "If there's another, he's most definitely on the down low."

"Yeah," I frowned. "I'm not trying to be the only one, Nina, but I've got to step out there."

"How are you gonna do that?"

I paused for dramatic effect and then reached into my pocket. I produced a small pink flier and gave it to Nina to read. She looked at it, read it slowly, and then looked at me.

"You serious?" she asked.

"I mean…yeah," I said.

"That's tight, Adrian! I am so proud of you!" Nina gave me a high five across the table. "But um, this meeting is tonight…like, in ten minutes!"

"I know!" I exclaimed. "You wanna come with?"

"Um…" Nina said. "You know you my boy Adrian. Just keep these chicks away from me if they try to push up on me."

I chuckled. "Of course, girl."

Fifteen minutes later, Nina and I stood outside of a classroom in the Intercultural Building. The hallway was swarming with all sorts of people, some going to late classes, but many headed toward the very same classroom we were eyeballing.

"This is it," Nina said. "Potomac Pride."

"Yup," I said. "Potomac Pride."

"You scared?" she asked.

"Yeah."

"Me too, boy. Them some big butch lookin' broads going up in there. You don't have to do this tonight if you don't want to, Adrian. You got your whole life to be out."

"Don't get scared now. I gotta do it," I said. "This is just one piece of the puzzle. I gotta be me, I can't live my life scared of what other people are gonna think or say."

"I feel you," Nina said.

"I mean, if I can pledge Beta, I can do anything. Ain't nothing worse than that, so this is gonna be cake."

"True, true."

"Yup."

"Right. So um…why you ain't walking in there?"

"I'm 'bout to!"

We laughed some more. I was about to launch myself headfirst in the Potomac Pride: the gay, lesbian, bisexual, and transgender student organization. I was scared, but I had to do it. I had to see what it was all about.

"Aight, let's do this," I said. Nina and I walked up to the door, and Nina let me enter first.

Inside the fluorescent-lit, hundred person classroom, about fifty students were already there. I looked at no one and walked briskly to the far side of the room. We saw a sea of mostly pale, mostly male faces. Some were preppy, some were punk. Nina and I were the only black people there.

"The fuck is this?" I asked to none in particular.

"I know, right?" Nina said. "This joint is quite colorless."

"Well, we do go to a white school," I said.

"I know, but um, damn, you are not the only gay black man at this school. I know you can't be."

I knew I wasn't either, but I for damn sure couldn't tell Nina everything I knew. Soon, the meeting was called to order by a tall and slender, blue haired fellow who stood at the front of the room.

"Good evening everyone!" the guy said. "My name is Lee Birney and I am the President of Potomac Pride. I am so glad to see so many of you out tonight for our first meeting of the year! Wow, welcome! It's really good to see old friends and new friends here tonight. Give yourselves a hand!"

They clapped. We stared.

"Wow, yeah, that's great," Lee continued. "Well, as I'm sure you know, Potomac Pride is the official gay, lesbian, bisexual, and transgender organization here at our beloved Potomac University. We serve as a social outlet for queer students as well as an advocacy organization. If ever you feel discriminated against because of your sexual orientation, whether it's in the classroom or out on the street, don't hesitate to tell me or another board member and we will handle it. But we'll get more into what we do as a club a little later. Right now, I think we should all get to know each other a little better. Let's see, over in the corner first, could you just stand and give your name and maybe tell us what you hope to gain from Potomac Pride this year?"

Of course, Nina and I were sitting in the corner. We looked at each other, and Nina rose first, straightening out her baby doll t-shirt.

"Hi, everyone!" she said cheerfully. "My name is Nina Bradley and I am a Junior in the School of Business. I am here to learn more about what Potomac Pride does and to support any friends who are members. Thanks!"

She sat down. Damn, she knew how to work a room.

I rose slowly and stood beside the desk, looking out into the room. I saw that a handful of black folks had tiptoed in while Lee made his welcome speech, so that put me at least a little at ease. I saw one brown-skinned boy I had never seen before, and two black girls who I thought might be sophomores.

"Hi," I said. "My name is Adrian Collins and I am a Junior Anthropology major in the College of Arts and Sciences. I am a member of Beta Chi Phi Fraternity, Incorporated, and I am here…"

Shit, shit, shit. Why did I have to say I was a Beta in a room full of homosexuals?

"I'm here because…I'm gay. And I wanted to join Potomac Pride. And I guess see what it's all about. Thanks."

I hurried up and sat my black ass right back down in my chair. Although the room as a whole was very friendly and smiling the entire time I spoke, I was still nervous. That was my absolute first time I had said I was gay in public. My heart raced the whole time everyone else spoke. I almost forgot to pay attention to who the black people were.

Lee was a friendly guy. He was a senior who I had seen around before. You couldn't miss his height, his hair, or his personality. He wasn't really a queen, though he was a tad feminine and dramatic at times. But as president of Potomac Pride, he was in control.

The meeting was soon over. As Nina and I prepared to leave, it seemed as though a swell of people started to surround us. The crowd was led by Lee, who extended his hand to me.

"Hey, buddy!" he said, squeezing my hand surprisingly tight. I guess I assumed with his unconventional appearance, I expected him to have a weak handshake. "Adrian, right?"

"Right," I said. "Good meeting."

"Thanks! And thanks for coming! I've seen you around campus forever, but I never thought I would see you here."

"Well, you know...It was time."

"Right on!" he said. This guy was a little too happy to see me.

"Let me introduce you to the rest of the board."

"Oh, um," I began. "That's really not…"

Before I knew it, the entire Potomac Pride executive board was introduced to us. I tried to get out of there, but they were determined to see just who this new Negro was and would I bring more. Near the door, I could see the black guy and the two girls introducing themselves to one another and making nice.

Nina grabbed me by the hand. "Well folks, we're really sorry, but we must be heading out now," she said. "It's getting late and my buddy and I have to get to a study group!"

"Aww, well hey, we'll see you at the party this weekend, right?" Lee asked.

"Yeah, sure," I lied with a slight smile. "Sounds like fun"

"Great! Thanks again for coming." Lee patted me on the shoulder and finally walked away. I could see the other black people in the room slightly giggling in my direction. Nina and I walked toward them.

"Hi," I said. The dude was on the short side, very young looking. Definitely a freshman. The women were familiar. One wore a head wrap, like Erykah Badu, and had very light skin. She was thick and about the same height as the dude. The other girl was tall and thin, built like a slim basketball player. She had shoulder length dreadlocks and was dark skinned.

"Brother," the light skinned girl said. "Come with us, it's gonna be alright."

I smiled and laughed. "Aight. I feel you."

Nina was confused.

"Nina, I'm cool," I told her. "I'ma gonna…yeah. You don't have to stay."

"You sure?" she asked, checking out the other black folks like they might have been toting weaponry.

"Yeah," I grinned. "I need to talk to these good people for a minute."

We hugged and I let Nina go. Me, the boy, and the girls walked down the hall to another section of the Intercultural Center.

"My name is Adrian," I began.

"We know," the light skinned girl said. "Adrian Collins. Who doesn't know you?"

I blushed.

"My name is Samirah," the light one said. "This is Cat."

"Hey," I said. "Sophomores, right?"

"Yup," Cat said. She was very pretty, and in some ways looked like a cat with her slanted eyes and round face.

"I'm a Freshman," the boy said. "My name is Morris."

"Nice to meet you," I said, shaking his hand. He smiled at me as I noticed the glint of his rainbow bracelet on his wrist.

"So, um, what's up with all the lily whiteness back there?" I asked bluntly.

"Chile," Samirah began. "It's always been like that, always gon' be like that."

We sat down on some wooden benches along a deserted, back hallway. The green walls and gray carpet made the place feel somewhat comfortable. We were away from the prying eyes of Potomac Pride and free in our own skin.

"I mean, I felt like a freak show or something," I continued.

"Yeah," Morris added. "I definitely peeped that. People were staring at me hard."

"You're black and male," Cat said softly. "What more do they need?"

"I don't get it," I said.

"It's like this," Samirah began. "Potomac Pride, by mission, is for everybody. Male, female, black, white, whatever. But historically, this is a white man's club. I joined when I was a freshman last year, and do you know I was the only black person in there?"

"Word?" I asked.

"Yup…well…Savion was there, too."

"Oh," I said.

"Who is Savion?" Morris asked.

"He was soooo fine," Cat said, rolling her eyes in the air in ecstasy. Samirah lightly nudged her with her foot. "Oh. Um, he graduated. This Dominican dude."

"Did you know him?" Morris asked me.

"He's my ex," I said.

"Oh," Morris said quietly. "My bad."

"It's all good. I didn't know he was coming to Pride meetings."

"Not many," Samirah continued. "We met and we were cool, but he and I both decided that Pride wasn't the way. I mean, I gave it a try, but…it's hard being an earthy type sista who doesn't drink and listens to Common…and these guys' idea of fun is a cramped house party, beer, and Madonna. It just ain't me."

"Yeah," I said. "Not really me either. I just can't assimilate like that."

"Me either," Morris said. "I mean, it's only the second week of school, but I expected something different. I didn't go in that room and feel overly welcome. I felt like…like meat."

"And I felt like a ghost," Cat said.

"These men don't know how to treat lesbians when it comes to the overall struggle," Samirah said. "Those white chicks in there ain't feeling Pride either, but they try. We probably need a whole 'nother organization, on the real. But anyway…I've also noticed that they don't know what to do with people of color unless they also assimilate. You'll see some other black folks at their parties every now and then. But they won't be the same folks you'll see at the next NAACP meeting or Umoja House party. You can bet on that."

"Wow," I said.

"So, when did you come out, big man?" Cat asked me.

"Um, today?" I joked. We all giggled. "I mean, I don't know. I knew I was gay when I first came here. I dated. I was in a relationship, but the time to come out just wasn't right for me until now."

"I think you're pretty brave," Samirah said.

"Brave? Naw," I said, slightly embarrassed.

"Dude," she said. "Don't blush! Everybody knows you. People like you. I know you might not be shouting it from the hills, but I think it says a lot that you showed up tonight. Last year this time, I didn't have anybody in that room that looked like me. This year, we're four deep. Now, we might never go to another one of these meetings, but at least we're here now."

And there we were. I was amazed to be sitting there talking with three other black folks who were in the same boat as me. We had to have talked for like an hour, just sharing stories and learning about each other. Samirah had a strong personality, like Nina. I guessed that they might like each other if they hung out. They were all normal people. Morris wasn't feminine, but he did wear a rainbow bracelet on his wrist. He was definitely more comfortable as a freshman than I would have been. The bracelet was what drew Samirah to him the first week of school. They struck up a conversation and decided to attend the Pride meeting in hopes of meeting other black people. Cat, who as it turned out really was a women's basketball player, had befriended Samirah the year before. I thought they might have dated, but if they had, they were just friends now. Samirah had convinced Cat to come to the meeting, too. I had no idea that either of these girls were Lesbians.

It seemed as though at least Samirah had an idea about me, though. She had known Savion, and who knew what he confided in her. I wasn't upset or anything, just curious. I let it go, though, and figured me and Samirah would just be friends regardless of whatever she already knew or didn't know.

"This was amazing," Morris said as we walked to his residence hall later that evening.

"Yes, indeed," I echoed. "I always kind of thought I'd just be the only one. You know?"

"Aren't you glad you don't have to be?" he asked sincerely.

"Hell yeah," I said. I noticed his rainbow bracelet for the second time that evening.

"Morris," I began. "Why do you need to wear the bracelet?"

"Why shouldn't I?" he asked.

"The question is why do you, not why shouldn't you?"

"Who cares?" he asked. This conversation reminded me of the debates that Savion and I used to have. Not wanting to recreate that drama, I took a deep breath and started again.

"I just was thinking that maybe wearing that bracelet would bring unwanted attention to you…have people make assumptions about you without getting to know you."

"Oh, sort of like how I assumed you were straight just because I've seen you wearing a fraternity jacket?"

"You thought I was straight?" I asked. "Why?"

"Why not?" Morris asked. "I've never met an openly gay fraternity member before. You're the first for me."

"Oh…well that's beside the point though, Morris. Aren't you afraid? That rainbow bracelet-"

"Means that I am proud of who I am. Period. I don't care what people think. If people see the bracelet and can identify with me because of it, then that's great. And if it keeps homophobes away, that's an added bonus."

"Interesting," I said. "Well man, I got your back, regardless."

"I appreciate that," he said with a smile. "You seem like a cool dude. I'd like to get to know you better some time."

He took me by surprise with his forwardness.

"That would be cool," I said. "I'd definitely like to hang out with you, Cat, and Samirah some more. I think you'd like Nina, too."

Although he deflated somewhat at my subtle rebuff, he still smiled.

"Yeah," he said. "Nina seems cool."

"I need to head out of here man. Again, nice meeting you."

"Same here," Morris said, giving me a hug. "I'll see you around.

His hug lingered for just a split second too long, but I wasn't mad. He was just a freshman, and for all he knew, we were the only gay men on campus. It was under very similar circumstances that I met my last boyfriend.

By the time I went to bed that night, I hadn't given a second thought to the magnitude of what I had done at the that meeting. I was myself, without any second thoughts.

I was definitely changing, growing into the person I always wanted to be, evolving into the type of man who could live with himself.

June 4

For the summer, I would be taking "Religions of the African Diaspora" while I worked for the Anthropology Department part-time. Through a combination of loans and a grant from the department, I didn't have to pay for my housing or my class. I had it made.

The phone rang early the first week of class, waking me up, but not my roommate.

"Hello?" I asked.

"Adrian, this is your mother," the shrill voice said.

"Oh," I said, disappointed. "Hi mom."

"You don't sound too happy to hear from me," she noted. I looked at the clock on my desk.

"Because it's seven o'clock in the morning and I don't have to be awake for hours, mom."

"Well, I'm sorry for calling to check on my son. I haven't heard from you in weeks."

"I've been busy…"

"Too busy to call your mother? Adrian, you haven't even been home since you picked up your mail that one day. And you didn't even come when you knew I'd be home, I would have given you some food to take to campus."

"I don't need any food. I have a meal plan for the summer and I have enough money to go grocery shopping."

"That's not the point, Adrian."

"Mom, every time I come home, we get into an argument," I admitted. "Don't you get that? I don't come home because I want to be happy."

"Well, whose fault is it that we argue? Every time you come home, it's all about you. You don't have any concept of what being in a family is all about."

"Okay, first of all," I began, sitting up in bed, "You might want to take a look in the mirror before you start talking about what a family is all about."

"Excuse me?"

"Excuse you?" I mocked. "Have you even thought about why we argue all the time?"

"We argue about your responsibility! Every time you come home, you sit on your ass and do what you want to do. Yeah, you get jobs, but you never chip in around here. But I always see you wearing new clothes, or buying a computer, or even now, pledging that damn fraternity. What about me?"

"You are a grown woman with a job! Isn't it enough that I am here on a full scholarship? All you have to do is sign the financial aid forms every year, and I am set. You pay nothing for my education. Not a damn thing. And don't you worry about my damn fraternity. This fraternity has given me the only real family I ever had."

"I am your real family, Adrian," my mother asserted.

"You are my biological mother, and that's it," I said. "When you drove my father out of my life, for whatever reason, you became a care-taker. All you did was push me to be an honor student, so that I could get into college. And now that I'm here, you make it sound like we're supposed to have this great relationship."

"I did not drive your father out of your life!" my mother shrieked. "He left!"

"How can I believe that?" I shouted back. "If he just left, as you say, why wouldn't he try to be part of my life? He's been gone since I was eight, and you won't even tell me why he left. So you must be the problem."

My mother was silent.

"Not much to say now, huh?" I waited for a response. "Look, I don't want to argue with you. All my life has been nothing but trying to live up to your standards, trying to be whatever you think a man is. It sucks going through what I've been through in my life and not feeling like I have a mother or father to talk to about it. Now just leave me alone. Let me do my thing, like I've been doing it since I was a kid. I have never depended on you for warmth, compassion, or your friendship. I don't plan to start looking for those things, either."

"Goodbye, Adrian," she said.

"Bye," I said. I quietly hung up the phone. I couldn't believe that I had said all of those things to her. It was years of anger and resentment, finally spilling over in one crazy argument. I felt a hand on my shoulder, and Isaiah's weight sitting on my bed.

"Are you okay?" he asked quietly. I looked into Isaiah's earnest eyes and felt myself well up with emotion.

"I just…I don't know why things are the way they are," I answered honestly. "I feel like…like…"

"It's okay, dude," Isaiah reassured. "Just relax, you'll be okay."

"It's not okay, though," I said. "I feel like I don't come from anywhere."

"Everybody comes from somewhere, dawg," Isaiah said.

"I mean…" I exhaled and tried to get myself together, fighting back tears. "I haven't seen my father since I was eight years old. And me and my mom don't get along at all. If I could just find my dad… talk to him…see why he left…"

"I hear you," Isaiah said. "My dad passed when I was young."

"I'm sorry," I said. "That sucks."

"It's all good. Been a while, you know. But you still got your dad somewhere. Do you…want me to help you find him?" I looked at my roommate and lightly laughed.

"It's not that simple," I said. "But thanks anyway. I'll be okay."

"Yeah. You still got your frat, if nothing else."

I smirked in response.

"Those are some cool cats," Isaiah continued.

"Yeah, they aight," I joked.

"So…" he began again. "Are you going to be okay? Because, you know, we ain't been living together that long, but I've known you for like two years now. I'm here if you need me, man."

"Thanks, Isaiah," I said. "That's tight. I apologize for waking you up."

"Man, no problem," he said as he stood up. "I gotta get up early most days anyway. Yo, you trying to take a jog with me?"

"Um…I don't know," I said, looking at my clock again.

"Come on man," he pleaded. "Just once around the campus, and right back home."

Potomac was a big campus when running around it, but I needed to burn off the energy. I'd never be able to get back to sleep with all that was on my mind.

I reached into a drawer and pulled out some blue jean shorts.

"What are you doing?" Isaiah asked.

"I can run in these, right?" I asked.

"You can't run in no jean shorts! Here man, take these." Isaiah reached in his own drawer and pulled out a fresh pair of blue basketball shorts.

"Thanks," I said.

We each changed and were soon out of the door.

From the front doors of Buckley Hall, we began our journey. The sun was up and the air was humid already, though the temperature was not yet unbearably hot as most summers were in DC. Isaiah kept a slow and steady pace for me. I was in shape, but definitely not to the extent as my roommate. Right next door to Buckley was the historic Potomac Hall, named after no one in particular, but the oldest building on campus. Its tall spires and clock tower were the signature of the campus.

We pounded the pavement and circled the building, passing our library and some campus apartments. Sweat began to bead on my forehead. I wiped it off and glanced at Isaiah, who hardly seemed to be fazed by the work out. We headed down the campus hill, passing a few maintenance workers along the way.

"Hey, Mr. Smith," Isaiah said to one of the men.

"Hey, young man," he said as we sped down the hill.

From the hill, we could see the entire southern end of the campus. Construction had been finished on it for a few years, but it still had a synthetic quality about it. We ran through the courtyard of the "New Quad" and noticed a few elderly priests sitting on benches.

"Hi Father Walsh," Isaiah said.

"Hello, Isaiah!" the priest said.

"You know him?" I asked in between breaths.

"Yeah man," he said. "Father Walsh is cool as shit."

"Cool," I said.

At the bottom of the New Quad, we began bearing to the right, near the campus power plant and the soccer fields. My mind was a little clearer by that point. I wasn't as alone as it seemed. Isaiah was right, I did have my frat, but that meant much more than just my line brothers.

My father was a member of my fraternity, Beta Chi Phi. In fact, he was a founder of the chapter at U. Mass. I was partially inspired to pledge Beta because of what I knew of the fraternity from him. If I closed my eyes really tight, I could even remember some of the pictures in his photo album. The one that sticks out is an image of my father with a huge afro, wearing burgundy bellbottoms and a gold shirt. He was doing some kind of synchronized line dance with some other men dressed identically.

My father's line brother, Mike McDaniel, was the one who pinned me when I was initiated. Beta definitely made my world smaller, because even though no one could find my father's whereabouts, half the fraternity knew who I was because I was the legacy of one of the earliest members of the organization. The fraternity was only thirty years old, so we legacies were few and far between. Mike had found me and decided to pin me, since my father could not be found.

My relationship with my mother was shot, and I had none with my father. If I was to feel complete, then I would have to be man enough to continue looking for my father and ultimately find out why he left. It was twelve years ago. Was he beating my mom? Did he have an affair? Was he a drug abuser? It hurt me not to know. I could not be mad at him for something my mom wouldn't even tell me about. I wanted to call Mike, but there was no point. My father had disappeared off the face of the earth and Mike made it clear that he had no leads.

We were home again, Isaiah invigorated; me, just tired, but mentally awake. Isaiah wasn't as annoying as I thought he would be. In fact, I thought that I could really come to like him as a person. He walked up the steps before me. Near the top of the stairwell, daggers sliced their way up the muscles in my leg.

"   Ah, shit!" I said. Luckily, I was already holding on to the banister. If I hadn't, I probably would have tumbled down to the landing.

"What's wrong?" Isaiah said, turning around to face me.

"I don't know man, my fuckin' leg just started hurting!"

"Okay. Don't move man, stay still."

"Okay," I said. I was trying to stay hard; I didn't want to seem like a punk around Isaiah, but my leg was hurting something awful.

"Where does it hurt?" he asked.

"My calf. It just feels knotted up."

"Aight," he said. He stood next to me on the stairs and put his arm around my waist, grabbing me toward him.

"What are you doing?" I asked.

"Just hold on," he said. I put my arm around his waist and let go of the banister. Next thing I know, Isaiah had lifted me up by the waist and was carrying up the rest of the stairs.

"Dude, I can't believe you are carrying me up the stairs," I said.

"What else was I supposed to do?" he asked, quite seriously.

He kept carrying me, effortlessly, through the door and down the hall to our room. Only then did he put me down.

"Still hurt?" he asked, fishing for his key.

"Yeah. I think it's just a cramp or something."

"Probably," he said. He found his key and unlocked the door. "You don't work out much, do you?"

I grimaced. "Not really?"

He laughed. "Aight, let me see you walk to your bed."

I limped, then hopped to my bed, then sat down. Isaiah closed the door behind him and walked over to my bed.

"So, what should I do, man?" I asked. The pain was definitely getting worse. My leg felt so tight, so sore.

"Hmm," Isaiah pondered. "Lay down on your stomach."

"Uh, okay," I said. I laid down with my head facing the window, and I could see the trees and tops of some of the campus buildings. I instinctually put my injured leg in the air, bending it at the knee in a right angle.

Isaiah unexpectedly started untying my shoe. I turned around and looked at him, puzzled.

"I'm gonna take your shoe off, let the blood circulate, then I'm gonna try to relax the muscle. Okay?" he asked.

"Yeah," I said. "That's cool."

My shoe was off and Isaiah started massaging my calf. I couldn't believe it. This man was massaging my leg in my own bed. He started at my ankle, moving my foot around in small circles. Then, he just worked the muscles in my calf in between his hands. I didn't get the impression that he really knew what he was doing, but it made me feel better. In fact, it was a good thing I was lying in my stomach, because Isaiah's massage was quickly erasing my pain and replacing it with an unmistakable pleasure. I closed my eyes as he rubbed.

"I wish you had told me you don't normally jog that kind of distance," he said softly. "I wouldn'ta made you run that with me."

"Naw, it's cool," I said. "I needed it. Needed to clear my head."

"I feel you," he said. He was using both hands on my calf, and my pain had dissolved. I didn't stop him from rubbing though. It wasn't that often that I had such an attractive man kneading my flesh.

My leg was now lying on the bed, loose and comfortably. I was in the zone, eyes totally closed, head resting in my folded arms like I was at the beach.

His hands were now totally off of my calf and rubbing the back of my knee.

"How do you feel now?" he asked, his voice barely above a whisper.

"Good," I said.

"Do you want me to stop?"

I paused. This whole scene could easily be seen as something else. Isaiah didn't know I was gay, and if he knew, this definitely wouldn't go over well.

"Yeah, I'm good," I said. "Thanks."

"No problem," he said, patting my calf to signify that he was done. "Anytime."

"I was never good at sports," I said, sitting up on the bed, in time to see Isaiah stripping himself of his sweaty shirt. He was facing away from me.

He laughed. "I hear that, man. I was practically born on the court. Mama squatted at half-court, and splat, there I was."

"You crazy, dude," I said. "You're a forward, right?"

"Yup," he said, turning around and kicking his shoes off. "Sure am. I know what you're thinking: I'm kinda skinny to be a forward."

"Skinny? I don't think so, homie."

"Yeah, I'm six feet, nine inches, 215 pounds. NBA forwards be like 230, at least."

"Oh," I said. He looked damn good to me, "skinny" or not.

"I'm sure Taina likes however you look," I continued.

He grunted.

"Don't mention her name," he said, sitting on his chair, still shirtless. "I'm so sick of her."

"Damn," I said. "Is everything okay?"

"Nope," he said, putting his hands in his face. "It's like this. Taina and I been together since we got here, just about. That's two years. She's like, making plans and shit. But I don't even know what else is out there. I'm a different person now than I was when I first met her."

"Wow, man. I had no idea there was any trouble."

"Yeah, it's crucial," he said. "Girls like her are in college to find a husband. I'm trying to find myself."

"That's deep," I said. "I always thought y'all were inseparable."

"Yeah, we were. But Adrian, I dunno dawg. I'm changing. A lot. I need space. Time to just work shit out on my own. I need her to be my friend, not my woman. You know?"

"Yeah, I feel you man."

"Yeah, I bet you do. You probably got all types of females sniffin' behind you on this campus!"

We laughed, but I said nothing.

"You're not dating Nina, are you?" he asked.

"Naw man…I'm not dating anybody."

"Why not?"

"Probably the same reasons you listed. I need to take care of me. When I was dating somebody, I was pledging. And I had my priorities all fucked up. But now…I don't know, man. If I could do it all differently, I would."

"Word." Isaiah said.

"Yo, let's get some breakfast," I suggested.

"You think you can manage, crip?" Isaiah joked. I stood up, shook out my leg, and took a few test steps.

"It's fine," I said. "Seems like you got the magic touch or something."

Isaiah smiled.

"Yeah, nigga. That's what I'm told. Let me take a shower right quick. And hell, so should you, funky ass."

We laughed. Isaiah was a cool dude. I was attracted to him, but that was the problem with Potomac. There were dozens of sexy men who were off limits to me. All I could do was hang back and take in all the scenery.

It was also somewhat startling to hear that he and Taina were on the rocks. It just proved that like me, nothing at school was always just as it seemed. As time went on, maybe I would learn even more about Isaiah that I would have never imagined. Maybe one day, we would be the best of friends.

September 12

"Brother Sergeant-at-arms, is the meeting room secure and free from outside intrusion?" Aaron asked Calen.

"Brother President, this meeting room is secure and free from intrusion. Every man present is a duly initiated Beta man, with all associated rights and privileges," Calen mechanically responded.

"Brothers, how shall we proceed?" Aaron asked all of us. We all rose to our feet.

"Let brotherly love continue," we responded with our secret motto, taken from the thirteenth chapter of Hebrews.

"Let us pray," Mohammed began. "Our Creator, we humbly ask that you watch over us as we perform the business of Beta Chi Phi. Allow us to proceed with a clear conscience. Allow us to be more than our brother's keepers: allow us to be our brothers' friends. We remember our five cardinal principles of Scholarship, Social Action, Service, Unity, and Faith, and know that of these, Faith is what allows men of different walks of life to come together under the banner of virtue. By all names we know you, we pray."

"Amen," we said in unison. Mohammed was the only Muslim in our chapter, and it was important to us that he led our prayers, if nothing else, to let him know that his beliefs were just as welcome as anyone else's.

"Brothers, please recite with me the creed of Beta Chi Phi," Aaron said.

"We, the Brothers of Beta Chi Phi Fraternity, Incorporated, believe in the unity of all people. We shall serve and speak for those less fortunate than ourselves. Through our scholarly endeavors, we shall elevate the Black and Latino communities to a level that transcends all prior inequities and subjugation. We, men of Beta Chi Phi, believe in the power of a higher being, and shall use the gifts bestowed upon us to fulfill the mission of our Fraternity."

"This meeting of the Sigma Chapter of Beta Chi Phi Fraternity, Incorporated, is now called to order. You may be seated," Aaron said.

I loved the way we opened Beta meetings. Being formal

reminded us all that we were in a fraternity, not just another club. Big things happened in Beta meetings, and our formal opening set the tone. We met just about every other Sunday in shirts, ties, and fraternity pins. Sigma chapter was lucky to have a chapter of mostly neos, all eager to work hard for Beta.

Aaron was a highly capable president. He pledged two years ago, and as a Senior, he had a lot of experience under his belt. His bald head and black glasses sometimes made him seem much older than twenty-one, but he also knew how to have fun when it came down to it.

"Brothers, I have some news to report," Aaron began. "Unfortunately, Brother Washington won't be staying on as our advisor this year."

"Awww," Jamal said sarcastically. The brothers laughed.

"Brother Washington got a new job in LA over the summer, so effective immediately, we have no advisor. But, the Cluster Chairman, Brother Bond, said he would appoint us one ASAP."

"God, nobody can be worse than Brother Washington." Tommy said.

"What was wrong with him?" Peter asked sincerely. "He seemed like a real nice guy, you know. He was at all the cluster workshops when we were on line."

"Yeah, right," Jamal said. "The man was soft. Didn't know anything and didn't fit in. It would be better to get an alumnus from our chapter."

"Too bad it's not up to us," Aaron said. "They're going to give us whoever they want. It's not like we can have an advisor who is going to be in pledge sessions with us."

"Now that would be interesting," Calen said.

"We need an advisor who will sign off on our paperwork and otherwise leave us the hell alone," Ciprian said. "Aaron, is there any way you can talk to Brother Bond about who we're gonna get?"

"I'll talk to him, but I can't guarantee anything. I have a feeling they're gonna stick us with just anybody for now."

The brothers moaned collectively. Aaron went back to the

agenda. Before too long, we had set up our calendar for the year. Our service projects and programs were being set into motion. We had a very strong group, even though there were only a handful of seniors among us.

"Gentlemen, I wanted to keep this part of our meeting toward the end, off the record." Aaron turned to Peter, who stopped taking notes.

"Brothers, every year, we formulate a chapter program that follows the national program. We fulfill our obligations to the fraternity not because we have to, but because we want to. That said, there are some unwritten rules you neos need to know. As you get older in Beta, you will see that all of a sudden, you have lots of new friends, people who weren't there before you were a Beta. You're an overnight celebrity. Why? I don't even know. We're the same people we were before we had letters. But for some reason, outsiders, including people who aspire to be Betas themselves, seem to think we have superpowers."

"We don't like that shit," Tommy interjected. He was our immediate past president, and now Dean of Pledges. "We want equals, not suck ups. Got it?"

We all nodded in agreement.

"You will see, sooner or later," Tommy continued, "that men you never knew will start offering to do you favors, for no good reason. I remember when I first crossed, this dude in my Biology class started calling me up and asking if I wanted to study. It was only two weeks left in the semester! I was like no thanks, dude."

All of the neos began to laugh, along with our prophytes. Soon, Tommy called for quiet again.

"At the same time," Aaron continued, "we all know that there are those of you that we took a shining to before the process began. There were others who we took a chance on during rush. You brought something else to the table. All seven of you, including Micah, worked hard to be where you are. If you want to put somebody on to Beta, that's fine. If they express interest, that's fine. But please, please, please be careful. Just because you like them doesn't mean the chapter will vote yes on them. It doesn't mean that they are made for the process.

If you are asking somebody to run you some errands, that's between you and them. Leave Beta out of it."

"Aaron," I said. "Like…I understand all that you're saying. We've all read the Beta manual over and over again. So, I don't think you have to worry about us following the rules – or really, knowing how exactly to break them without getting caught. But…say a dude is interested in the frat. When can we invite him to projects and stuff?"

"Whenever you want to," Aaron said. "Everything but meetings and pledging is open to the public. By all means, tell them to come, so we can get to know them as well. That's how we met most of y'all."

"But leave your faggot friends at home," Jamal said out of nowhere. "God knows Sigma Chapter can't afford another mistake."

"Excuse me?!" I said sharply. "What the hell are you talking about, Frat?"

"Don't call me your frat," Jamal said.

"Gentlemen, settle down," Aaron said.

"Naw, fuck that, we're speaking off the record," Jamal said, standing up. "I'm gonna say what's on my mind. Aaron…you, me, and Tommy all know that Sigma Chapter made a mistake in letting Adrian cross, but you're too afraid to say it. Sigma Chapter has never pledged a faggot before, and I am sickened when I realize our line helped let that shit happen."

The entire room was as silent as a crypt. Nobody could believe what they were hearing, except me.

"Jamal…" I said. "Don't do this."

"Don't do what, Adrian?" He looked at me dead in my eyes, the first time he had done so since the night he tried to beat the life out of me. "You should have dropped that night me and Craig found out your dirty little secret. Too bad your Dean was too much of a bitch and let you stay. He was too afraid you might snitch if he let you drop. Try to sue us or something. But I am not afraid of you. I will tell you to your face that your lifestyle is disgusting. You are an abomination to everything we stand for in this fraternity."

"Jamal, you need to sit down," Tommy said.

"Shut up, Tommy," Jamal said. "Your piss poor leadership got us into this mess in the first place. Do you even know where he was last week? Do you know where the campus queer was last Wednesday night?"

"Probably minding his own business, like you need to, Frat," Calen said. "Sit your wack ass down. You're just mad cuz Adrian can pull more bitches than you do."

"Oh, okay Mr. Dumb and Dumber," Jamal shot back. "Do you even remember the founders' names?"

"Jamal, sit down now!" Aaron said sternly.

"He was at a Potomac Pride meeting," Jamal continued. "A big gay meeting for our big gay frat brother."

I threw my middle finger up at him.

"Whatever. Brothers, I am putting it to you now. Either we reign in this renegade now, and shut him up before he can do more damage to this chapter, or we can watch everything we worked for fall apart. Sigma Chapter runs Rock Creek and Potomac. Don't let this fag ruin it."

"You are out of control," I said. "You don't even go to Potomac, how do you know where I was? And yeah, I did go to a Pride meeting, so the fuck what? You know what, Jamal, I have tried and tried with you! You haven't even looked me in the face since I was online. I raise my hand toward you in brotherhood, and you ignore me. Like it or not, we are in the same fraternity, and there's no debating the matter. So suck it up and get over it. We don't have to be friends, but we are brothers. And you need to start acting like it!"

"Fuck you!" Jamal shouted. "You are no frat of mine." A surreal quiet fell over the room as Jamal and I glared at each other for seconds that seemed like weeks. By now, most of the Brothers either cradled their heads in their hands or folded their arms in disbelief.

"Brother President," Mohammed said, breaking the oppressive silence in the room.

"Yes, Mohammed?" Aaron answered.

"I would like to place a motion on the floor," Mo said.

"By all means," he replied.

"I move that Brother Jamal Jackson be put on probation from

the chapter for unbrotherly conduct."

"What?" Jamal screamed. "You foreign little bitch! I made you! How the fuck a neo gonna say I need to be suspended and I'm the only one who remembers what being in a fraternity is supposed to be about?"

"There is a motion on the floor to put Brother Jamal Jackson on probation from Sigma Chapter for unbrotherly conduct," Aaron continued. "Is there a second?"

"Second," Calen said.

"As you all know, the Beta manual states that chapter probation is an automatic thirty days. Is there any discussion on the matter?" Aaron asked.

"I can't believe you wack niggas are even entertaining the motion," Jamal said. The veins in his neck were stretching against his skin.

"Is there any further discussion?" Aaron asked. Silence.

"Hearing none, the motion on the floor is to place Brother Jamal Jackson on probation for unbrotherly conduct. All in favor signify by raising your hand."

Mohammed, Calen, and I were the first to raise our hands. Tommy, Peter, and Ed followed. Six votes for probation.

"All opposed?" Aaron asked. Ciprian raised his hand while Jamal slouched in his chair with his arms folded. The idiot forgot to vote no in his own defense.

"By a vote of six to one, Brother Jamal Jackson is put on probation from Sigma Chapter for thirty days," Aaron announced.

"Yeah, fuck Sigma Chapter," Jamal said. He stood up, overturning his chair and letting it drop to the floor. "Fuck all of y'all, and fuck you Adrian. I'd sooner die than acknowledge you as frat." He bolted out of the room, slamming the door against the wall as he left. Ciprian ran out of the door after him.

"Brothers," Aaron said somberly. "We need to circle up. Come on, hurry up."

We stood up and made a circle of seven people, without Ciprian and Jamal.

"Adrian, I just want to tell you something," Aaron began.

"I don't…I mean, I've never known a gay person before. Ever, in life. Neither has Jamal. Neither have most of us. So…it's hard for us. We don't get it. It's strange for us. But as for me, personally…I'm sorry for what…"

He stopped. His eyes were glassy.

"I'm sorry for what we did to you when you were on line," he said. "We were afraid, man. We were wrong and we never apologized properly."

"Yeah," Tommy said. "It shouldn't have happened, and we should have had more control over Craig and Jamal. It was all just… it was a surprise to all of us. For what it's worth, man…everybody in this circle loves you."

"So do I," Ciprian said. He came into the circle and stood in between Peter and Ed. "Jamal's not coming back, though."

Then, it was Tommy's turn to be filled with emotion. Tommy, Aaron, and Jamal were line brothers, but the time had come for both men to put line loyalty to the side.

"He needed it," Tommy rationalized through silent tears. "He was the renegade one. He got all wrapped up with Craig and just… went in a whole new direction. It's like we don't know him anymore."

Crying was contagious, even among men. We held each other tightly in that huddle for what seemed like hours.

"We can't let this chapter be split apart any further, Brothers," Aaron said. "We are one. Remember our motto, 'let brotherly love continue.' Don't let it stop, men, don't ever let it stop. We've got to love each other like blood. Adrian, be yourself, but be a Beta. Do what you think is right. We're all new to this."

"Thank you, Frat," I said. "Trust me, I'm new to all this as well. But I'm gonna do my best. Hey, let's sing that song we love so well, so we can get out of here."

"Good idea," Aaron said. "This meeting of Sigma Chapter is now adjourned. Let us sing our fraternity hymn."

We sang our beautiful hymn without Jamal. He really didn't come back. I had never been the victim of so much hatred in my life. At the same time, my brothers were there for me. There's something to be said for our pledge process – for us, adversity was a unifying agent.

"We all need to…hang out, or something," Ed said as we made our way back to Potomac, stuffed into his tiny car but still numb from the events of the evening. "Just our line. We need to get back to basics. I don't want what happened to our prophytes to happen to us."

"True," Calen said. "We need to stay tight. We need Micah to come back, too. He really balanced all of us out."

"He still stays in Virginia," I said. "It would be nothing for him to come back. I'll call him this week."

Ed let us off at the front gates. Calen and I bid him farewell and we walked back to Hurley Village. The sun was setting and the campus seemed to be filled with a nice orange glow. It reminded me of when I used to date Savion.

"You okay, frat?" Calen asked. "Don't be too upset about what happened, okay?"

I put on a smile for Calen. "I'll be okay. He's just an asshole. I didn't take what he said to heart."

"Good. I was hoping we wouldn't have a repeat of that night…"

"Yeah. That wasn't a good night."

"I think about that night, Adrian. A lot. I think about the lot of shit we had to do when we were on line."

"Me too."

"Would you do it all again?"

I looked at my LB and shrugged my shoulders. We stopped in front of the entrance to the student center. Calen hugged me, and then gave me the fraternal handshake.

"You not going home?" he asked.

"Naw, not right now. I'll be home soon, though."

"Aight, bro. I'll see you later, then."

I pushed the heavy glass doors of the student center and walked in. Sunday evenings there were quiet. The bookstore was closed, as was the food court. The only people there were studying in the lounges or buying food in the convenience store. I walked toward a stairwell beyond the study lounges. Pushing the doors open, I smelled the stagnant air. I hadn't been up these stairs since the summer.

I walked up two flights and pushed the doors at the top of the stairs. They still opened as easily as they had over the summer. On the other side of the doors was not a roof, but an esplanade. The school had put grass, trees, and benches on top of the student center. The view of the rest of the campus was breathtaking, yet so few people made the journey up the stairs to this secluded spot.

I had missed the sunset. The sky had gone from deep orange to violet, and I couldn't see the sun on the horizon. I walked to the edge of the esplanade, to the waist-high wall. I leaned over and stared beyond the football field, dorms, and parking lots, into the far off houses and apartments, across the Potomac River below.

"Adrian," a voice called. I turned behind me and saw him, reclining on a bench, wearing a white t-shirt and blue windbreaker pants. I walked toward him.

"Hey." I sat close to him.

"What's wrong, boy?" he asked me.

"It was a rough meeting."

"I'm sorry."

"It's not your fault." He put his arm around my shoulder.

"You sure you wanna do that?" I asked.

"Of course."

I sighed. We stared into the night in silence. Occasionally, I would hear the swish of Isaiah's pants as he changed his position. He inched his way closer to me. I let him.

"I knew if I stayed up here long enough, you'd come back eventually," he said.

"Up here? To the esplanade?"

"Yeah...this is where...this is how I found out...this is where a lot of stuff happened."

"Yeah," I said. I put my head on his shoulder, closed my eyes, and remembered.

June 17

I loved working for Professor O'Bannon. She was probably the nicest and most brilliant woman I had ever met. In my fraternity, you had to be endorsed by a faculty member, so Professor O'Bannon was my number one pick. She happily obliged. She had also selected me to assist with some of her research over the summer. I wanted to be where she was, teaching and doing research for social change. I hadn't decided in what area I would do my field work, but I was leaning toward urban minority communities.

During the summer, I brought my photo album to share with her when we had some down time at the department.

"And this was our Probate Show," I said as she slowly turned the pages of the album.

"Oh wow," she said with wonder. "Adrian, is that you? The fourth one?"

"Yup!" I said excitedly. "That's me."

"Wow, you look so…hardcore!" she exclaimed. We laughed. Professor O'Bannon was in her late thirties. She had a husband and a young son, whose pictures I always saw displayed prominently on her desk. She was so proper, but could be so fun when she wanted to.

"Okay, so who are all these guys?" she asked politely.

"Well," I began. "That first one is Peter. He goes to Rock Creek. Remember how we have joint chapters?"

"Right, I remember," she said. "He looks like he lifts weights."

"Yeah, he takes pretty good care of himself. The number two is Ciprian. He also goes to Rock Creek."

"What a handsome young man," she said.

"Please don't tell him that," I laughed. "He's a good guy, though. From Atlanta."

"Ciprian is an interesting name," she added.

"Yeah," I said. "He was named for his grandfather's church, New Cyprus. They messed with the spelling, and there you have Ciprian."

"Neat," she said.

"I know. Then we have Micah, who just graduated from

Potomac in May. Did he ever take your classes?"

"I don't think so," she said. "But he does look somewhat familiar. Was he active on campus?"

"He sure was. He was active in the NAACP all four years he was here. Then there's me, then behind me is Mohammed."

"Adrian," Professor O'Bannon said with a hint of astonishment in her voice. "He looks…middle eastern."

"He's Algerian. International student. He goes to Rock Creek."

"So…is he…I mean…"

"What, Professor O'Bannon?"

"Well, you know," she began. "It's an African American fraternity. How does he adjust, not being American and all."

"Hmmm. Well, I can't say it's easy for anybody to adjust to such a uniquely American concept. But, he does okay, I guess."

"Oh, okay," she said. "Just curious."

"The last two guys both go to Potomac," I concluded. "Ed is number six, and Calen is number seven."

"Oh, I know Ed for sure. He's had one of my classes. Very bright young man."

"Definitely," I said. "And Calen and I are going to be housemates in the Fall."

"Wonderful!" she exclaimed. "Another benefit to being in your organization. Well, Adrian, I am definitely glad that I was able to help you become part of such a fine fraternity. I hope that it's everything you want the experience to be. Anytime you all need some help on campus, just let me know."

"Thanks! I appreciate it all, Professor O'Bannon. I definitely couldn't have done it without your help."

"Anytime!" she said, closing my photo album and handing it back to me. "So, are you going to – oh, can I help you?"

Isaiah appeared in the door frame of the office.

"Hey!" I smiled. "What are you doing here?"

"I went to the front desk, and nobody was there, so I just walked around until I found you all…I didn't mean to interrupt your conversation," Isaiah said apologetically.

"Oh, it's quite all right!" Professor O'Bannon stood up to introduce herself. Compared to me and Isaiah, she was an absolute Smurf. "I'm Sally O'Bannon, how are you?"

"Hello, Professor O'Bannon!" Isaiah said brightly. "I'm Isaiah Aiken, Adrian's roommate. He speaks very highly of you!"

"Oh my, I'm so flattered! Wow."

"I don't mean to interrupt," Isaiah repeated.

"Oh no, by all means. Adrian, why don't you go ahead and take your lunch break. See you in about an hour?"

"Sure!" I said. "We can talk about those periodicals from the library when I get back."

I left her small office and went into the hallway with Isaiah. As we walked toward my cubicle, he started laughing softly.

"What's up?" I asked.

"She's a nice lady," he said.

"Yeah, I love her man! She's the coolest." We stopped at my cube and I put my photos back in the drawer. "So, um…what brings you here?"

"Oh, I just wanted to know if you had any plans for lunch," he asked.

"Oh," I said. "No, I don't. What are you trying to do?"

"I dunno, maybe the Faculty Club," he suggested.

"The Faculty Club?" I repeated. "I ain't got no money for no Faculty Club. I thought you were talking about Taco Bell or something."

"Don't worry about it," he said, winking. "I got you."

"What? Man, I can't let you do that."

"Nigga please, let's go." Isaiah walked out of the cube and I had no choice but to follow.

The swanky Faculty Club was located in a quiet corner of the student center. When we got there, I saw that Isaiah and I were grossly underdressed for the ambiance. He had on a Baltimore Ravens football jersey, baggy jeans, and Timberland boots. I was wearing khaki shorts, a red polo shirt, and sandals. There were very few patrons already in the restaurant, so we could see clearly that each table was set with white linen tablecloths, floral centerpieces, and cloth napkins.

"Dude," I whispered. "I don't think we're dressed right for this place."

He looked at me with one eyebrow in the air, as though I had clearly bumped my head and forgotten who he was. The hostess quickly walked up to us.

"Table for two, Mr. Aiken?" she asked.

"Yes, please," he said. We walked past the sign advertising the coat and tie rule of the establishment. I zipped my lips and followed Isaiah's lead.

"Isaiah…how is it that we're able to waltz up in this joint looking like commoners?" I asked after we had been given our menus and the hostess was out of earshot.

"Look at the wall," he said quietly.

I turned to my right to see a wall covered with picture frames. In each frame was a group picture of men in suits in various locations on campus, like the front gates or steps of the library. I looked closer and saw that these were group pictures of the men's basketball team.

"Oh," I said.

"Yeah, coach always brings us here. He likes us to be cultured or some shit," Isaiah explained as he opened his menu.

"I see," I said, opening my menu as well. "Seems like we're both in exclusive fraternities."

Isaiah gave me a puzzled look.

"You know. You play basketball. You get to travel. Get good seats in restaurants. All that."

Isaiah laughed. "It's not all that simple. Yeah, we get good shit sometimes. But you know, I haven't spent a summer at home in years. Most of my Christmas break is here. It's cool to get nice things in exchange for the sacrifice."

"Don't you get a free education?"

"Of course," he said. "Division I, baby. Gotta love those athletic scholarships."

"Maybe some folks think what you miss out on – holidays and summers – is the price you pay for a 'free' education."

"Maybe. I like the way your mind works, boy. You're always

thinking about all the different facets of a situation."

"I guess. When I was a freshman, people said I was argumentative. Militant. Whatever."

"I wouldn't say that. I think you're no more opinionated than anyone else here. That's why I stay pretty quiet in class. I don't like debating with these people."

"Potomac kids are the worst," I said. "Always debating something, anything."

Isaiah silently agreed.

"Good afternoon gentlemen, my name is Sandra!" A middle-aged, but still bubbly blond waitress came to assist us. "Are you ready to order?"

Isaiah looked at me, slightly nodding as if to repeat the woman's question.

"Sure," I said. I was afraid to order. Everything was so expensive! Sensing my indecision, Isaiah chimed in.

"Try the linguine Florentine," he suggested. "It's got shrimp in there."

"Okay," I said. "Linguine Florentine for me, please. And ginger ale to drink."

"I'll take the jumbo crab cakes and a Coke," Isaiah said without hesitation. The waitress took our menus and we waited.

"Thanks for lunch, Isaiah," I said. "I probably would have just gotten some potato chips or something."

"Adrian, don't even mention it, man," he said. "You've been a good roommate so far. And a good person. You deserve a nice lunch."

"Thanks. I need to put on some weight, too. I lost too much this past year.

Isaiah smiled. He really was a good man, too. It was a shame he and Taina weren't as close as I thought they were. I'd always thought they made a good couple.

"How's the summer league going?" I asked.

"Pretty good. It's good practice for us. It reminds me of when I was home in Baltimore. The rec center used to have summer leagues, too. My mom always made sure I went so I could stay out of trouble."

"That's cool," I said. "My mom wasn't into sports. She wanted me in those books so I could get good grades and come to college."

"Mama knew good," Isaiah said.

"I guess, man. I'm just not close to her though. I wish I was. But it just ain't happening."

"It's okay," Isaiah said. "Everything is gonna work out."

"I hope so. Hey, there's supposed to be a Beta Barbecue in a few weeks in Kalorama Park. You wanna come?"

"Sure man, that sounds fun. Is your girl coming?"

"Who, Nina?"

"Yeah, Nina. Your girl."

"I keep telling you man, she is not my girl. She's just my friend."

"And you say she's just a friend," he sang.

"Shut up, she is."

"Aight, aight, I believe you. So…you said you were dating somebody when you were on line for Beta."

"Did I say that?" I said uncomfortably.

"Yeah, you did." he said. "What was she like?"

"Oh, you don't know her."

"Well I didn't say I knew her, just want to know what she's like."

"Why do you wanna know that?"

"I dunno, I just want to see what kind of person can keep up with Adrian Collins, that's all."

"I don't know. Maybe nobody can keep up with me. Maybe that's why I'm single."

"Damn, so you saying ain't no girl out there that can keep up with you?"

"I don't mean it like that, man. I mean, everybody's got issues, and maybe mine are too much for most people to deal with."

"There's somebody out there for everyone. You might get the wrong ones the first couple times, but you'll find the right one."

"Yeah, I guess. And even when we think we have the right one, maybe the match wasn't really there at all."

"No doubt," Isaiah said. "I can relate to that."

Luckily, our food came quickly and the conversation shifted to more frivolous topics: hip-hop, sports, and the weather. I did my best to avoid questions involving women. I didn't want to have to knowingly lie to Isaiah, but I didn't think I was ready to come out to him, either. It was hard. Isaiah was as friendly as he was handsome. I hated not being truthful with him. It was like lying to my line brothers all over again. God, why couldn't I learn a lesson the first time around? Look at how much I had given up to hide my secret before - look at how much I had lost when it was finally revealed. I couldn't risk my friendship with Isaiah by continuing to hide. If he was to be as close to me as Nina was, he had to know.

We reached a lull in our conversation as I pondered what I should do.

"Hey," he said as I scraped the remaining bit of pasta from my bowl.

"Yeah?" I asked.

"You got some sauce right here" he said, pointing to the left side of his chin. I picked up my cloth napkin and dabbed at the left side of my own chin.

"No, other side," he said.

"Oh," I said, and then wiped the right side.

"Naw, you missed it. Here, I got it." He leaned forward with his own napkin and wiped the dot of sauce from the edge of my lip. We locked eyes and I froze.

"There you go," he said, smiling. "It's gone."

"Thanks," I said, averting my eyes in shame. I felt like Isaiah and I shared a certain intimacy that perhaps we shouldn't have. He was so calm, so sure. He couldn't have known that I was gay. At the same time, I couldn't figure out why he had done that. He couldn't possibly always be so…close with his other friends.

"What's wrong?" he asked.

"Isaiah…I think maybe there's something you should know… about who I dated."

"Okay," Isaiah said. He put his napkin on the table and leaned in closer to hear what I had to say.

"I don't really have a perfect way to say this, man." I paused.

He stared intently into my eyes.

"The reason I don't talk about…relationships and stuff. Well…like, you know how you and Taina – no, not like you and Taina, more like… I mean, I'm trying to say I don't…like…girls. Like that."

"What?" Isaiah asked. "Dude, what are you trying to say?"

"I'm…not…heterosexual," I said.

Isaiah blinked.

"So, you're gay," he said.

"Yeah," I said. "I'm gay."

For the first time that summer, Isaiah averted his gaze.

"Oh," he said. He coolly picked up his Coke and sipped it until it was gone. He clanged the ice around in his glass a few times, titled the glass back, and crunched on a few ice chips.

"Are you okay with that?" I asked. He looked at me.

"Mmm-hmm," he uttered, not even looking at me. I felt something deep inside me fall away. Something wasn't the same. I shouldn't have told him.

"Would you like dessert?" Our waitress asked as she suddenly appeared.

"No, thank you," Isaiah said without even looking in my direction. "We'll take the check."

I glared at Isaiah, to no avail. He might not agree with my life, but he didn't have to be rude.

"Is something wrong?" I asked. "I mean-"

"No," he said sharply. "Everything is fine."

"I-"

"I'm just surprised, that's all," he added.

"Okay," I said.

"Not trying to be rude," he said. "But you've got to get back to work soon. So we need to skip desert."

"Yeah, you're right," I said as the waitress came back. She handed Adrian the check and began to depart.

"No, wait," he said. "We're in a hurry, here you go." He handed her a few twenties and told her to keep the change.

"Let's go," he said. He stood up and began to walk quickly out of the restaurant. I could barely keep up with his huge strides. We were soon in the wide hallway of the student center. Isaiah seemed intent on leaving me behind. I struggled to catch up to him. All of a sudden, halfway down the hall, he stopped and turned around. I stopped short to avoid running right into him.

"These doors…" he said, motioning to a pair of large double doors, leading to a stairwell. He was struggling to find the words. I just looked at him and waited until he finally asked "Do you have time for me to show you something?"

I waited until he looked at me.

"Sure," I responded.

He pushed the doors, which emitted a metallic screech as they opened. I was hit with a wave of air that had been stagnant until the doors were opened. It was old, musty air that had not moved in hours, perhaps. Isaiah began walking up the stairs, and I followed his purple jersey and blue jeans closely behind. The only noise made was the sound of his Timbs and my sandals on the concrete of the steps.

Two flights later, we were as high as the stairs would take us.

"Adrian," Isaiah began, slowly enunciating every syllable of my name. "I've got something I want to say, too. Come with me."

He flung open the door and let me walk through first. What I saw was nothing out of the ordinary: it was just the esplanade on top of the bookstore, little used because nobody ever felt like walking up the stairs to see it. It was a green, grassy area bounded by red brick, and dotted with a handful of trees and benches.

"Come on," he said. I followed him as he walked toward the edge of the esplanade, where a brick wall safely kept visitors from falling over the edge. We both stared out over the campus, watching people slowly come and go. You could see over half of the campus from this vantage point.

"Adrian…man…" Isaiah began, "I don't care that you're gay."

"For real?" I asked softly.

"Of course not, man. I didn't mean to be a jerk before. I'm just shocked as hell, man. Nobody's ever really, like, showed me that kind of trust before. You know what I'm sayin'?"

I nodded. "Yeah."

"Adrian, you are a good person. I have always – and I mean always – had the utmost respect for you, even when we were freshmen. You were always everything I wanted to be, but couldn't be. You got to do everything you wanted. You see all this, man? All these dorms and buildings and people? You run this school, man."

"Wow. I wouldn't say all that, but I do appreciate it, for real."

"Man, you just don't understand," he continued. "It's like these past two years I wished I could have a friend like you. And now, for some reason, we got to be roommates. And every day, I learn something else about you that makes me like – that makes me respect you even more. As a man. As a black man. As a friend. You feel me, dawg?"

"Yeah," I said. "I feel you."

"I brought you up here because it's the only thing I could think of to give you in return. This right here…this is my refuge. This is where I go when shit pisses me off so bad that I just have to get away. Nobody knows that I go here. Not even Taina. It's not private, but it's my special place. That bench over there, see it? That's my bench. I sit over there and I think. I've spent entire nights here sometimes. Adrian, I wanted to show you this place because it's all I've got to give. You've shown me your most private side, and I wanted to show you mine."

"Isaiah, I don't even know what to say, man. Thank you so much, for real. I didn't expect you to say all this, and I definitely didn't expect you to buy me lunch. I really appreciate it man. I do. I feel better now that you know. I've been feeling like, you know, like you haven't been able to really see who I am. You never know how somebody is gonna react to something like this. I've had people damn near kill me for who I am. So every time I say something, it's a gamble. But man, you just don't know…I really do appreciate you saying all that."

"And now, I really do see you, man," Isaiah said. "And that's dope as hell. Thanks man."

Isaiah extended his hand to me. I grabbed his hand back and shook it; he drew me into his embrace. A weight had been lifted from my shoulders, finally. Now that Isaiah knew, my guard could be down around him. I could share any and all aspects of my life with him if I wanted to. He could see the real me, a side that only Nina and Savion had seen before. I was ready for a new friend, someone else to trust, to respect, to love. I was happy to know him, to befriend someone I didn't have to befriend due to circumstance; someone I had chosen as a friend and had chosen me in return.

After a few seconds, I was ready to end our embrace, but Isaiah still held on tight. Isaiah was different. Now that the veil had been lifted, he could truly see me, and hopefully, I would truly see him.

"Aight, let's get you back to work, man," he said with a smile as he let me go from his embrace. We started walking back toward the stairwell, past his bench. "And now you know where to find me if there's ever a time you need me. If you can't find me anywhere else, by phone or by email…if I'm not in my room, you can bet that I'm right up here, thinking. Adrian, you my dawg. Aight?"

"Cool," I said. "No doubt."

October 9

"You nervous?" Aaron asked me. We were all seated in a hallway behind Grayson Hall, a large auditorium at Potomac. We were dressed identically – not how we had to dress while pledging, but in nice black slacks and burgundy button-down shirts.

"Yeah," I said. This was our first step show as a chapter since we neos had crossed. Our probate show was a little different – that was something we had to do. This Homecoming Step Show is something we wanted to do, and hopefully win. First prize was a thousand dollars for the chapter. We needed that money desperately for our programs and service projects. If we didn't win this money, we would most likely have to keep coming out of pocket for our expenses.

We had practiced for this show ever since our first chapter meeting of the year. Since it was a Homecoming show, only the organizations with members on campus were allowed to participate: us, the Alphas, the Kappas, and Lambda Upsilon Lambda for the fraternities; the AKAs, Deltas, and Lambda Phi Chis for the ladies. It was anybody's guess as to who would bring home the trophy.

Although it felt different to step with people who didn't pledge with me, I saw it as way to bond with the men who had made us Betas. It was also weird that not all of my line brothers would be stepping with us. Micah, of course, had graduated. Calen couldn't make step practice because of his football schedule. And Mohammed…well, stepping wasn't really his thing. He would be helping us with the music. The pressure was on for the six of us to obliterate the competition.

"Don't be nervous," Aaron said. "It'll be fun."

We made sure to invite all of the Betas from the metropolitan area to support us. This spirit of competition kept all of the organizations on their toes. If nothing else, if people didn't know you for your service projects or your programs, you had to come correct at a step show. Especially on your own turf.

Aaron and I snuck around to the wings of the stage to size up our competition. On stage were the Kappas, wearing cream suits and crimson shirts. I had to admit, they did look good. Setting everything off were their trademark red and white canes. While Aaron focused on the precision taps and clacks of the Kappa canes, I slowly scanned the audience to see if all of my guests had made it. Close to the front row, I saw Nina, smiling. No matter what letters they wore, Nina loved her some men. Hopefully, now that people were slowly, really believing that we were in fact not a couple, her prospects might actually improve.

Nina sat with Morris, Cat, and Samirah. We were all becoming a close-knit crew in the weeks since the Potomac Pride meeting. I wasn't sure at first how Nina might feel being around lesbians, but to my surprise she had no problems being around them. "More men for me," she said.

I scanned the mezzanine of Grayson Hall as well. I saw a mass of burgundy and gold and knew that I had found the Beta section. They seemed to be bored by the Kappas, but that was to be expected. We weren't exactly known for being supportive of our fellow fraternities. We were indifferent at best and combative at worst.

I saw Isaiah sitting with his basketball teammates. Isaiah was different when he was with them. The quiet one. He, too, looked bored. I knew that in his heart, he was probably only there to see me.

As the Kappas ended their routine, the crowd gave them a rousing round of applause. Judging by Nina's face, it was well deserved.

"Dude," Aaron said, pulling me backstage. "They didn't drop their canes one single time!"

"Are you shitting me?" I said. "Damn."

We were up against stiff competition indeed. A flawless Kappa routine was a tough thing to beat. The AKAs took the stage next, and the Betas lined up in the hallway.

"Hey, let's pray," Peter said. Mohammed and Calen were already at the sound booth, so just the six steppers remained. We made a circle and held hands. As we prayed, we heard the cacophony of skee-wees, the call of AKAs nationwide. No sooner than we were done praying, it seemed like the AKAs were already passing us in the hallway and wishing us luck.

"Come on up," the stage manager told us. We walked through the doors and waited in the wings.

"And now, ladies and gentlemen, I would like to introduce you to the Sadistic Sigma Chapter of Beta Chi Phi Fraternity, Innnnnncorporated!"

The stage went dark. The six of us held onto the shoulders of the brother in front of us as we inched out on stage in the darkness.

"B…C…P!" Peter shouted. We instantly locked our arms together and held our heads to the sky as we did when pledging.

The stage lights came on and the audience saw us in our severe pledge stance. I saw nothing but ceiling, but I could feel the energy of the audience as they screamed for us. After five seconds, our music began to play. The montage began with a reggae song that everyone was familiar with. After four counts, we began to lock step to the rhythm of the music. The crowd loved it. We brought our line from the back of the stage to a straight line facing the audience. Our music then blended seamlessly to a hip-hop song. In four counts, we unlocked our arms and made space in between ourselves. We then began our signature "party walk" – a unified step that we performed in one single file line at parties. We strolled from our line to our positions on stage. I moved swiftly across the stage, stomping my feet and flailing my arms in time with the music and in perfect precision with my brothers.

When the music stopped, the crowd roared once more. We stood still with the "Beta Grill" on our faces, that unmistakable grimace that conveyed our seriousness to the audience. Over the howls, I could hear a solitary: "I see you, Adrian!" I had learned long ago not to smile or smirk when wearing my Beta Grill, even though Nina's scream of approval was appreciated.

We had formed three rows of two with Peter and myself making up the front row. He began the first step slowly, and the rest of us came in right on time. Stepping didn't come easy to most of us, but with practice, we usually got all our steps down pat. After we cycled through the first step once, we repeated it with a chant:

> *We…are…the…mighty Betas…*
> *And we…can't…be…stopped.*

And if you try to step to us
You're gonna get, get, get…get rocked.

That step immediately transitioned into another step, one that was much more complicated and crowd pleasing. The Kappas had a higher degree of difficulty in their steps, which would add points to their final score. Since we usually preferred not to utilize props in our routines, we had to make every step count.

In our new position, we were two rows of three. We ended our first step in our fraternal hand sign and waited for Tommy to step out and give his monologue.

"Ladies and gentlemen, the Brothers of Sigma Chapter, Beta Chi Phi Fraternity, Incorporated, welcome you to our house. Beta Chi Phi was established in 1970 at Boston University by five strong and dedicated black and Latino men. Sigma Chapter performs many community service projects and implements programs to benefit all minority communities here at Potomac University and Rock Creek College.

"Tonight, we want you to sit back and relax, but pay attention to the message we are sending tonight. Being in a fraternity is not about stepping, hand signs, and parties. It's about brotherhood, service, academics, leadership. But y'all might not hear me. Do y'all hear me?"

The crowd uttered an adequate "Yeah."

"Man, Adrian, they don't hear me," Tommy said while taking his place back in line. "Why don't you tell them what we're about?"

I stepped to the front of the stage and looked out at the audience.

"I…never shall cry…" I sang, in the tune of "I Know I Been Changed." "I…never shall cry. I…never shall cry, cuz I'm a Beta Chi Phi until the day I die. Sing Brothers…" The brothers repeated the verse with me as I walked slowly back to my place in line.

We stomped a slow, steady beat to match the somber mood of the song. After we sang the first verse, we began a second, and added sharp hand movements and claps. This was possibly one of our best steps. Although it was simple in rhythm, it was fraught with emotion. We had to convey to the judges that we intended on winning the show.

When that step ended, we immediately picked up the pace with one of our most complex steps. We had learned it from Jamal before he left the chapter. He had been our chapter step master, but Ciprian had stepped up to the challenge in his absence.

Our fast and furious step ended with all of us in a straight line at the front of the stage.

"Brothers!" Ed shouted.

"Yeah?" we replied.

"Brothers!" he repeated.

"Yeah?" we said.

"Let's give the ladies what they came for!"

Each of us smiled, as was part of the routine. The music began, and in keeping with our roots, it was a popular Latin beat. We began an improvised merengue on stage as we unbuttoned our burgundy shirts to the waist. Underneath, we each wore gold sleeveless t-shirts. The ladies in the audience screamed in approval. As I made eye contact, I saw all my friends clapping and shouting in approval. I looked up into the mezzanine and saw Isaiah sitting still, but smirking. I smiled, removed my burgundy shirt completely, threw it to the side, and quickly took my place for our final step.

We were now all just wearing the gold t-shirts. Luckily, about a million push-ups a day ensured that we were toned enough to pull off such a move. The audience was still rumbling even though the music was long over. Ciprian started off our final step, an extremely complicated set of stomps and claps that involved clapping underneath our own legs as well as the leg of the brother next to us. It also had a special twist on the end that we had practiced endlessly for weeks.

When it came time for the twist, me, Ciprian, and Aaron were supposed to leap into the air and Ed, Tommy, and Peter would place us onto their shoulders.

We nailed it. It was scary, but I hid my fear as I performed the hand motions of the step while Tommy performed the stomps. The crowd went wild, and every Beta in the audience was on his feet. We ended our performance with every man's arms fixed in the fraternity sign, the Beta Grill back on our faces.

The lights went out and amid the roar of the audience, we ran backstage.

"Oh my God, y'all, that was so tight!" Ciprian exclaimed.

"Hell yeah, man!" Peter said. "You hear that?"

We paused and listened. The crowd was still applauding.

"Yo man, we might have won the whole thing," I said. We walked past the Alphas who had yet to perform. They were a rag-tag looking bunch.

"Hmm," I said. "Good luck, gentlemen."

"Thanks," one of them said sharply. The rest just ignored me.

"You're such a bitch," Ciprian laughed.

We sat in the audience after our performance, there being only limited space backstage. Our brothers had saved us seats among them, and I sat next to Micah, my line brother who had graduated soon after we crossed.

"What's up man?" I asked. "Long time, no see!"

"Yo man, y'all were so fuckin good!" he said. "Man, I wish I coulda been down there!"

"Man, no you don't…you know how much we had to practice? That's shit's for tha birds!"

We laughed, but we couldn't talk too much since other teams were performing.

"Did you see my father," I asked Micah quietly.

"Naw, I haven't seen him," he replied.

"I didn't see him from the stage," I said.

"How are y'all doing?" he asked.

"Eh," I said. "Something is better than nothing, I guess."

"I feel you," he said.

Soon, it was time for the team to take the stage and receive whatever prize we were owed. Each fraternity and sorority stood in a single file line, still dressed in whatever they had worn to perform in. We stood between the Kappas and the Alphas, and the LULs stood next to the Alphas.

They gave out the sorority prizes first and the Deltas won. For the fraternities, the Alphas came in fourth, to no great surprise to those who had seen their routine. The LULs came in a respectable third.

"In second place," the hostess began.

We were wound up tighter than a pledge on Hell Night.

"In second place," the hostess repeated, "is Kappa Alpha Psi Fraternity! First place goes to the Betas!"

We were elated and astonished. The Kappas were just astonished. Like gentlemen, we shook their hands as they accepted their trophies. They had really given a great show, and we almost didn't understand how we had beaten them. But who cared? We won, and that was way more important than figuring out the points.

All six of us went to the front of the stage to claim our trophy and our check, amid much shouting of our fraternity call and cheers from the audience. All the rest of the Betas in the audience rushed the stage as the remaining organizations cleared it. Every brother there was full of the same energy, even those who had never met us.

Spontaneously, we broke out into Beta chants and strolls, as though this were a Friday afternoon on the quad. It was a sight to behold, fifty men in burgundy and gold. As we chanted and walked around this circle, I noticed a man in his fifties wearing an old burgundy coaches' jacket. Beyond the gray beard and belly, I could see who he was.

My father.

I ran across the circle so that I could chant next to him.

"What's up, dad?" I gripped the man as he beamed at me.

"Good job, son," he said. "I was sitting near the back on the lower level."

"Thanks for coming," I said. We continued to chant and sing for a while. Finally, we made our circle tight and sang our hymn. Once it was over we finally began to disperse.

"After party at Adrian and Calen's!" I heard somebody yell.

"What?" I said. No one heard me. My dad had his arm around my shoulder and he was still beaming. We walked to the stage stairs, where we were approached by my friends.

"You were so good, Adrian!" Nina said.

She, Cat, and Samirah gave me a group hug.

"Thanks," I laughed. "Are y'all coming to the after party? Apparently, it's at my house."

"No doubt" Nina said. "You know I am, I dunno about these guys."

"Oh, hell yeah," Cat said. "You know I got to hear some good hip-hop before I go to bed!"

We all laughed.

"Hi, Mr. Collins," Nina said, shaking my father's hand.

"Hello, Nina," he said.

"Dad, these are my friends, too," I said. "That's Morris, and this is Samirah and Cat."

"Nice meeting you," he said. They smiled and nodded in agreement.

"Adrian, I'm gonna get back on the road," my father said. "But I wanted you to have this before I left." He took off his jacket and gave it to me.

"What?" I asked.

"It's yours," he said. "Keep it."

My mouth fell open. Giving someone your paraphernalia was seen as the ultimate gift in my fraternity, especially when it was your crossing jacket.

"Thanks, dad," I said while giving him a hug.

"Awwwww!" Nina said. "Stay right there, I'ma take a picture."

"Put the jacket on!" Morris said. I slid it onto my arms one at a time. It felt...historical. My dad had been a charter member of Delta Chapter twenty-five years go. This jacket was older than I was!

We smiled like we were both neos as Nina flashed the camera. Right before she snapped, I noticed Isaiah standing in the aisle about ten feet away, taking the scene in, but not participating.

"Alright, dad...be safe." I said. "And thanks."

"Anytime, son," he said. He leaned in and whispered in my ear "There's something in the pocket for you."

I reached into the pocket and felt the familiarity of a folded up piece of paper. I knew exactly what it was.

"Thanks," I said. My father nodded and walked away.

"I guess we should let you go get ready for the party," Samirah said.

"Yeah," Morris said. "I'm trying to go all the way in tonight."

I hugged all of my friends one last time as they filed out of the auditorium. Isaiah walked slowly toward me, with that same smirk on his face. His eyes got wide for a second, and then I felt someone large behind me grab me and put me in a headlock.

"Good job, frat!" Calen said. His mood, as usual, was very jovial. I wrestled my way out of his headlock and grabbed onto his waist, as though it would do any good. Wrestling Calen was like wrestling a tree. We play fought for another moment, and then gave up.

"I'm out playa," Calen said. "The boys are getting the house ready."

"The boys?" I repeated.

"Yeah man…the boys."

"Oh!" I said. "The boys. Okay then, I'll see you there in a little bit."

Finally, Isaiah and I were alone. Well, as alone as we could be with the bustle of the step show winding down.

"That's a really nice jacket, Adrian," he said. "I saw your pops give it to you."

"Thanks…I totally didn't expect it," I said.

"I could tell," he said.

"Where's Taina?" I asked.

"I don't know," he said. "I don't care."

I sighed.

"What?" he asked.

"Nothing," I said.

"Adrian, you know I gotta do this on my own time, aight? Just like you gotta handle your business on your time. Just be patient. You know I ain't going nowhere."

"Yeah," I said. "I know."

"Aight then…" he said. "Yo, let's go to your crib. I'm trying to get my party on, too."

He smiled. I smiled back.

"Aight…let's go." I walked with him out the door. I turned back to face the stage one more time.

"You did good," Isaiah said. "Real good."

July 3

It looked like rain.

We sat on the curb in front of the school like three orphans, waiting on Micah to pick us up and take us to the Beta Barbecue. It wasn't very warm outside, and the sky was overcast. On my left was Isaiah, our blue-jeaned legs just barely touching each other as we sat. On my right was Nina, silently resting her head on my shoulder as we waited.

"For all this, we could have walked to Kalorama Park," I said. "It's not that far away."

Nina grumbled.

"It's okay, dude," Isaiah said. "Ain't your fault your line brother's an hour late picking us up."

I frowned. "Yeah, I know. I'm sorry anyhow."

We waited some more.

"It'll still be going on when we get there," Nina said. "I mean, it won't be over until dark."

"Yeah," I said.

It was about four o'clock and we were hungry for some good summertime barbecue, hot dogs, watermelon – anything at this point. Micah was never late normally, so I knew he had a good excuse.

"Here he comes," Nina said, noticing his car rounding the bend. He was smiling. As he pulled up to the curb, we barely waited for the car to stop before we got in. Isaiah opened the back door for Nina and I got in front.

"Dude," I began.

"I know, I know," Micah said, smiling wide. "I am so sorry, frat. Traffic was so bad getting across the 14th Street Bridge. But we on our way now, aight? Don't be mad."

I rolled my eyes and smirked. Micah said his hellos to Nina and Isaiah and they made small talk.

"Are you okay?" Micah asked me softly as we neared the park. "You're kinda quiet."

"I think so," I said.

"Not feeling well?" he asked.

"I feel fine," I said. "It's just…something doesn't feel right. But I'll be fine."

He raised his eyebrow at me but kept his eyes on the road. We were at Kalorama Park, in a quiet neighborhood in DC, within fifteen minutes. Miraculously, we found a parking space right at the park's edge. We hopped out of the car and walked a short path up the hill toward the center.

As urban parks went, Kalorama was nice. It was bounded on all sides by palatial homes and elegant apartment buildings, but even with the surrounding architecture, the park was large. As we topped the hill, we saw a small sea of burgundy and gold clustered around a few picnic tables. Even more people lingered under a shelter. The sky was still overcast, but at least we would be dry if it rained.

I still didn't feel right. It wasn't the weather and it wasn't my health. I felt off. I almost felt like something was about to go down, like that prickling you get in the back of your neck right before a fight. I tried to ignore the feeling as we walked down the path toward the benches.

I could see a few brothers I recognized approaching us from the main event. They threw our signs in the air and emitted a low "B-Chi." Micah and I raised our signs in response, bellowing "Chi Phi."

It was my Dean, Steven, who had just graduated. He was with one of our brothers from Philadelphia, whom I had met when I was pledging. His name escaped me, but I didn't want to tell him I had forgotten it.

"What's up, baby boy?" Steven said. We hugged and gripped each other tightly.

"I'm glad you could come down for this, Steven," I said.

"Man, I would not miss this for the world," he said. "I've been to every one since I crossed."

As I greeted our Philly brother, Isaiah and Nina reacquainted themselves with Steven. They all remembered each other from school. While Philly brother made small talk, my attention was drawn to those picnic tables. There was something down there…from my vantage point, a few brothers were listening intently to one brother. I couldn't make out who any of them were, though. I needed to be down there.

"Excuse me, Brother," I said. I began walking past him.

"Dude, where you going?" Steven called. I heard him, but I couldn't respond. I had to get to those tables.

The sky seemed to turn grayer with every step. My heart was racing but I didn't know why. I had to see what was down there. I felt a hand grab my arm, and I stopped.

"Wait," Steven said.

"Huh?" I snapped out of my trance and saw Steven grabbing my elbow, preventing me from moving.

"Adrian, you're my neo," he began. "Just…wait. It's not gonna go down like this."

"Steven, what are you talking about, I'm just trying to see what's going on down at the tables," I said.

"I know," Steven said. His dreadlocks were getting long, definitely long enough to have back in a ponytail if he wanted, but he still chose to let them fall in his face a little bit.

"Just wait, though," he said. "I'm not going to let it go down like this." Micah appeared next to him.

What was going on? I felt out of it, like everything was a dream.

"Micah," Steven instructed, still sounding like a dutiful dean of pledges, "Take Adrian to that picnic table over there by the edge of the park. I'll be back. Just sit with him."

Micah nodded and led me about fifteen yards away to a grove of trees set apart from the rest of the picnic. I sat down, water welling up in my eyes.

"I know what's happening," I said. Micah said nothing.

"I don't know, frat," Micah said. "I'm just…here…I don't know anything."

Nina and Isaiah walked over toward me, but they were intercepted by one of my line Brothers, Peter, who was already at the picnic but hadn't said hello yet. He guided my friends over to the main area politely. I could tell by their body language that they were confused. Isaiah almost didn't want to move, but he followed Nina's lead. As they walked away, Steven returned. At his side walked a man, a grown man, wearing sunglasses and a big straw hat. The hat had a burgundy band with Beta Chi Phi printed in gold Greek letters. The man was my complexion, but had a full beard. I knew who he was.

I could barely see now. I looked at the ground in hopes that neither Micah nor anyone else could see the tears.

"Are you okay?" Micah whispered. I shook my head.

"You've got to be strong," he whispered sharply. "This is your moment, frat. You can handle this. I know you can."

He touched me on the shoulder and stood next to Steven.

"Adrian," Steven said. I looked up into his eyes. Somehow, I could find strength if I looked hard enough into my Dean's eyes. When I was online, I could gauge whether we would have a good night or a bad night just by glancing into his eyes. His eyes reiterated what Micah had said. I had to be strong.

I stood up, still looking at Micah, and not the man.

"Adrian," he repeated. "This is our Brother…Adam Collins."

I looked at the man's feet first. He wore brown leather sandals. His toenails probably could stand being clipped, but his feet didn't look grotesque or anything. His shins were bare and shiny, as though he applied a healthy coating of lotion on them before leaving the house. He wore plain khaki shorts with stuffed pockets, probably keys and a wallet, who knows. He had a belly that a gold Beta t-shirt angrily stretched around. The screen printing on the shirt was faded – he probably dug deep into his closet for the relic.

Then, I finally looked into his face. I felt as though I was staring into my own future. We resembled each other so much that it was frightening.

His sunglasses were removed and his eyes, too, were watering over.

"Son," he said, voice trembling.

"Hi," I said. I couldn't move. I couldn't be angry or sad. I just stared at him as he stared at me, uncertain what the next move should be.

"We call him Lazarus, Brother Collins," Steven said. "He's my neo. He's a good brother."

"That's good to hear," my father whispered. He slowly raised his arms toward me. All I asked for in over ten years was finally right here in front of me. All my answers, all the love I needed over the years was here. The man I needed all through junior high school and high school was right here. The man that should have pinned me the day I became a Beta was right here, ready to embrace me.

I shouldn't have forgiven him. I should have walked away, back to Micah's car. I should have spat on him for being gone when I needed him the most. I was left with an overbearing mother and a tough world. He made me into what I was by his absence.

But I couldn't ignore the shame and regret that I could see in his eyes. I didn't know this man, but I knew that he was my father. If we were to rebuild our relationship, I had to reach back to him.

I raised my arms and took him into my embrace.

We stood there for seconds, holding each other. We were the same height. He was not the big and majestic man that I remembered. He was just a man.

Micah and Steven slowly walked away and left me and my father alone under the grove of trees.

We let go of each other and wiped the tears from our own eyes.

"Come on, let's sit down," he said. We sat on the opposite sides of the lone table. I faced him, but I could also see the action of the picnic. Isaiah and Nina were being entertained by some of the Sigma chapter brothers.

"So," I began, gaining composure and focus. "Where the hell have you been?"

"Wow," he said. "I'm happy to see you, too, son."

"Yo, cut the bullshit," I said pointedly. "You left us when I was eight years old. I wanna know where the fuck you been at for twelve years."

He frowned.

"Adrian, that's really complicated," he said. "I understand your frustration, but I was hoping we could-"

"Listen, man, if you don't tell me why you abandoned us right now I will leave this fucking picnic."

"Okay…" he said. "Okay."

He folded his hands on the table and began to tell me his story.

"Your mother and I…we loved each other. Very much. But sometimes things just don't work out."

"Dude, I am a grown man," I said. "I know sometimes things just don't work out. Clearly they didn't work out for you and mom. But what is your reason for abandoning us? No contact whatsoever."

"Adrian…I left because your mother asked me to leave. And she asked me to leave because…because I had an affair."

"You had an affair?" I repeated. "With who?"

"A friend from college. Your mom knew her. They weren't friends, but she knew her."

"Damn," I said. "I figured it was something like that."

"She never told you?" he asked.

"No," I said. "She just told me that sometimes…people can't work out their problems. But she never said anything bad about you, not once. I think…I think your absence spoke volumes."

My father deflated in his chair.

"I know," he said. "I know I wasn't a good husband to your mother and I know I wasn't a good father to you. And I apologize for that, Adrian. I do."

"Where were you all those years?" I didn't want to acknowledge his apology right away. I wasn't so sure I could or would forgive him.

"I was ashamed and embarrassed," he said. "I had failed as a husband, so I left town. I thought I could stay with the woman I was having the affair with, but she wouldn't have me. She never…she never really loved me like your mom did. So, I was alone. Alone in New Jersey as a single man, pretty much past his prime."

"So, you played my mom, and then you got played yourself," I said. "I guess there's some justice."

"I…I moved around so much those first few years," he continued, ignoring my verbal assault. "I thought about you all the time. But, I thought I would do more harm to you and your mom if I tried to stay in your life."

"Dude, you did more harm by staying out of my life," I said.

"That's probably the dumbest fuckin' reason I've ever heard for a father being absent. You spent the first eight years of my life with me, then all of a sudden you think you suck as a father, so you leave and don't even say where you are? Do you know how many young, black boys out there need fathers? And you had a son and just left me! You wrote me no letters, no cards, nothing!"

"I thought your mother would move on," he said. "She was still young, still so beautiful."

"Yeah, well she didn't," I said. "She was a single mom struggling to make do with what she had. No child support, no alimony. I think that she basically had a 'fuck-it' mentality and that she didn't need anything of yours to be a good mother. And she was a good mother. I can't say that I agree with her all the time, but at least she was there for me. She was there. Which is a hell of a lot more than I can say for you."

I got up to leave the picnic table.

"Adrian, wait," he said.

"You make me sick, old man," I said. "How dare you show up at this picnic and think everything is going to be okay? I spent the past twelve years without you. Don't you think I can handle my life without you now?"

"I know you don't need me, Adrian," he said. "Please, sit down. Please. If you do walk away, I understand, but I don't want you to leave until we're finished. I don't want you to leave at all."

I sat down again and folded my arms.

"Listen. I fucked up, Adrian. I fucked up bad. I missed the most important years of your life because I ran away from a problem. I shouldn't have left you. I thought I was leaving your mother to raise you in peace, but I was wrong. I should never have left you alone. I was wrong. I apologize, Adrian, and I want to do whatever it takes to make it up to you. That's why I'm here, now."

"I don't understand what you want from me," I said. "It's been twelve years. You ambushed me at this picnic. Is everything supposed to just be okay?"

"I know everything's not going to be okay at first, Adrian, but I want you to know that I care about you. You're my son and I am proud of you. I know I can't teach you anything or show you anything new – you're a grown man. But I want to be there for you now. I don't want you to keep traveling through life thinking I don't care, because I do care. I care, and I love you."

"How can you love me and you don't even know me?"

"I love you because you are my son. I knew you before you knew yourself."

With that, I was silenced. I allowed my father to continue.

"Adrian, I hope you one day know the feeling of being a father. There was nothing in the world like holding your mother's belly and feeling you kick. I'll never forget the day you were born. I even remember the first time you threw up on me. I was a nervous father, and I was never very good at being one. But I loved you just the same. Me skipping out on you…that was foul. But I always thought I was doing you a favor. I thought your mother could do better. I thought any man might be a better step-father than I could be a father. But I know I was wrong. I came back down here to try to make it up to you somehow. I wanted to…I wanted to let you know that over all these years I still love you. When I found out that you had pledged Beta…I knew then I had fucked up. I felt like all this time had passed and now you were my frat brother as well as my son. I knew then…I knew I had to come back to see you."

"I…I almost expected to see you there when they took the blindfold off me…the morning I crossed."

My father looked down at the ground. "I should have been there. I'm sorry."

I looked around me and saw that the throngs of people were still there. Nina emerged from the crowd with two plates of food. I welcomed the break in intensity.

"Hey," Nina said to both of us. "You hungry?"

"Kinda," I said, taking a plate. "Nina…this is my father."

Her eyes opened widely.

"Oh my," she said, extending her free hand. "Pleased to meet you."

"Likewise," he said. "Please, join us."

Nina looked at me first.

"Sure, that will be a good idea," I said to her. "Could you bring Isaiah, too? So he doesn't feel left out."

"Cool," she said. "I'll go get him. Oh, Mr. Collins, do you want some food?"

"No thanks, baby," he said. "I already ate."

As she walked away, I hissed at my father "I really wish you wouldn't call her baby."

"Is she your girlfriend?" he asked.

"No," I replied sharply. "She's just my friend."

"That's how it starts, you know," he said.

"Dad, stop."

"Well, at least you feel like you can call me dad…"

"Don't push it."

Nina was back, with Isaiah in tow, as well as Steven, Micah, and Peter. We all stood up and I properly introduced my father to Isaiah, who looked just as shocked as Nina had. The influx of people created chatter that I needed to prevent me from becoming overwhelmed.

I was upset at my chapter brothers. They had clearly known that my father was already at the picnic and had done nothing to warn me. They thought they were doing the right thing, but it was all wrong. I needed to meet my father on my terms, not theirs. I ate in silence, glancing at my father occasionally. He looked sad, but there was nothing I could do about that. I didn't know how I was supposed to feel.

It finally began to rain, and we were on the outside of the shelter.

"Ah, shit," Steven said. "This sucks. Let's get under there."

Everyone started rushing to the shelter. My father and I stood up and faced each other.

"Come on, Adrian, you're gonna get soaked," he said.

"I…I'm gonna go home," I said.

"Are you sure you want to do that?" he asked.

"Right now, I'm sure," I said. "But…I need a way to contact you."

He hurriedly reached into his pocket and produced a card. Without looking at it, I stuffed it in my pocket so it wouldn't get wet.

"Dad, I really appreciate you coming to see me," I said. "Just… give me some time, okay?"

"I can do that, son," he said. Without waiting, he gave me another hug.

"I'll call you," I said.

"Please do," he replied. He slowly turned around and made his way under the shelter. Nina and Isaiah had hung behind under the trees to wait for me.

"You not staying?" Nina asked.

"Naw, I'm rollin' out," I said. "I can't really deal with all this right now."

"Damn, Adrian, I'm sorry," she said. "Come on, I'll go get Micah."

"Naw," I said. "Don't do that. I want you to stay and have a good time. Okay?"

"No dice, Adrian, I'm rolling with you," she said.

"Nina," Isaiah interrupted. "Why don't you stay here and enjoy yourself. Micah can take you home. I mean, it makes no sense for you to go all the way back to campus when Micah can drop you off at your house. I can take Adrian back to campus."

"But, it's raining," she said.

"We'll catch the bus," he said.

"Yeah," I agreed. "I want you to stay."

"Okay," she said, giving me a hug. "Take care, boo."

As she ran back under the shelter, Isaiah and I began walking through the rain toward the street.

"You ain't gonna say goodbye to your frat?" he asked.

"Naw man…I gotta get out of there." We got to the pavement and just began walking. We weren't that far from a main avenue, so we just walked briskly down the street, past some elegant apartment buildings and houses. The rain started to lighten up a bit, and by the time we got to Columbia Road, it had stopped entirely.

"Ain't that a bitch?" I mused. Isaiah simply laughed.

We caught the bus home, mostly in silence. Once we got back to campus, Isaiah broke the ice.

"I've got an idea," he said. "How about we order some Chinese food and watch *Friday* or something? I think…well, maybe…it might be nice to just chill out tonight, you know? Just unwind and not even think about everything."

"I think that's a good idea," I said quietly. "I'd like that a lot."

And that's just what we did. Isaiah didn't know it, but all I truly needed was some time to do nothing, to say nothing, but just unwind. Have no worries. I let Isaiah order the food while I took a shower and let the hot water massage my back.

Much later in the evening, when our bellies had had enough lo mein and sesame chicken, Isaiah slid in the disc into the player and we both sat on my bed to watch the movie. I was comfortable in his company, feeling protected by him sitting near me on my bed. He was becoming a good friend to me, evidenced by how in synch he was with my feelings at any given moment. He was like another Nina to me, only male.

Before *Friday* had finished, the comfort of Isaiah's friendship had lulled me to sleep. The next morning, I woke to see that Isaiah and I had not moved all night, our bodies still wearing the previous day's clothes, and the television screen shining a simple, blue screen.

October 14

"Girl, why don't you just tell her?"

Samirah and I ran into each other late one night at the deli near East Campus. We were enjoying a leisurely stroll when she finally revealed to me the crush that she had on Cat.

"Adrian, I don't think I can do that," she said. "I mean, we're friends. That would be like Nina trying to holla at you all of a sudden."

"That's different, though," I said. "There's no chance of me and Nina hooking up. With you and Cat, there's always the possibility. I mean, who knows? Don't they say all great love affairs start off as friendships?"

"So they say," Samirah said.

"Don't be afraid," I continued. "You and Cat are both cool people. I'm sure she won't freak out if you tell her."

"I guess," she said. "I might have to keep this one inside for a little longer, Adrian. I think I value our friendship too much to try to pursue something with her."

"I feel that," I said.

We had walked about halfway across campus by this point, passing by the statue of St. Ignatius. The campus was never illuminated well enough for my taste, but at least we weren't in a high-crime neighborhood. Potomac was one of the wealthiest neighborhoods in DC, and the residents made sure that the rest of the city stayed as far away as possible. There was no subway station in the neighborhood, and the century-old trolley tracks remained in the ground, making many of the roads difficult for cars to pass through. The neighbors had somehow made the entire neighborhood declared a historical landmark, so by law, the trolley tracks had to remain. This was a good way to keep the neighborhood exactly how the neighbors wanted.

"I know somebody who has a crush on you," Samirah said with a sing-song voice.

"Who?" I demanded, smiling all the while.

"I'm not telling you," she said coyly.

"Well, that's fine," I joked. "It's not like I'm getting any anyway."

"Okay, I'll tell you," she relented. "It's Morris."

"Morris?!" I exclaimed. "Are you serious?"

She nodded her head excitedly.

"Wow," I said. "He sure doesn't act like it!"

"He's shy," she explained. "But he just thinks you're the best thing since Wonder Bread."

"That's really nice to hear."

"So…what do you think?"

"About Morris?"

"Yeah."

"He's a nice guy, but I guess I don't know him well enough to really think of him in that way."

"Would you go on a date with him?" she asked hopefully.

Morris was a nice kid. Although he was two years younger than me, that wasn't a problem, as Savion and I had also been two years apart in age. Morris was out, proud, and handsome. I never thought about him sexually, though. There was too much going on in my head to seriously give dating anyone more than a passing thought.

"Samirah, he's nice. But…I can't date anyone right now."

"Oh, are you seeing somebody else?" she asked.

"No. I'm just not where I need to be yet, mentally. I mean, I just got out of a relationship."

"Adrian…you broke up with Savion last April. It's October."

"I know. But still…I know that I got a lot of growing to do before I can move on. Plus, there've been other things going on…I've just got to take inventory, you know?"

"Yeah, I guess I can see where you're coming from," she said. We stopped walking where the path to Hurley Village diverged from the path to the Student Center.

"I wish you'd think about Morris, though," she pleaded one last time. "He's a really good guy."

"I appreciate it, girl. And maybe I will think about it – when I'm ready to be on that level with somebody again. But for now, we both need to go study! We ain't in college to be chit-chattin' at all hours of the night."

She hugged me tightly.

"Aight, boo," she said. "Go get your study on!" She walked toward the student center stairs.

Instead of taking the red brick path through the Hurley Village courtyard, I decided to walk around the outer buildings. I could still access my building since it was near the back of the complex. I just felt like doing something different.

I stepped off of the brick and onto the grass, walking slightly up a hill. To my left was the first low-rise building, to my right, a long fence separating my path from the lacrosse field. Walking this path reminded me of being deep in the country, when I used to visit my grandmother in North Carolina. If I didn't look to my left, all I could see was grass and trees. I walked slowly, taking in the scene, thinking about nothing in particular, stopping briefly to stare out deeper into the darkness. The bright lights of the city struggled to escape from behind the dense trees on the far side of the field.

"Yo."

I gasped and jumped back, turning to face the voice that accosted me. I saw a hooded figure in the darkness, but I couldn't make out his face.

"What?" I asked. "Who are you?"

He slowly lowered his hood from his head. It was the same hateful frat brother of mine, Jamal.

"Jamal, man, what do you want?" I asked.

"I came to talk to you," he said. "I saw you talking with that bull dyke and I followed you back here. Look man, you know it's your fault I got kicked out the chapter."

"Jamal, man, first of all, you didn't get kicked out, you got put on probation. Second of all, that shit's not my fault, that's your fault. You can't go around talking to people any kinda way."

"Man, fuck that, Adrian," Jamal said, inching closer to me. "If I can't be in the chapter, then you don't need to be in the chapter either. Simple as that."

"Jamal, let me tell you something. I pledged hard to be a Beta, just like you did. And I will not walk away from Sigma chapter just because you tell me to. Now, we can either walk into that chapter meeting like brothers, or we can walk in there like enemies. But if you want to be in the chapter, I'm not the one stopping you. Aight?"

I turned around and began to continue walking toward my apartment. In the next heartbeat, I heard three short footsteps pound the grass, and then I felt a sharp blow to my shoulder, knocking me off balance.

That bastard hit me. I stumbled to one knee, and while I tried to turn around, Jamal's fists kept coming down hard on my body. Somehow, I was able to elbow him to the jaw. As he held his face and stumbled back, I was able to stand up, shed my book bag, and face him with my fists up.

"Aw hell naw, mufucka." He came at me again like a madman, but this time I was prepared. I deflected each swing he tried to land. I didn't want to hurt him. Deep down inside, as much as he hated me, I really didn't want to harm my brother.

One of his blows finally landed right on my cheek. With that, I said to hell with brotherhood and intended to do as much damage to him as possible, at least enough to slow him down so I could get to safety. I was convinced he would kill me if I gave him a chance.

I jabbed at his face and landed one square on his chin. I swung my left arm up toward his torso, driving my fist deep into his gut, just as he had when I was his victim the previous spring.

He grunted in pain and began to cough.

"Damn, Adrian," he panted. "Damn. I ain't know you had it like that."

"Get out of here, Jamal," I spat. "Go back to Rock Creek and leave me the fuck alone."

"Aight, nigga," he said. "You got it."

He straightened out his black hoodie and coughed once more. This time, I wouldn't let him out of my sight until he left. He extended his hand to me.

"Come on, Adrian," he said. "Don't leave me hanging. Let's squash this shit right now. You got it."

I extended my hand back to him and we shook. He smiled.

"See?" he said. "That wasn't so hard, was it?"

He yanked my arm violently and hit the side of my head with his left hand. I saw stars and stumbled to the ground. I had let the bastard fool me again. I tried to block his blows all the way down, but he was getting the better of me. If I could just get back to my feet, we would be on even keel again. But he knew better, and did his best to keep me pinned to the ground while he jabbed at me.

All of a sudden, a pair of long, strong arms yanked Jamal off of my body and about six feet off the ground. Somebody was coming to my rescue. As I scrambled backwards to get my bearing, I could see that my rescuer was a six and a half foot, light skinned friend.

Isaiah.

"What the fuck you think you doin', man?" Isaiah asked angrily. He shook Jamal violently with every syllable. He seemed to dangle him in the air like a rag doll. Jamal was so shocked that he couldn't speak.

"I said, what the fuck you think you doin'?" Isaiah threw Jamal against the chain-link fence, not letting go of his sweatshirt. I finally stood up; in shock that Isaiah was able to come from nowhere to help me.

"I-I-I was just t-t-t-talking with him, man," Jamal stammered.

"You were just talking?" Isaiah mocked. "Looks like you were putting your hands on him, weren't you?"

"Naw, man," he said.

Isaiah slapped him with the back of his hand. The sound echoed across the open field.

"And you gonna fuckin' lie to me, too? What the fuck you think this is?" I had never in life seen anyone as angry as Isaiah was at that moment. He grabbed Jamal by the throat with his left hand and squeezed it to hold him steady. He cocked his right hand back and then punched Jamal squarely in his cheek. The sound of fist hitting flesh broke the eerie silence around us. Isaiah pummeled his face again and again, five, six, seven times and more.

"Isaiah," I said. "Please."

He paused. "Adrian, this nigga is not going to mess with you anymore. I ain't gonna let him."

He looked at Jamal again; whose nose was now oozing blood. He released his grasp on his neck and then let him slide down to the ground. He was conscious, but no longer trash-talking as he did when he was fighting me.

"You little bitch," Isaiah spat venomously. He kicked Jamal in the stomach, hard. Jamal started vomiting onto the grass and onto himself.

"Isaiah, that's enough," I said. I walked up to him and softly touched his shoulder and whispered: "Please stop."

Isaiah was huffing and puffing, his adrenaline soaring. He didn't look at me. He was focused squarely on Jamal.

"Get out of here, bitch," Isaiah commanded. "Now."

Jamal clung to the fence and tried to use it as leverage to stand up. He got about halfway up when Isaiah got tired of waiting. He grabbed Jamal under his arms and stood him up straight.

"Go," he commanded, standing about two inches from Jamal's face. Jamal eyeballed me one last time and then hobbled back down the grassy path where he came from.

"And don't come back, bitch!" Isaiah yelled after him. "You come back again and you'll end up dead!"

"Isaiah!" I said sharply. He finally turned around and looked at me. "Are you okay?"

I nodded.

"Are you sure?"

I shook my head.

"Come here," he said, extending his arms. We hugged each other.

"I will never, ever let anything bad happen to you. Ever."

I buried my head deep into his chest, feeling his all-too-familiar heartbeat, as soothing and comforting as it always had been. His hands rubbed back and forth over my back.

"Isaiah…thank you." I let go of his embrace and stepped back, noticing his plain, gray t-shirt.

"It's October," I began. "Why are you out here with just a t-shirt on?"

Isaiah smiled.

"Always trying to deflect attention from yourself, huh?" he said.

I forced a smile back at him. I noticed that there was a spot of blood on Isaiah's shirt, where I had rested my head.

"Damn," I said. "Blood on your shirt."

I touched my cheek and looked at my hand. It wasn't much, but Jamal had indeed cut the skin. Isaiah looked at my face closely then looked at his shirt.

"Let's go to my place," I said.

"Aight."

I turned back to the dark path toward my building and felt Isaiah's hands on my shoulders. As I walked, he walked. At my apartment within minutes, my hand shook slightly as I unlocked the door.

It was after midnight, so said the clock on the microwave. My football-playing roommates tended to go to bed early since they had to be up at the crack of dawn, so Isaiah and I all but tiptoed through the living room and down the stairs. I let Isaiah into my room, while I went into the bathroom and washed my face. Gazing into the mirror, I didn't look so bad at all. Sure, I was bruised, but compared to Jamal's face, I was a GQ cover model.

Isaiah had worked him over. Even with all I had experienced as a pledge, I had never seen rage like I saw in Isaiah that night. I wished it hadn't all transpired that way, but maybe this was what Jamal needed in order to leave me alone once and for all: to receive the beating that he thought I was going to get at his hands.

I dried my face off. The cut was so small that no bandage was necessary. I went back into my room and saw that Isaiah had taken his t-shirt off and was rifling through my closet. I saw the shirt on my chair and I inspected it.

"Don't worry about it," he said, gazing at me from the closet. His chest was still beautiful, slightly paler than his face and arms, but still perfectly chiseled. "I got plenty more shirts. Some of them are probably in this closet."

"Are you cold?"

"Naw," he said. "You know I don't feel the cold."

"Then why are you looking for a shirt to wear?"

"I was just…oh. Ooooh…" He let his sentence trail off and then smiled widely, like a kid on Christmas morning.

"You're home," I said. "You ain't got nothing I haven't seen before."

"I know that's right," he said. He stepped away from the closet and let his hands fall at his sides. He had on his signature baggy jeans that slung low on his hips, even with a belt. I could see those perfectly cut lines leading from his torso to the hidden regions that his black boxers struggled to hide.

"Can I hug you again?" he asked sincerely. I looked into his eyes. His unmitigated rage was replaced by a genuine longing that I had not often seen in him or anyone else for that matter.

"Of course," I said. He came to me and reached his arm around my waist. The next thing I knew, I was being lifted up off the ground. I hugged him back to steady myself. I laughed and rested my face in the cradle of his neck and shoulder.

"Why you laughing? I missed you, man," he said in between his own giggles.

"I missed you, too," I said. He placed me back on the floor. "Hey. How did you know where I was? I mean…I almost never take that back path. If you hadn't come when you did, I really think…he might have…"

"Don't even think like that," Isaiah said. He sat down on my bed and started to take off his shoes, a pair of black and red Air Jordans that I didn't even think they made anymore.

"I saw you and Samirah talking from like a hundred yards away, down by the library. I knew you were headed home, so I figured I'd meet up with you when you got here. Well, I peeped the dude – Jamal – walking about fifty yards ahead of me. I wasn't tripping, really, he looked like anybody else. But I got concerned when you went up the back way to your crib and he followed. By the time I caught up to you, y'all had already started scrapping."

"Damn. He really planned on doing something to me."

"Yeah, he was looking kinda crazy," Isaiah concluded. He began to gaze into my face again.

"If you hadn't been there," I said quietly.

"Shhh," he interrupted. His hand touched my shoulder and rested there. "I was there. I always will be."

I let my eyelids droop until they closed. His touch was still like fire, even after so much time had passed. As long as my eyes were closed, I could imagine anything I wanted to. We could be back in Buckley Hall, just the two of us, with no housemates sleeping in rooms on either side of us. There would be no Beta Chi Phi, no basketball, no Savion, and no Taina. I felt his hand slowly slide down the length of my arm under it rested on my own hand. I sensed him moving toward me, closer and closer on the bed until I could feel his breath on my cheek.

"We can't. You know we can't," I finally said, refusing to open my eyes.

"Fuck," Isaiah said. I felt his weight suddenly leave the bed and I opened my eyes. He was pacing the room, his face anguished.

"Why you keep doin this to me, Adrian?" Isaiah demanded. "You know how I feel. I know how you feel. Why can't it be how it used to be?"

"You know why," I said. "I'm not going to live that kind of life, Isaiah. I'm not going to be another stereotype that people write books about. I deserve better and you deserve better."

"I know you're not a stereotype, Adrian! Goddamn it! I just fuckin' beat a nigga's ass for you! What more do I have to do to prove how I feel?"

"You don't have to prove anything!" I retorted. "I expect that much from a friend. Wouldn't you do the same thing if it was one of your teammates out there getting his ass beat by some homophobe?"

"Yeah, but…" Isaiah said.

"But what? What makes me any different? We are friends first and foremost, and I don't want that to change by anything else that happens."

"Anything else?" Isaiah asked, eyebrows raised high. "Adrian, 'everything else' has already happened. Let's not kid ourselves, aight?"

"That's not what I mean," I said. "Listen, just sit down."

Isaiah sat back next to me on the bed.

"We have to remember what we said in August, man," I said. Isaiah rolled his eyes.

"You and this fuckin' pact. You put more weight on some words we said months ago than the feelings you havin' right here…" He placed his hand over my heart. "I know what you're feeling, man, cuz I feel it too. I am scared. I am scared shitless, man. But…"

He grabbed my hand and placed it over his naked pectoral.

"I know that deep down…in here…I have something that overrides all that fear. That shit wants me to be here, with you. That shit makes me want to protect you. That shit is real, Adrian, and I don't want you to keep blocking it. Let me share it with you, man. You gotta let me share it."

His voice was cracking and his eyes were welling up with tears.

"I'm not Savion," he concluded. "I plan on being here."

I looked at the floor. I didn't know what to say to all that, so I said nothing. He stood up and went back to my closet to find a shirt to put on.

"No," I said. "Turn the light out."

Isaiah looked at me quizzically and did as I asked. He remained standing by the light switch as I began to take my shoes off.

"You can sleep here tonight," I said. I saw his frown change from a smile, then to a forced grimace to prove that he was still hard.

"Oh, stop being silly," I said. We both laughed out loud in the darkness. "Come here."

He gleefully ran to my bed and tackled me into the mattress.

"Ow, ow, ow," I said. "Careful."

"Oh shit, what happened?" he asked.

"Nothing. I'm still kinda sore from where he hit me in the shoulder that first time."

"That bastard…"

"Let it go…let it go."

Isaiah was now on top of me on the bed. He was touching my face, just as he used to, his smile never diminishing.

"Let's get some sleep," I suggested.

"Sleep?" he asked.

"Yeah…" I said. "Sleep. That's what we both could use. For now at least. Okay?"

He shrugged.

"Yeah…you're right. Sleep is good." In the darkness, we took our jeans off and rested under the covers in just our boxers. For old time's sake, Isaiah held me, just as he did for many nights the previous summer. There was no rubbing, no caressing, no unwanted advances. Just Isaiah's comfort and closeness. For now, that's all that we could have, even though we were teetering on the edge of breaking our pact, which was by now, a distant jumble of words that at one point made sense, but now…now they were becoming more meaningless with each passing day.

October 30

It was the night before Halloween, a Saturday night, and all good Potomac children were changing into their most ghoulish ensembles. For the night, I was transforming into Freddy Krueger. I had the black slacks and tattered red and black striped sweater on already. It was snug, making me look lithe and sinister. Once the glove, mask, and dirty brown fedora was on, my transformation would be complete.

But until then, I simply waited. My housemates and I, plus Nina, were all going to attend a screening of *The Exorcist* together, and then go party on Wisconsin Avenue with all the other Halloween revelers. Next to Homecoming, Halloween was probably the biggest deal on campus.

I read some case-studies while I waited. My anthropology classes were going really well, but statistics was kicking my ass. At least I had gotten all of my general requirements out of the way my freshman and sophomore years.

It was quite hilarious to catch a glimpse of myself in the mirror dressed as one of the scariest horror figures from my childhood, yet poring over a thick college text book.

"If mama Krueger could see me now," I mused aloud. Just then, the phone rang. I answered after two rings.

"Hello?" I said.

"Adrian? Is that you?" my father said.

"Hey dad, what's up?"

"It's been a few weeks. How are you?"

"I'm okay, you know. Nothing's really going on. How are you?"

"I'm good," he said. "I was just thinking about you. Are you doing anything for Halloween?"

"Yeah, actually. I'm just waiting around so me and the fellas and Nina can go see *The Exorcist.*"

"Sounds fun."

"Yeah, it is. I try to see it every year. This is the first time we're dressing up for it, though."

"Dressing up?"

"Yeah, like, we're going in our Halloween costumes."

"Oh, that sounds like fun."

"Yeah, it should be."

"You talked to your mother lately?"

"Not…lately. But I spoke to her a few weeks ago. She's good."

"When's the last time you've been home?"

I paused.

"Are you there?" he asked.

"Yeah, I'm here. Um…last time I was home…was last Spring, I guess."

"Adrian! Are you serious?"

"Yeah, dad. You know me and mom aren't really…you know. We don't talk much."

"Oh, well that's gonna have to change, son."

"Um…no offense, dad, but you don't know her like I know her."

"I don't doubt that, Adrian. I am sure she's a much different woman now than she was twelve years ago. But, she's still your mother. I don't want you to have a bad relationship with her."

"I know. But she's just so…I can't explain it. It's like in that time you were gone, she and I weren't close. She just kept pushing me and pushing me. Anything below an A was like a personal affront to her. By the time I got to college…"

"You resented her."

"Yeah. I guess I do, dad. I feel like I got here with all the book smarts I needed to get by, but I didn't feel like I had anyone to relate to back home when I just needed someone to talk to. That's what it is…I just don't feel like she understands me or tries to understand me. I'd just rather be around my friends."

"I understand," my dad said. "But Adrian, you know she only pushed you because she loves you. She probably tried to instill values in you that would make you a success at whatever you do. She probably… she probably thought that was the best way to make you a man since I wasn't around."

"Maybe," I said. "But dad, you just don't know. I hate going back home because there's always an argument. If it's not one thing, it's another. I haven't even…she doesn't…"

"Adrian, she doesn't know about me, does she?"

"Naw, not really," I said.

"Adrian. Come on, man. That's not good."

"I know, I know. But you know that's just gonna be another argument."

"Don't make it worse by waiting, man. Your mother deserves to know that I'm in your life."

"Dad. I know. I still have to do it on my own time, though."

"Adrian…sometimes, a man has to do things on everybody else's time but his own. I waited twelve years to see you because I wanted to do things my way. Don't make the same mistakes. Okay?"

"Okay, dad. I understand."

"You sound preoccupied or something. You sure everything's okay?"

"Yeah…I've just been thinking a lot about something, dad."

"What is it?"

"I've been thinking a lot about you and mom, and why you split up. You know, I thought maybe I'd never be able to forgive you for betraying your loyalty to her…to us. But I can see now that sometimes, two people don't stay in love. Or, maybe they do, but true feelings can also be had for other people."

"Well, Adrian, yeah, but…"

"No dad, wait. I have to say this. Dad, I love you, and I forgive you for what happened. I don't know if mom ever will or if she should, but I know…I know that you can be with one person and still have feelings for someone else."

"Adrian…are you in a situation like that now?"

"Kinda…"

"Don't do it, son. I appreciate your forgiveness, but I gotta tell you, if I had it all to do again, I wouldn't. I loved your mother and I messed up a really good thing by cheating on her. Now here I am… alone. And that's what I deserve. If I hadn't done what I did, my life would be so much different. And so would yours!"

"Dad, I can't control who I love. The person who loves me can't control it either. It's just really tough dad. I'm just so frustrated. But…I'll be okay."

"You sure? You know you can talk to me about anything. I don't want to see you in a bad situation."

"I know, dad. I appreciate it. And maybe I can tell you more when we have some more time. But right now…"

"Yeah, you've got to head on out with your friends. But before you go…do you have everything you need? Textbooks? Spending money?"

"Dad, you give me more than I could ever even spend in a semester! And it's really appreciated. Thank you."

"You're my son. I'm going to take care of you."

"I appreciate it. I really do. But I'll be fine until Christmas, seriously. I'm saving most of what you send me."

"Good. Save it and get your mother something nice for the holidays."

"I will."

"And how is frat?"

"Beta is doing well here. We've had a few programs, but nothing major yet."

"Alright. Well, if you all need anything, New Jersey isn't too far for me to drive down."

"Thanks dad. Take care, okay?"

"I will, son."

It was amazing that I hadn't spoken to my dad in over a decade, and now he was giving me fatherly advice. He didn't fully understand my ins and outs as a person yet, but he loved me just the same.

"Yo, Adrian, you ready?" Calen called out from the kitchen.

"Just about!" I called back. I reached into my drawer and pulled out my Freddy mask. Looking eerily similar to the charred flesh portrayed in the movies, I slid the mask over my head. I then grabbed the brown fedora from my closet. I looked in the mirror and startled myself. Adjusting the mask and hat, I looked just like the demon from all those films.

Finally, I pulled a black glove with gray plastic knives and slid it over my hand. In the mirror, I was Freddy.

"Ha ha ha!" I shouted maniacally into my mirror. "What's the matter, Adrian? Am I not the man of your dreams?"

I was being silly, but it put me in the mood for the evening. I opened my door and shut off the light to my room. Creeping up the stairs, I could hear my three roommates laughing and joking with one another. Closest to the stairs, I saw Calen dressed in all black from head to toe with black boots. Although he was facing away from me, I saw that he was wearing a plain white hockey mask. He was supposed to be Jason from the Friday the 13th movies. I could not pass up the chance to startle him.

I crept up behind him and tapped him on the shoulder

"Oh shit!" he said.

"You like this shit, right?" I asked.

"Hell yeah, nigga!" Calen said from behind his mask. "That shit is tight!"

I looked around my living room and saw my other two housemates standing around. Brad was dressed as Michael Myers from the Halloween films. He carried with him a long plastic knife, but not as long as Calen's faux machete. Orlando probably had the best costume. Wearing a long, flowing black coat with brown fur about the collar and cuffs, he simply held a hook in his hand. He was Candyman. Orlando was rather menacing in appearance even without the hook, so Candyman was an excellent choice for him.

"My, my, my," Nina said from her seat in the corner. From head to toe, she was a knockout. She had pressed her curly hair until it was bone straight. Although her face was caked with pale makeup, her beauty still shone through. She had on a long black dress that was tighter than anything I had seen her wear before. There was no split.

"What is this, the four horsemen of the apocalypse?"

"You got it, Miss Morticia!" Calen said, eyeing Nina up and down. "You got Freddy, Jason, Michael Myers, and Candyman up in this piece. Yo, take my camera and get a picture of this!"

Calen handed Nina his camera while we got in our most menacing poses.

"Say cheese…or…well, just growl and look scary!" Nina instructed.

I splayed my gloved hand outward, Orlando brandished his hook, and Brad and Calen raised their blades.

The camera flashed, and we were ready to go.

"Aight, Potomac, here we come!" Brad announced as he threw open the door.

"I'm hungry," Orlando said as he hesitated at the door.

"Nigga, you know we ain't got no food!" Calen bellowed

"That sucks," Orlando said. "Big ass 'fridge and can't even keep no food in it."

We stormed out of the apartment and headed down the path toward Grayson Hall, where the movie would be shown. About twenty feet away, I heard a shrill voice behind me.

"Guys!" Nina said, shuffling her feet about an inch at a time. That was just about as much as her tight dress would allow her to move. We practically fell over with laughter.

"It's not funny!" she whined. "I need help!"

"I got you, girl," Calen said. He raced over to her, picked her up, and swung her over his shoulder.

We continued our laughter as we marched toward Grayson Hall, Nina slung over Calen's shoulder the whole time.

We had one hell of a time getting Nina up all of those steps, but we quickly settled into our seats on the mezzanine of Grayson Hall as *The Exorcist* began. We were a few minutes late, but we still found good seats. Orlando, Calen, and Brad found three seats together near the middle of the back section, while Nina and I sat together in the very last row. Although it was dark, we could see that the room was packed to the brim with Halloween revelers of all types, most of which were dressed in costumes and were already inebriated. It was a little chilly in the room, but keeping my Freddy mask on kept me warm. Nina had brought a shawl to cover her Morticia Addams get-up.

Although I had had nothing to drink, I was still enjoying myself, smiling wide under my mask. That is, until five minutes into the film, when Taina and Isaiah arrived. Together. Holding hands.

I only noticed them because the side door they came in shut with a loud clang while the room was silent. Everyone on the mezzanine turned sharply to the left. Taina was wearing an all white ballerina-type outfit, with white tights and a snug white top. She also wore a golden halo and small angel wings on her back. Isaiah was wearing nothing out of the ordinary, except for a pair of devil's horns on his head. I rolled my eyes so hard under my mask, they could have snapped right out of their sockets.

I shrank in my chair at first, so they wouldn't see me. Then I realized that I was in costume and there was no way either would recognize me, so I continued to stare. Taina led Isaiah by the hand across the front row until they sat in empty seats almost directly ahead of Nina and me, only ten rows in front. I was in a prime position to see what they would be up to.

I alternated between the screen and the back of Isaiah's head. He and Taina were watching the movie quietly, without too much movement from either of them. But then I noticed Taina leaning her head against Isaiah's shoulder.

So desperate, I thought to myself. She was such a goodie-goodie, I could see why Nina couldn't stand her sometimes.

As if on cue, Isaiah put her arm around her.

"The fuck?" I asked, not realizing I was speaking out loud. Immediately, I turned to Nina to see if she had heard.

To my surprise, she was staring me square in the face.

"What's wrong with you?" she hissed.

"Nothing," I whispered back, returning my attention to the movie.

"You're lying," she whispered. "You think I don't know you?"

"Nina, hush. Watch the movie."

"Nope. Come on." She stood up and began shuffling into the aisle. Taking a few inches at a time, she turned around to notice me still sitting there.

"Let's go!" she whispered. I left my seat, unconsciously fiddling my gloved hand at my side. As she shuffled along, I took one last look at Isaiah and Taina, who were still cuddled together in their seats.

We stood in the empty lobby of the auditorium and Nina carefully sat down on one of the ornate mahogany benches.

"Whew!" she sighed. "I'm thinking being Morticia this year might not have been the best move."

I smiled underneath my mask and sat next to her.

"Adrian, take the mask off," she said. I first took my hat off and laid it to the side. With both hands, I slid the mask above my head and cradled it in my hands. I looked at Nina waiting for her question.

"You're kicking it with Isaiah, aren't you?" she asked.

"Man," I began, looking past her, around her, to the side – anything to avoid her stare. "Why you gotta ask me that, girl?"

"Damn," she said, her voice devoid of her usual whimsy. "Why?"

"I didn't say I was kicking it with him," I countered.

"Don't bullshit me, man! You know good and well that out of anybody on this campus, I know you. I know when you're lying. I know when you ain't up to no good."

"Don't do me like this, Nina. It's not like that at all."

"Then tell me what it's like."

"Well, what do you want to know?"

"Are you kicking it with Isaiah or not?"

"Anything but that…"

"Boy, if you don't tell me-"

"Yes."

"Yes, you been kicking it with Isaiah, yes?"

"Well, not currently. But…we have."

Nina stopped and stared at me until I would look her in the eye once more.

"You…"

"Yeah?"

"…and Isaiah…"

"Yeah?"

"…hooked up before?"

"Yes!"

Nina shrieked and fell out on the floor. Her smile was wide; I had taken her by complete surprise.

"Whooooooo!" she said, arms flailing about.

"Stop acting silly!" I demanded, helping her up. She had gone limp, as though filled with the Holy Ghost in the middle of a Pentecostal church service.

"Stand up!" I said. "This is serious, I don't know what to do."

"Whoa," she replied. "Whoa, whoa, whoa! Isaiah is gay?"

"Yeah…well, no…kinda…I don't know!" I buried my face in my hands.

"Wait, you hooked up with the nigga but you don't know if he gay?"

"Naw, I know he's gay," I said. "Well, bi. We hooked up… damn, where can I begin?"

"Calm down, boo, just calm down. I know you're upset. You know you ain't been right since the school year started, but I ain't wanna say anything."

"You could tell?" I asked.

"Kinda," she said. "Adrian, you're changing. I don't know if it's good or bad, but you're definitely changing. On one hand, we've been hanging out less – and that's fine! Don't get me wrong about that. Shit changes and we all get busy. You hang out with your frat brothers, of course. You made some more gay friends – that's good! I even think Morris is sweet on you or something, he follows you around like a puppy."

I blushed.

"You know it's true! At the same time, I can tell you ain't thinking about no Morris. But I know you. I know that if it ain't him, it's somebody. You always like somebody, even if you ain't really kickin' it with them."

"You know me well," I said.

"Right. Now, when the school year started, I was just waiting to see who the latest crush would be, or who you might start talking to. But there was nobody. When you met Morris, I was like ooh, this is gonna be interesting. But nothing. And you stopped talking about dudes altogether. And as much as we talk about dudes…come on, you knew I was gonna think something was up."

"I hadn't even noticed I changed, girl."

"Oh wait, it gets better. Cuz then I started getting observant. It seems like every time you're with Isaiah, y'all be on some touchy-feely shit. Like, when you are around your frat brothers, maybe y'all will play wrestle or something. But you and Isaiah? Please, one of you always has your hand on the other's shoulder."

"Yeah…we do that," I said sadly.

"But I just thought 'well maybe that's just the type of friendship they have.' But then I noticed the looks! Every single time you two are in the same room together, you are scoping him out. And when you're not looking, he scopes you out!"

"For real?" I asked hopefully.

"For real?" she mocked. "Of course! Homie, you been my ace boon coon since freshman year, I would never make up some BS about this whole thing. You two look like something was going on, and to me, it's obvious. But that's because I know you. I'm just…shocked, I guess."

"Yeah, I would be too," I said.

"But not only that…I'm supposed to be your girl! How could you not tell me? Did you think I would tell somebody? I don't talk to nobody but you!"

This was the first and only aspect of my life that I had not clued in Nina on, and it had backfired. Not only was me and Isaiah's relationship transparent, now Nina thought I couldn't trust her.

"It's not like that at all. I trust you. I really do. But it's just that me and him…we have a complicated relationship."

"Well, I'll say," she said quickly.

"But please know that I still trust you. I always have and I always will. The reason I didn't tell you is because…well, because we decided not to. He asked me not to, and I didn't."

"I see," she said. "Well, how did this all start?"

"I don't want to say too much," I said.

"Well it's all out in the open now, no need to hold back."

"Yes, there is," I said. "He and I…we're different."

"Different?" she asked. "Yo, I'ma tell you how I see it, same as I would anything else. From my vantage point, you are cavorting with just another one of these jive ass niggas on the 'down low.' A nigga that don't know what he wants, so he samples a little of everything until he gets tired of it."

"That's not it at all…"

"Isn't it?"

"No. It isn't."

"Then tell me what it is," she said, folding her arms and waiting for an answer. I sighed and tried to find the words that I couldn't say to her for months.

"Isaiah and I…got together over the summer. But we haven't been together since then."

"You got together. Like, when? How?"

"It just sorta…happened."

"I don't understand. How does something like that just happen?"

"It just did, alright? Damn."

"Okay, calm down! I'm just trying to understand."

"I know. I know. But I can't explain how something like this happens. We were just friends. Then one day, it all changed. There were feelings there…feelings that we acted on. And then…then we decided that we couldn't keep going on like that when the fall semester started. We both had things we needed to work out. One of those things was…her."

"Taina?"

"Yeah. He wasn't with her when we got together. It always seemed like they were well on the road to breaking up, like for real. Believe me; I would never have let it happen any other way. But now… now I gotta go and see them up in my face all the time. It's like he doesn't know what he wants!"

"Cuz he a jive ass nigga!" Nina interjected. "Don't you see what he's doing? Just like all these other bisexual black men, he wants to have his cake and eat it too. You can't tell me he's not fuckin' Taina and then trying to sneak in your bed, too."

"He's not like that," I said. "You just don't understand the type of relationship we have."

"I understand that he's hurting you. If he has the balls to walk around campus hand in hand with this girl, right in front of you, then he doesn't care about you!"

"He does. I know he does. Nina, you just don't understand." There was so much that I wanted to tell her. This thing with Isaiah went back further than this summer. It started the first day that I met him and dubbed him "The Finest Boy on Campus." It was those moments in Philosophy class our freshman year when I would just stare are him from afar. It was that day I got tipsy at a party sophomore year and he helped me stand up. It was the day he congratulated me on becoming a Beta. It was the whole of last summer. It was the night we first kissed. And it was that last night we were together, when we promised each other the space we needed.

Nina didn't understand how I felt when I woke up so many days that summer and his face was the first thing I saw. She didn't know what it meant that Isaiah had literally rescued me from an attack. I had feelings for Isaiah that rested deep in my soul, deeper than physical attraction or animalistic lust.

"I love him." I finally admitted.

"Oh lawd," she said. "Lawd, lawd, lawd. What are we gonna do with you?"

Nina gave me a hug and patted me on the back.

"It's killing me to see him with her. He keeps telling me it isn't what I think... that I should know where his heart his. I feel so stupid for even giving him this 'space' to begin with. I should have just told him it's either her or me, no space, no in-between time to figure it all out. Girl, I know I sound crazy, but…he has spent the night with me before, since this summer. We didn't have sex, but we still…we shared the same bed. I miss that intimacy. He's still been there for me, just like he always was. But I'm starting to crack. I need him to be there for me like he was this summer. I can't keep seeing him with her."

"I know…Adrian, listen." Nina grabbed me by the shoulders and looked deep into my eyes. "I know you didn't tell me this because you promised Isaiah you wouldn't. And that's okay with me. But it is eating you up inside, can't you see that? You started off this year determined to be who you are! Nobody was going to stop you. You are a strong, black, gay man. And I love you. And your frat loves you. And I don't know…maybe Isaiah loves you, too, but he's scared. I see the way he looks at you. It's like…when you're not looking, he's longing. I've seen that in him since the first day of school. I don't want you to get your hopes up, because lord knows I want to see you happy again."

"I want to be happy," I said. "And I am happy. But I know there are other things I need to take care of, still. I got a father I barely know slipping me money like it's supposed to make up for twelve years. I got a mom I barely speak to. I got so far to go. He and I…we needed this time. It was my idea, too. My stupid ass idea to take a step back until we figured it all out."

"That is not a stupid idea. If we all took a step back sometimes, do you know how much better off we could be? You are growing up! So many people are proud of you and you don't even know it. Isaiah is just one piece of everything…trust me. If it's meant to be, everything will work out."

I hugged her again without saying a word.

"You gonna be okay?" she asked.

"Yeah," I lied. If I told her everything would be fine, maybe I wouldn't have to deal with it anymore. "Let's just go back in there and watch the movie."

Nina shuffled her way to the door and waited for me to open it. I grabbed the handle, breathed a few times, and then slowly cracked it open to minimize its metallic squeak. We crept into the darkness and found our seats once more.

Everything Nina said was appreciated – she was my best friend – but I didn't believe her. It wasn't going to work out. I would just have to go back in that auditorium and endure having to see them together. Even as Linda Blair's head spun on the screen before us, Taina's head never wavered from her man's shoulder.

It was a scene I was familiar with, only my head was on Isaiah's shoulders and his hands were around me.

I would persevere, even if all I truly had with Isaiah were memories.

***

I got home before any of my housemates and stripped off my costume. Sitting at my desk in just boxer briefs and a t-shirt, I dug into my desk drawer looking for the scrap of paper that might change my life.

I found three. I don't know what I hoped to accomplish, but I felt a profound emptiness in my gut that only someone else could fill.

I dialed.

I waited.

"Hello, you have reached the voice mail of Savion Cortez. I'm sorry I'm not available to take your…"

Click.

I balled up his number and finally threw it away.

Next number.

I dialed, and almost instantly:

"Hi, this is Eugene. Leave a message."

Click.

His number, too, was thrown away.

Next number – third time's a charm.

I dialed, I waited.

"Hello?"

"Morris…this is Adrian."

"Hey man, how are you?"

"I'm good, man. Listen, what are you doing tonight?"

"Well, it's kind of after 12, so I'm not doing anything really."

"Want to come over?"

"Um…sure," he replied. "Where do you live again?"

"Hurley Village," I said. "Right by the Lacrosse field."

"Alright. I'll see you in ten minutes."

"Cool…peace."

I hung up the phone and reclined in my chair, cupping my erection.

I'd forget about Isaiah the best way I knew how.

July 17

I asked him what he wanted for his birthday, and I could have sworn he said "you."

When I said "What?" he said he didn't care and that just hanging out would be fine.

When I asked him if he wanted to go to a bar or something and invite his friends, he said he didn't really have any close friends, just a lot of acquaintances. It was then that I learned Isaiah treated basketball as a job and his teammates as coworkers. He preferred to separate his basketball life from his personal life. Maybe that's why he was a phenomenal basketball player.

So on July 17, I took Isaiah down to U Street in DC for dinner and drinks at the Kaffa House, which was really a reggae joint that had the occasional live music. It wasn't exactly great for a full meal, but we had some chicken wings and two big plates of nachos.

Kaffa House was not much more than a hole in the wall, but the lounge turned into a completely different world when the sun set and the place was packed with all sorts of people, some dressed in military fatigues and wrist bands in the colors of African liberation, and others dressed simply in jeans, t-shirts, and wild afros. The women all reminded me of different versions of Nina: strong, natural, urban.

That night a local R&B band called Urban Ave 31 performed. I had seen them before but Isaiah was a virgin to their unique sound. It was neo soul at its finest: a beautiful band with a rich, soulful sound; a lead singer whose range went from baritone to a falsetto that rivaled Prince, a huge percussion section, and a style that was laid back. The lead singer wore a simple pair of baggy jeans and a Che Guevara t-shirt, the standard of any self-respecting conscious black man. They brought a quiet energy with them, quickly putting minds at ease and hearts pumping with their flow.

After two songs, Isaiah was in love. After three songs, we were both on the floor dancing with the rest of the party goers. I wasn't sure that I had ever seen Isaiah so happy prior to that point. Part of it might have been the Black Russians he was tossing back. I was happy with my Long Island Iced Tea that I seemed to nurse all night long.

Before we left, I picked up an Urban Ave 31 CD that was for sale and stuffed it in my back pocket to give to Isaiah later. If he loved them live, he'd definitely appreciate the CD. He was a hard person to gauge sometimes, so when you noticed what he liked, you had to run with it.

"Yo man, let's get out of here," he said. He was giving me the "club whisper" -- when you get real close to somebody's ear but talk real loud to speak over the noise around you.

"No doubt," I said, nodding in case he couldn't hear me. I walked toward the door and felt Isaiah's hand on my shoulder, steadying himself.

"Are you okay?" I asked.

"Yeah," he said, still smiling wide. We stumbled out onto U Street. Isaiah was still singing one of the band's songs as we crossed the street and hailed a cab back to Potomac. Surprisingly, the first cab that came along stopped for us.

"Dude, that never happens around Potomac," Isaiah said.

"And you know this," I replied. He opened the door and allowed me to enter the cab first.

"Potomac University, main gates, please," I told the driver as Isaiah slid in next to me.

"Dude, that was so much fuckin' fun," Isaiah said. "I gotta hand it to you, you sure know how to show a nigga a good time. Thanks a lot."

"Aw man, it was no problem! You are cool people, you deserve it. And once again, happy birthday. How does it feel?"

"It feels real good man," Isaiah said. We rode down U Street and saw the streets start filling with people as the clubs and bars closed down. It was a warm night, as all summer nights should be. The drinks made me feel buzzed, but I was still in control of my faculties. Isaiah, on the other hand, was definitely feeling his four or five drinks. It was his birthday, though. He deserved to be a little tipsy.

"Hey, I wanna tell you something," he said. I turned to him and took in his gaze. He leaned in close to me and began to whisper in my ear.

"This was probably the best birthday I ever had," he whispered. His lips brushed against my ear with each consonant he formed. Even in the July humidity, I shivered.

"I'm glad," I replied with a grin. He took my hand, squeezed it once, and let it go. He quickly turned away and watched as the clubs and closed stores became houses and apartment buildings. We were nearing home.

That chill stayed with me for a while. I was definitely still attracted to Isaiah, even though I tried not to be. He was my friend now, a good friend, at that. There was no way we could be anything more. But still it seemed as though every time I thought he was being a friend, there might have been more behind his actions.

His buzz was wearing down by the time we got out of the cab and paid the driver.

"You a good man, Adrian," Isaiah said as he put his arm around my shoulder. I believed that he was still tipsy and needed my support to walk.

"You're a good man, too," I said. "You okay? Can you walk aight?"

"Yeah," he said. "But a little support never hurt."

We laughed all the way to our room in Buckley. I turned the light on, but Isaiah turned it out right after.

"What'd you do that for?" I asked.

"Turn the lamp on instead, that overhead light is too bright."

I felt my way to the far corner of the room and turned on the negligible light of the little-used floor lamp we had.

"Is that good?" I asked.

"Perfect," he said. He stood by his closet and stared at me.

"Dude, what's wrong?" He was almost looking past me. Something was clearly on his mind.

"Nothing," he said. He kicked off his boots and unbuckled his baggy black jeans. They fell to the floor, showing off the legs of his jet black boxer briefs. His gray t-shirt was so long, you could barely see his underwear. I averted my eyes after I realized I was staring.

I turned around and started to unbutton my short-sleeved linen shirt. I removed it and tossed it to the floor. The pile of clothes under my bed was growing. I needed to wash soon.

Before I could grab a t-shirt to sleep in, Isaiah grabbed me softly on the shoulder. I turned around and our naked chests faced each other. I looked up into his eyes.

"We need to talk," he said.

"Okay," I replied. "What's up?"

"When you're ready...come over to my bed." He let my arm go and backed away. All he was now wearing was those black boxer briefs against his pale skin. He turned around and walked to his bed. His entire body was built perfectly and it seemed like he insisted throwing it in my face. He lay down with his eyes wide open and his fingers interlaced behind his head.

I sat in my chair, took my shoes off, and laid them down under my desk. I stood up and took my jeans off. I was naked, save for my dark blue boxers. Grabbing a t-shirt from my drawer, I slipped it on and then walked over to Isaiah's bed.

"What's up?" I asked. He pulled himself up to a sitting position and gestured for me to sit down. He moved his legs up, making space for me.

"Adrian, I like you a lot," he began, "As a person. As a friend. And I want to thank you for taking me out to U Street tonight."

"Wait," I interrupted. "I almost forgot." I went back to my side of the room and dug into my back pockets. I slid the CD out carefully and walked back to Isaiah, holding it behind my back. I sat down and then quickly produced it urging him to take it out of my hands.

"What's this?" he asked.

"It's Urban Ave 31," I said. "The band from tonight. I got it for you, since I didn't really give you anything tangible for your birthday. So…happy birthday. Again."

He looked at the gift and smiled again.

"Thank you, Adrian." His voice was barely above a whisper. He refused to look back up at me. He just held the CD in his hands and closed his eyes.

"Isaiah," I said. "It's okay."

I stroked his bare arm because I didn't know what else to do. When he finally looked up, I could see a tear flowing from his eye.

"What's wrong?" I asked.

"I hate my birthday," he said. "I've hated it ever since I was eight."

"Oh... I'm sorry," I said.

"Adrian…" My name got choked in his throat and he couldn't get any more words out. He dropped the CD to the floor and broke down.

I hugged him. He cried and cried until my shoulder was soaked with his tears. I didn't know what to say or do – I didn't understand what upset him so – so I just held him. He grabbed onto me tightly as we sat on the bed.

"I…I'm sorry," he said, wiping his eyes with his hands.

"Dude, it's okay."

"I wanted to tell you…I've never been big on my birthday since I was a little kid."

"That's okay," I said. "Lots of kids-"

"Naw," he interrupted. "Not like that. See…you know I'm from Baltimore, the west side. Me and my mom never had a lot, but we did okay. Had a little house, I had my own room and all that bullshit. Mom worked for the city. Everything was cool.

"My dad…I mean, he was around and shit, but he wasn't one of those work nine-to-five type of fathers. But he was a good man. He never did anything bad to me or my mom. And when I needed him, he was there. He loved basketball – that's where I got it from. Most kids went to the park, we went to the court.

"On my eighth birthday, my mom decided to throw me a birthday party. You know, one of them parties that start at three o'clock in the afternoon and goes on until midnight. My whole family was gonna be there, and everybody in the neighborhood would probably roll through.

I'm sure all your birthday parties were like that, too. That's just how black folk do, right?

"It was getting close to three and my dad still wasn't home. We all knew he was probably at the basketball court, so my mom sent me around the corner to go get him. It was real hot that day. I remember that part well. I got to the end of my block, by the little Chinese store, and I turned the corner, to the left. I walked to the middle of the block, and across the street was my elementary school – the school where my dad played ball. I saw him there, and he…"

Isaiah stopped and took a deep breath. He had stopped weeping but his voice still wavered.

"He was in an altercation with this dude, this young cat. They were yelling at each other, hard. Viciously. I had never seen my dad that angry at anybody before. There were some other dudes there, but it didn't seem like they were part of it. They were just watching like I was.

"They were cussin'. I ran across the street and stood outside the fence. I yelled to my father that my mom wanted him to come home, but he didn't respond. I called out to him a second time, and he turned around and told me to go home, that he'd be there in a few minutes. He kept arguing with this dude and, to this day, I can't tell you what they were saying. All I remember is profanity."

"I called out to him a third time, and he turned the face me. Next thing I know, this other guy…he pulls out a gun from his belt and just starts blasting. This nigga didn't just shoot once. He shot his entire round into…my father."

"Oh my God," I said with every bit of sincere anguish. "You saw the whole thing."

"Yeah," he continued. "Some street nigga shot my father to death right in front of me. Then the coward ran. I never even saw his face good. I remember my father's face, though. He sorta just winced in pain and fell to the ground backwards."

I grabbed Isaiah's hand and he clenched it as he continued.

"I screamed out for him. The blood was everywhere, even spurted onto me as he was shot, but I didn't notice right away. The shooter ran away. So did everybody else who was out there. I don't know why I didn't run around the fence to help him. I couldn't move. I couldn't walk. My knees just got weak and I couldn't do a damn thing. I held onto the fence, but I just kinda sat down on the sidewalk and watched my dad bleed. His…his eyes never really closed. He looked at me and his lips moved, but I couldn't hear what he was trying to say. Then, he stopped moving. I just cried. I couldn't do anything and I cried."

"Isaiah…oh man…"

"I don't remember much else. I think one of the neighbors scooped me up and took me home. I know my mom was hysterical when she saw the blood on me. Adrian, I just can't remember anything else after that and before the funeral. But the next time I saw my dad, he was in his casket. That's when I knew it was real and he wasn't coming back."

Isaiah stopped talking and let the tears roll down his face freely, without fighting them.

"So, homie, that's why I don't usually celebrate my birthday. My birthday reminds me of my dad and how he died. I never really let myself celebrate until now."

"Isaiah, I'm so sorry," I said. "If I had known…"

"If you had known, you would have let me stay at home all depressed and shit, like I normally do. But I didn't tell you on purpose. I wanted to see if I could get out there and actually enjoy the day for a change. If you had known, things would be different. But you let me be myself. Thank you for that. I appreciate it."

Isaiah hugged me once again. I hugged him back.

"Isaiah…for real…I do want to say I am so sorry you lost your father that way. I really am. That's a horrible way to lose your dad and you didn't deserve it. For what it's worth, I can tell your dad really had a positive influence in your life, and…well, if you are a reflection of even a little bit of who he was, then he was a great man indeed."

He smiled at me.

"Thank you," he said.

"And, really," I continued, "I just did for you what anyone would do for you. You're a really cool person man, and I'm really glad I've had the opportunity to come to know you this summer."

He laughed almost silently and reclined.

"There's still a lot you don't know about me, homie," he said.

For some reason, my heart began to race.

"Like what?" I asked.

"Come here," he instructed. "Come look at the ceiling with me." He grabbed my hand and guided me down to the bed with him. He scooted over to the wall, making room for me to lay on my stomach next to him. I then turned over to face the ceiling. Up there was something, I had never noticed before: a loose leaf sheet of paper that had been tacked up on each of its corners, with writing that I couldn't read from this distance.

"What's that?" I asked.

"My goals," he explained. "Every now and then I revise them and tack them to the ceiling of wherever I happen to be laying my head. I think about them right before I go to sleep. Wanna know what they say?"

"Sure," I said.

"Well, one goal is to play professional basketball."

"I think you can reach that goal."

"I hope so. Then I got all types of goals under that one, like buy my mom a house, make sure my friends and family are taken care of, all that shit. Another one I got is to maintain a 3.0 grade point average. It's hard, but I do it."

"Damn, I barely have a 2.9 as it is," I remarked.

"For real? I woulda pegged you as a 3.5 kinda nigga," he said.

"Yeah, right," I said.

"Then, one of my goals is to be a good friend. I'm always trying to work on that, how to be more thoughtful and considerate. And… my biggest goal is to just be myself."

"That shouldn't be too hard, eh?" I asked.

He turned his body on its side and rested his weight on his shoulder. Looking into my face, he simply said "It's harder than I could ever think." He then lunged off the bed and turned the floor lamp off.

"That was bothering me," he explained while walking back to the bed. He climbed over me and reclaimed his position. "But yeah. Sometimes it's tough trying to be all things to all people. Potomac expects me to be this basketball prodigy, so I have to play that role. All the females expect me to be this perfect boyfriend, so I have to be this strong, silent type when I'm around Taina. And then I'm black, and male, and people have expectations of that. I wonder a lot when it is I can just be me."

"You don't have to worry about that when you're around me, man. I like you for who you are. Don't ever feel like you have to adapt or change to suit my needs."

"You mean that?" He was still resting on his elbow and listening to me intently.

"Of course I meant it," I said. "Although, I gotta admit, I thought I was getting the real Isaiah all this time."

"Well, you were," he said. "Just not all of the real Isaiah."

"Hell, I've seen you in your drawers. What more is there?" Isaiah smiled broadly.

"Do you really wanna know?" he asked.

"I don't think you really want to hear the answer," I joked.

"Don't start nothing, man," he said with a laugh.

"Hey, I'm innocent," I said. "You're the one inviting strange gay boys into your bed."

"You're not even in my bed," he said. "You're on it. Now, if I pull these covers up, you'd be in it."

He pulled his thin blanket over the two of us.

"See?" he said. "Now I have a strange gay boy in my bed."

"You're silly," I said.

"Yeah, kinda. But I don't even see you like that, Adrian. You ain't some strange gay boy. When I think of gay, I think of these white boys on campus with the leather pants and the blue hair. I don't think about people like you and me."

"Yeah, I feel you. It's kinda hard for me to relate to a lot of gay folks I come across because…well, I don't think I act a certain kind of way. I'm just me, you know?"

"I understand." He paused. "You totally missed that, didn't you?"

"Missed what?" I asked.

"Never mind," he said. He turned over and faced the wall.

"What? What did I miss?" I asked. Isaiah turned over and faced me again.

"Just go to sleep, man," he said with a smirk. "It'll hit you in the morning."

I began to slide out of bed when Isaiah grabbed my wrist.

"Stay," he asked.

"Stay?" I repeated.

"Yeah," he said, slowly releasing my wrist. "Don't leave. Stay over here tonight. I could…I could use the company."

"You sure?" I asked. "Not a lot of space in here with them big ass legs you got."

He laughed and purposefully threw his leg over my waist.

"What, this big ass leg?" We laughed some more.

"Man, you better get these big ham hocks off of me. You crazy." I grabbed his thigh under the covers and tried to move it, but it was impossible.

"What if I fell asleep like this?" he asked.

"Fine with me," I said. "I'm already over here, what can I do?"

"Naw," he said. "I wouldn't do that to you."

He moved his leg back to his slim portion of the bed and I again got comfortable. We faced each other. The laughter stopped and we just stared at each other.

"If anybody we knew walked into this room right now…" I began.

"I wouldn't care," Isaiah finished. He put his arm around me and pulled me close so that he could whisper, letting his lips tickle my ear. "Because I am chillin' with somebody I care about. And I don't give a fuck about what anybody else thinks."

My heart raced under my cotton shirt. Although the precise words were not spoken, Isaiah's hidden truth became crystal clear. I was under his sheets, sharing his bed, wearing nothing but underwear, and allowing his arm to cradle me. This was a situation I had dreamed about but didn't even realize that it was happening until it happened.

When I think of gay…I don't think about people like you and me.

He had told me his truth with just two simple words:

…and me.

My mind had a thousand questions, but I knew that the time for questions had passed. I was, in a rare moment, without words, without sounds…without any thought other than utter shock.

"Are you okay?" he whispered.

I nodded.

"Let's go to sleep," he suggested. He closed his eyes and left his strong arm resting over me.

"Wait," I said.

"What? Is everything okay?" he asked.

"Yeah," I said, turning around in my space and positioning myself in the valley of his long body. When I was done, we were as spoons in a drawer, my back pressed against his torso, his thighs against my thighs.

"That's better," I said.

He slid his left arm between me and the mattress and wrapped his other arm around my body until his hands met and interlaced at my chest. His chin rested lightly on the top of my head.

"Now…that's better," he said.

Every now and then, I felt his hands rubbing my arms throughout the night, but on the whole, how we fell asleep was how we stayed all night. When we woke up, we spoke nothing of it, as though it was the natural thing to do, and to sleep any other way would be uncivilized.

November 5

The air was brisk, so I decided to wear my black pea coat for old time's sake. It reminded me of being on line once again. It kept me plenty warm, though. I found myself sitting at the bus stop in front of campus waiting for the infrequent Saturday bus to roll around. I was going home for the day to visit with my mother. I hadn't seen her in months, and I thought I owed her a nice visit. I also planned to tell her all about my father. I hoped it wouldn't be a dramatic meeting but who could tell with my mother and me.

It was fairly early that Saturday morning, so I didn't expect to see anyone I knew before I left campus. That all changed when I noticed Taina, dressed in a pink coat and beret, sashaying down the street with a huge grin on her face. She waved from about fifty feet away.

Although I was thinking "Damn, why her? Why now?" I simply waved back and smiled. I was used to enduring her irritating conversations. To her credit, she wasn't a bad person. It was just awkward being nice to the girl Isaiah was dating when I knew how we felt about each other.

"Hey, boo! How are you doing? You sure are up early!" she said, giving me a hug when she approached me.

"Yeah, I'm on my way to my mom's house," I explained.

"Aww, isn't that sweet!" she exclaimed.

"That's quite the…ensemble…you've got there," I pointed out.

"I know, right?" she said, doing a spin for me. "I got the jacket from Urban Outfitters, but I got these cute shoes from this outlet back Rochester. You know, I just love me some pink, so I had to set it off with the hat, too."

"Of course," I said. I was so not interested, but I knew that for as long as we talked, the conversation would somehow be about her, so I might as well get used to it.

"So you're gonna go home for a bit?" she asked.

"Yeah, gotta hang out with my mom for a while," I repeated. "I haven't done that in a long time."

"Yeah, I guess being local you kinda lose track of the time, huh?"

"Exactly," I said. "So what are you doing out so early?"

"Well, I've got to go down to this art gallery downtown for class, so I figured I'd get it out of the way first so I can go shopping. There's supposed to be a Macy's down where I'm going."

"Cool. That should be fun, but why are you going alone?"

"Well, my girls didn't want to come out this early. And I don't mind going by myself, anyway."

"I see." I looked up the street for a bus I knew wasn't due for another few minutes, praying that it would materialize.

"Adrian, let's sit down on this bench," she suggested. "I've got something to say to you."

"Okay," I said. What I really wanted to say was "oh no" or "oh shit." The good news was that as bad as I wanted Isaiah, we had barely touched each other all semester, not even a kiss. If she called me out on it, I could just deny everything. Yeah, that's what I would do. Admit to nothing and insist that she was crazy.

"Isaiah told me everything," she said calmly, pulling her jacket down and fixing her hat.

"What!" I exclaimed.

"It's okay!" she said reassuringly. "I just wanted you to know that I think you are very brave for coming out. I know it's none of my business, but when he told me you were gay, I couldn't believe it! But then I kinda realized that hey, you haven't changed as a person. You're the same Adrian everybody knows and loves! You just happen to prefer dudes. And that's fine!"

"So, he told you that I'm gay? That's it?" I asked.

"Yeah," she said. "What else would he tell me?"

"Oh!" I said, relieved. "I mean, I just didn't know what it might have been. But yeah, I'm gay. There's no secret about that."

She smiled. "And like I said, I think that's awesome. I am sure there are plenty of men at Potomac who are looking at you as an example. Maybe even a role model."

"Thank you," I said. "Maybe so."

"And you know," she rattled on, "I think that you coming out is what's needed nowadays. Seems like so many men are out here playing both teams and not telling their women they go both ways. Bringing all types of diseases back into their relationships. Just lying and cheating, all of them! What do they call that, the Down Low? Well it's awful low down if you ask me. But then again, you're not one of those types of men anyway."

I faked a smile.

"Sure," I said. "I know where you're coming from."

"Yeah," she said with a sigh.

"Everything okay with you?" I asked.

"Yeah," she sighed again. "It's just rough living the single life again, but I guess it's good that me and Isaiah are able to be such good friends."

"Wait a minute…what?" I asked. Surely I had misheard her.

"Isaiah didn't tell you that we broke up?" she asked.

"No, not at all," I said, trying to mask my excitement. "We haven't spoken in a while."

"Oh," she said. "Well, it hasn't been that long. Maybe about two weeks."

"Two weeks? But I saw you two together on Halloween. Well, the day before, when they showed *The Exorcist* in Grayson Hall."

"Well we're friends, silly! Friends can go to the movies!"

"Oh, okay," I asked. "I just wouldn't have guessed."

"Yeah," she said. "I mean, it really all began over the summer. We sorta started drifting apart. And finally, we just decided to let it go…date other people."

"Just like that?" I asked.

"Just like that," she affirmed. "But Adrian, I gotta tell you I am so glad he found a friend like you. I worry about him sometimes. He never seemed to bond with his teammates, and if he's not hanging out with me, then he's just content to be by himself. And I don't know, I don't think that's very healthy. But like I said, he has a friend like you to broaden his horizons!"

"Aw, thanks. He's a good man. I'm sorry you two didn't work out." Lies.

"Don't worry about it," she said. "Hey, is that your bus coming?"

The big red, white, and blue vehicle pulled in quietly to the bus stop.

"It sure is," I said. "Are you getting on this one?"

"Nah, I think I'm going to walk down to Foggy Bottom and catch the train from there. Give me a hug, boo!"

I gave her a quick embrace and then went to the waiting bus.

"Have fun at home!" she called out.

"Thanks!" I replied as I stepped up to the driver and placed my dollar and change into the steel box.

As I walked to the back of the bus, I saw Taina crossing the street and walking away from the campus and into the city. I couldn't believe it was official and Isaiah hadn't told me! What could he be waiting for?

Two bus rides and a train ride later, I was at home – my mother's house. My key still worked in the front door, so that was at least one good sign.

I pushed open the door and looked around the foyer. Mom had left all my mail piled neatly on a table near the door. Pictures of me as a child still adorned the walls in nice frames. Everything was as I had left it, for the most part.

"Adrian?" she called. I looked through the foyer and saw my mother in the kitchen. She was cooking, as she usually did on Saturdays.

"Hi mom," I said.

"Well come on in," she said, wiping her hands on a towel. "You can put your coat in the closet." My mom was a stickler for such things while I was prone to just leave my coat on the back of a chair or on the couch.

I walked back into the kitchen and hugged my mom. She didn't seem to expect it, but she hugged me back. Her hair had gotten longer since the made the decision to go natural and keep her hair in twists. We didn't look much alike. Her skin was a deep, dark brown, while mine was a shade or two lighter, similar to my father's. Me and my dad shared sharp features, while hers were round, from her nose to her cheeks. She was taking good care of herself, and I thought she was still a pretty woman. The only difference between my mom now and my mom back in the day was a few more pounds in her hips.

"I was just making some chicken salad," she said. "You want some?"

"Sure," I said. I hadn't had any of her chicken salad in years. I sat down and took in the kitchen. It was still immaculate, although it had the seasoned feel of a country kitchen.

"So how's school?" she asked as she chopped up the apples that would go into the chicken salad.

"Good," I said. "I got an A in my class from the summer and all my classes this semester are going really well too. Well, except for statistics, but I'm still passing."

"That's good," she said. "I'm glad the fraternity isn't distracting you too much."

"Nah, not at all, really. It's something to do, but it doesn't keep me up late at night. Anymore, at least."

"You know your cousin Belle is getting married next summer," she said after a few minutes had passed.

"Belle is getting married? Wow. She's not that much older than me."

"I know," she said. "Pretty soon she'll be making your Aunt Pat a grandmother."

"That's crazy," I said. The little television on the kitchen table was begging to be turned on, but I resisted. I hadn't watched TV in ages. There just wasn't any time for it in college.

"I found Dad," I blurted out.

"Yes, I know," she said.

"You know? How do you know?"

"Adrian, I am your mother. I know everything. Now here, take this sandwich."

Bewildered, I got up and took the chicken salad sandwich my mother had placed on the kitchen counter.

"There are some chips in the pantry if you want some," she

added. I looked in the old wooden cabinet and found some plain Utz potato chips.

After I got settled in my chair again, I asked her my burning question.

"How did you know?"

"You think I'm not going to know when your father blows back into your life?" she retorted.

"Mom, I'm just asking a question, gosh."

She sat down to the table with her own sandwich.

"He called me. Not too long after he saw you. Maybe a month later. He told me all about it."

"Oh," I said, ashamed that I hadn't had the nerve to tell her earlier.

We ate the remainder of our lunch in relative silence. Once I finished the last bite of my sandwich, I decided that if I didn't say anything then, I would never say it.

"Mom…I apologize for the way I talk sometimes. I don't mean to lash out at you. I definitely was wrong when I accused you of driving dad out of my life. I didn't know what to think, so it just made sense to blame you. I'm sorry."

"Apology accepted," she said. "I'm glad that Adam is in your life again."

My mother seemed a bit more cold and clinical than usual, even for her.

"So that's it?" I asked.

"Adrian, what goes on between you and your father is just that – between you and your father. He and I are divorced. Yes, we talk to each other now because he has chosen to step to the plate and participate in your life. But I really don't want any part of that."

"I see…"

"Son, it's not personal…yes, I do have some bad feelings toward your father. You know now why he left, right?"

"Yeah. He cheated on you."

"Exactly. And I never once told you why he left, why we divorced, because it wouldn't be right. Adam had every opportunity to tell you himself those twelve years he was nowhere to be found. Who am I to badmouth a man to his own son? That's why I was silent. Yes, you deserved to know, but how could I tell you such a thing and not make it a personal attack."

"I understand. I see why you did that. But mom, don't you see where that also caused a lot of tension between us? You pushed me so hard after dad left. So hard. I had all types of unanswered questions. But you only responded with silence…and pushing me even harder."

"I did the best I could, Adrian!"

"Mom," I said calmly. "I know. I think you were a great mother to me. I am not here to accuse you of anything. I am just trying to explain the arguments that we have now that we never had before. When I got to college, I started learning a lot about myself. And the past few months…the past year, really, I've learned more than I ever thought I would. After dad found me, I realized that my issues with him weren't the only ones I had in my life. He helped me understand that just knowing him isn't going to set things right. I knew that I would have to eventually apologize for blaming you all those years. And again, I am sorry. I won't talk to you about him if it will upset you."

"Well," my mother said uncomfortably. "I'm glad you've been doing some thinking and learning these past few years. And…I won't apologize for pushing you so hard. But…I do apologize if you ever felt you couldn't talk to me. I've definitely noticed your detachment, but I chalked it up to you growing up…you know, doing your 'man thing' that I might not ever understand. But I always trusted you to make the right choices in your life, because that's just how I raised you."

"Thanks mom. I think I've been making okay choices. I hope so, at least."

"You're a good kid," she said. "I know you're doing the right thing with your life."

I smiled slightly.

"Did you decide on a major yet?" she asked after a few moments.

"Anthropology," I said eagerly.

"Oh," she said. "That's... interesting."

"Yeah, I really love my classes, too. And my mentor is Professor O'Bannon, she's kinda young but really smart."

"Anthropology," she repeated. "So…what kind of…job…are you going to get?"

"Oh, I don't know," I said. "I think I want to do non-profit work in the inner-city after I graduate. The frat works with kids sometimes and I think I like that so far. And my course of study is leaning toward urban ethnography."

"Ethnography?" my mom asked.

"Yeah…the study of cultures. I don't know if I'm destined to be a scholar or anything. All I know is that I really like what I'm learning. By the end of this year, I'll select my research topic for my senior thesis. Then all next year, I'll be immersed in whatever it is I'm going to study. I'm really excited about it."

"I see," she said. "Well, I hope it turns out to be lucrative for you in the long run."

"Yeah, we'll see," I said.

For my mother, it all boiled down to the bottom line. She cared about me being happy, but she was more concerned about me getting paid. Her dream was that her only child would never want for anything. I knew she was disappointed with my major, but I hoped if she saw how enthusiastic I was about it, she'd at least think I had made the right choice for myself.

"How are all your friends doing?" she asked.

"Well, you remember Nina, right? Well, she's doing really well. She finally decided to major in Marketing. I made a few new friends, too. Of course the frat. Isaiah, the guy I lived with this summer – he plays basketball for the school. And a few others."

"Well that's nice," she said. "Listen, let's go to the grocery store and pick you up a few things."

"Wow, mom, we don't have to-"

"Oh hush now, I insist. You have to eat! And I am sure those burly boys you live with can barely keep anything in that fridge."

"Yeah, you're right," I said. "We have a nice little kitchen, but we never have time to cook."

"Well then," my mom said. "It will be nice to have a well-stocked pantry for a change."

So, almost as quickly as I had come into my mother's house, I had left, grabbing only the few pieces of mail that had accumulated since my last visit. We drove off to the grocery store in my neighborhood and got plenty of cans of soup, boxes of spaghetti, cereal – anything you could think of that four young college men would need.

The back of mom's Corolla was filled with bags. She decided to drive me back to campus so I wouldn't have to get on the train with all those groceries.

"You know, you're lucky to go to college so close to home," my mom said as we neared Potomac.

"Yeah, I know," I said.

"But I'm glad you're able to live on campus," she added quickly. "Every young man should have that experience. And besides, Potomac is beautiful."

"I agree, mom. But it's nice, you know…to be able to come back home when I want to."

I glanced at my mom as she drove. A smile seemed to creep onto the side of her face.

Finally, we were back at PU. It was early afternoon and the campus was definitely more abuzz than it was when I left. Students were walking back and forth across the busy road connecting Potomac to the outside world.

"Is this close to your apartment?" my mother asked.

"Not really, but I can manage the bags, I think."

"Okay. Well, Adrian…Thanksgiving is in a few weeks. Do you want to come to your Aunt Pat's house for dinner?"

"Yeah," I said. "I actually thought I would come home for that weekend anyway."

"Oh, okay," my mom said, trying to hide her smile.

"Thanks for everything mom." I gave my mom a quick hug and then opened the car door. I started unloading the bags onto the sidewalk. Somehow noticing a familiar presence close to me, I looked up and saw Isaiah hovering above me.

"Hey," he said.

"That's my mom," I told him without a prompt.

He smiled widely and then stepped to my mother's car, waving wildly at her. She rolled down the passenger side window.

"Hi, Ms. Collins!" Isaiah said.

"Hi!" my mom answered. "Are you one of Adrian's roommates?"

"I was his roommate from the summer. My name is Isaiah."

"Oh, okay! Well, take care of my boy, Isaiah."

"Will do, Ms. Collins. Have a good day."

"Thank you!"

I shut the back door and waved goodbye to my mom as she drove on down the street.

"Well, aren't you a people person today," I said snidely to Isaiah while gathering my bags.

"What's that supposed to mean?" he asked, gathering the remaining four bags for me.

"I'm just messing with you," I said. Although there were plenty of people walking about campus, I was lucky that Isaiah was around to help bring my bags home. We began the trek to Hurley.

"I saw Taina this morning," I said.

"Word?" Isaiah asked, not particularly looking in my direction.

"Mmm-hmm," I continued. "Says you're 'just friends' now."

"Yep," he said.

"So…why didn't you tell me?" I asked.

"Cuz…I'm not finished," he answered.

"Finished?" I asked. "Finished what, breaking up with her?"

"Come on, man…don't tell me I have to remind you what this pact was really all about. It was never just about me breaking up with Taina. It was about me…it was about her. It was about you. It was about the life."

"Yeah," I said. "You're right. I just thought after that happened, maybe things would fall into place."

He smiled.

"Things are falling into place. You'll see."

I was puzzled.

"Is there something else you're not telling me?" I asked.

"Patience is a virtue that you taught me," he said. "Remember what I told you. I'm not him. I plan on being here. I gave you time. I need some too. But in the end, you know where my heart is, right?"

We were now standing in front of my apartment.

"Yeah, I guess," I answered.

"You guess?" he replied incredulously. "So now I see I need to remind you." He looked to his left and to his right, surveying the complex. He then looked at me in my eyes and leaned in close.

He kissed me.

It was neither a long kiss nor an extraordinarily passionate kiss. It was, however, a kiss nonetheless, in broad daylight, on campus, between a star athlete and a fraternity man, in all of its two-second glory. I was in shock.

"Take that one for the road," he said. "And don't you ever forget where my heart is."

July 31

From my perspective, the summer league basketball games were really only good for some eye candy. There were no cheerleaders, no band, and a sparse crowd. At least the games themselves were free and the concession stand was open.

I watched Isaiah's team play one of the other teams in a close match. Isaiah's boys were mostly Potomac players, along with a handful from Howard. Other players in the league were from suburban colleges. It was an interesting little tourney. It gave the players a lot of practice, created some variety and diversity among the teams, and gave some Junior College prospects the opportunity to show their stuff to several college coaches.

He was a power forward, always alert and in motion. I didn't really follow basketball outside of my school's team, but I could tell that Isaiah had talent. His eyes practically glowed when he played. It was a look I would come to recognize in him only when he was on an emotional high.

He was driven. He was not only a good player, he was a team player. Never hogging the ball, he was perfect on offense and defense. I could see now that his dream to play ball professionally could very well become a reality.

His team easily won the game. I noticed that Isaiah wasn't big on rejoicing his victories; he merely high-fived his teammates, who sort of just dispersed after the final buzzer. There couldn't have been more than fifty people in the whole gymnasium. I sat on the second row, away from any of the other spectators. Isaiah had his game face on until he noticed me in the stands. It was then that his grit turned into a smile.

"You came," he said.

"Of course," I replied with a smirk. I stepped down to the sidelines where Isaiah stood. "You're pretty damn good."

"Thanks," he said, standing about five inches away from me. I had to look upward just to stare back at him. Beads of sweat rolled down his face onto his collar bone.

"What are you trying to get into tonight?" I asked.

"Whatever you want to get into," he said.

"I get the feeling you might want to make it another Blockbuster night," I said. He smiled and looked at the floor.

"I'm down for whatever," he said.

"I knew you'd say that," I said. "I'll see you back at the room." He winked at me and walked away.

What the hell were we doing?

The past two weeks had been…different. The night of Isaiah's birthday marked a new beginning for us. I had seen him at his most vulnerable, and just when I thought I couldn't get any closer, we had shared his bed. I saw him in a new light now that he had let me know the deal in his subtle way. What we shared was something genuine and pure. We had few inhibitions. Sleeping with him – and only sleeping – was becoming common place.

It was about nine in the evening when I got back to the dorm room, with a DVD I thought Isaiah might enjoy, some snacks, and two cans of ginger ale. It should be a low-key evening. The room was a little stuffy, so I turned the thermostat down a tad. I popped the disc in, turned the lights down, and waited.

About ten minutes later, Isaiah came in. We said nothing to each other. It was a game we had begun to play a few days earlier: how long could we ignore each other without the other saying something.

After about thirty seconds, Isaiah walked up to me and spoke.

"I lose," he said, taking me into his embrace. I hugged him back. There was something about Isaiah that made me like him.

"Your place or mine?" I asked, referring to our beds.

"I like yours," he said. "In the corner. Makes it more cozy or something."

"Sounds good," I said.

"So what are we watching?" he asked as he took off his sneakers.

"Push play and find out," I said, taking a seat on my bed. Isaiah moved the television at an angle so that it faced my bed, and then he pushed the button on the DVD player. He sat down on the far side of the bed and let his toes tickle the small of my back. The movie opened to a shot of the city of New York, with a piano playing a tune familiar to both me and Isaiah.

"Uh-uhn," Isaiah said. I turned to him and simply nodded. The opening titles quickly established that we were about to watch one of me and Isaiah's favorite films from our childhood: *The Muppets Take Manhattan.*

"Dude…you are something else," he said. "I can't believe you remembered I love this movie."

I smiled and got up to extinguish the only light in the room. When I sat down again, it was in the space that Isaiah had pat on the mattress, the space in between his legs. I happily slinked my way to that spot and rest my head against Isaiah's chest once I got there. He immediately encircled my body with his arms and legs.

We were at peace. The most that happened at the outset was an occasional arm rub from Isaiah. I never initiated our touching. I felt like by leaving him in control, I could just continue to live out my dreams of being in his arms without having to deal with the 'hows' and 'whys.'

We laughed nearly the whole movie. Being in college was so serious most of the time. College was girlfriends and boyfriends and homework and pledging. Watching the Muppets poked fun at our own humanity. I mean, it was a frog and a pig getting married on Broadway for God's sake. How could anyone not find that ridiculously absurd?

After about an hour and a half, the movie was over and I got up to turn the TV off. There was still light shining into the room from the lights on the main quad. It was a good substitute for moonlight.

In that brief instant, Isaiah also stood up and followed me to the middle of the room. As soon as I turned around, he was standing there.

"Damn," I said, somewhat startled. He smiled and rested his hands on my shoulders. Stepping backward ever so slightly, he guided me back to my bed until he had no room to move. He sat down and allowed his hands to trail down my arms on his way down.

"You wanna get in bed?" he asked.

I nodded instantly. I knew the routine by now. We would share a bed and probably fall asleep holding each other, like we had almost every night since his birthday.

Isaiah climbed under the sheets first, his white cotton shirt becoming one with my white sheets. His navy blue Potomac basketball shorts were a sharp contrast to the crispness of his shirt and the paleness of his thighs. I followed, still wearing my khaki shorts and silkscreen printed frat shirt.

We settled in, as we always had, with Isaiah spooning me. His arms neatly folded around my body as though they belonged there. I pressed myself against him and felt, as usual, the hardness between his thighs. I caressed his arms as they caressed me and slowly, making microscopic movements, rubbed myself against his entire body.

I heard him exhale and the warmth of his breath traveled across my ear. I wasn't sure how much longer I could go on sleeping with him like this without one of us taking the next step.

As though he heard my thoughts, Isaiah's hands began to wander, for the first time, beyond my arms. Ever so slowly, his hand traveled down my side and over my thigh. His hands were huge, but gentle.

He searched for the button and zipper on my khakis. I guided him to the location, and in one swift motion, my shorts were wide open. He retreated from them, however, and began caressing my arms again. He held me tightly to his body. I felt the weight change on the bed – he was moving to focus on another area of my body, but what would it be?

The answer surprised me. He buried his face deep into my neck and began to kiss me deeply. I moaned with pleasure and surprise. The touch of his lips was gentle, but powerful. I knew that this was something he had been waiting on for a long time and so was I. His lips parted and I felt his warm tongue on my flesh. He flicked it further up my neck until he reached my ear. He softly bit my earlobe and traced each curve with the tip of his tongue.

I was in heaven. Isaiah was as talented as he was attractive.

He retracted his tongue and began giving me closed mouth kisses to my cheek. I finally laid flat on my back and let him lay on me. His weight was a lot to handle all at once, but I could take it.

With his body hovering over mine, we looked at each other in the face. Eye met eye, cheek met cheek, and lips were millimeters away from meeting for the first time. With every breath, I tried to lean forward so we could have that first kiss.

But he kept retreating with each centimeter I moved forward. When I was sitting almost all the way up trying to pursue his lips, he began to giggle.

"Stop playin.'"

"Aight," he said. "Is this what you want?"

He pushed me softly back down to the bed and kissed me once on the lips. His hands rested on my shoulders, keeping me down.

"Yeah," I said.

"How about this?" He kissed me again, this time longer.

I nodded.

"Mmm-hmm," he said. "What about this?" He kissed me once again on the lips, this time using his lips to force mine apart. His tongue slid into my mouth, and we kissed deeply. He let go of my shoulders and my arms slid up around his waist. I drew him into me so I could feel him, taste him, smell him, all at once, to feel like we were one body once again.

His tongue filled my mouth the more we kissed. My hands roamed the span of his back as he kissed me. He was so broad, so strong. My hands finally settled on his ass, encouraging his hips to grind into me as we kissed. I caressed the smooth mesh shorts as though they were his own skin.

Isaiah's hands searched my whole body for the first time. His ten fingers found the bottom edge of my t-shirt and slid it over my head, exposing my torso to him. His kiss progressed from my lips to my Adam's apple and down my collarbone to my pecs. My nipples were already rock hard by then, so he couldn't resist tasting them for himself, to see if they were as sweet as they looked.

I was in ecstasy already. His tongue was out of this world. There was no way I could believe this was the first time he had been with a man. But at that point, I really could have cared less if I was his first or his last, as long as when I pinched myself, I wasn't dreaming.

His tongue continued its path down my abdomen and rested at my navel. While he kissed it, his hands slid my shorts and my boxers off in one tug. He backed up a bit just to get my clothes off of my feet, but he got right back to work worshiping my flat stomach.

I was now completely naked, much to my amazement. Not so surprising was my rock hard erection. To Isaiah, this was a serious matter. His kiss continued as he raised my knees and kissed my inner thighs. With each peck, he got closer and closer to my balls.

He stopped, sat up, and peeled his t-shirt off his back. His chest seemed more massive than it ever had before. It made a perfect V down to his waist, where his shorts were slung low. I raised my body to try to touch him, but he stopped me and slowly pushed me back down. This was Isaiah's show, and he was going to have it his way.

He continued licking the inside of my thighs until his tongue began to caress each of my balls. I was on fire. I hadn't had this much action in months and Isaiah was a pro. Without making me suffer too much, he finally took his hands and placed my penis in his mouth. It wasn't warm – it was hot. He slowly licked my penis like he was kissing my mouth again – passionate, powerful, intense. I caressed his head and ears as he feasted on my manhood. Isaiah enjoyed what he was doing, as though he had waited a lifetime to do it and might only have the one chance.

He reached up and played with my nipple as he sucked my organ. It was nearly more than I could handle. I pried his face away from my crotch and pulled him on top of me, kissing him deeply and tasting myself on his lips. My fingers found his ass underneath his shorts and felt the bands of his jock strap. I reached under the waistband and pulled it down to his knees, along with his shorts. Our penises now rested on one another as we kissed each other on our mouths, our faces, our necks.

He wiggled out of his garments and proceeded to grind on me. My legs were splayed wide open to accept his weight and his manhood. To feel his entire body grinding mine in steady rhythm was beyond comprehension. Every single nerve ending between us was charged with electricity from head to toe.

Strong arms gripped me like a vice when our rock hard penises rested in a perfect groove in between us. He thrust into me hard. The friction between us was the most amazing thing I had ever felt. I was lost in the sensation. He thrust into me again and began to grunt, his voice barely emitting a human sound. With each grind, Isaiah brought me closer to the edge. His supreme session of oral sex left me ripe for the plucking.

He thrust into me continuously, grabbing around my torso for leverage as he grinded into my body. I grabbed handfuls of his ass with both of my hands to drive him deeper onto me. There was no penetration, but enough physical stimulation to make us climax.

I came closer and closer to climax the more Isaiah grinded.

"Ah, ah…Isaiah, I'm gonna come," I warned.

"So am I, nigga," he said. "Let that shit go."

With a few more thrusts, Isaiah and I exploded. The orgasm rocked my body in waves with each spurt of semen that left my body. Seconds after my orgasm, Isaiah followed. His hot juices escaped his body and dripped onto my thigh.

We huffed and puffed in unison until we were spent. He collapsed on top of me and we held each other, still intertwined like a brown pretzel on my bed. Breathing slowly, but deeply, we fell asleep just like that.

Ten minutes passed and Isaiah woke up. He kissed me on my neck and peeled himself off of me, slightly waking me up in the process. I heard his footsteps as he walked on the bare tile of our bathroom. The water was turned on. I tried not to move at all.

After a few minutes, Isaiah emerged from the bathroom, naked, with a hot washcloth in his hand and a towel over his arm. He knelt on the floor and gently wiped my pelvis clean. Its warm dampness woke my appendage. I took the towel from his arm and dried off. Once I was done, he took the towel from me and kissed me on the lips. I relaxed and allowed his tongue to enter my mouth. With a smack, Isaiah backed away and put the used towels in the bathroom.

"How you feelin'?" he asked as he climbed back into bed.

"Great," I said. "You?"

"Awesome." He put his arms around me and kissed my neck. I sighed.

"What are we doing here?" I asked playfully.

"You really wanna know?" he asked me.

"Yeah…" I said. "I wanna know what's on your mind."

Isaiah pulled away from me and sat in the middle of the bed. He pulled me toward him until I sat in his lap, straddling him. I rested back on my hands as I looked in his face. He grabbed me by my backside and held me steady.

"I've had my eye on you since I first met you," he declared.

"What?" I said.

"Yup. I remember the first day I saw you. It was the night of the first day of classes and it was about seven o'clock. I went to the cafeteria with the fellas from the basketball team. We already knew each other from the summer and stuff. Anyway…I went into that cafeteria and you know how you get food from that little side area? Well, I loaded my tray up and when I came back out, the first thing I saw was you."

"Me? Where was I?"

"You were sitting at the window eating by yourself.   I was like damn, that nigga is fine."

I laughed out loud.

"I'm serious," he said, leaning in and kissing me quickly on the lips. "I saw your face and was like 'damn, that nigga need to be in movies.' Your hair was a little longer than it is now. Your skin was real smooth-looking. And your eyes. Man…they're so dark, I could just get lost in them. Everything about you was sexy to me. My heart was racing all fast…I didn't know what to do. I had half a mind to go introduce myself or something, but…I was already sittin' with the fellas. And anyway…Nina came out of nowhere all boisterous and shit and sat down with you. So…that's how I first noticed you."

I smiled hard.

"You remember all that?" I asked.

"Yup," he said. "If I thought hard enough, I could probably tell you what was on your plate."

"So that was the first day you saw me," I said. "Well then, I bet you also remember when I first met you."

"Yup. Philosophy class, that very next day."

"But I bet you don't know the nickname I gave you after I met you."

"Nickname?" he asked. "You gave me a nickname?"

"Well, more like a title. 'The Finest Boy on Campus.' I called you that so much, every time I said your name, Nina would say 'Oh, you mean Isaiah – The Finest Boy on Campus?'"

Isaiah smiled and looked away bashfully.

"Why you ain't say nothing?" he asked.

"What?" I asked. "What was I supposed to say? 'Hey big daddy, what you got goin' on tonight?' Please, man. I was definitely not even out then, much less was I gonna approach somebody like you."

"Somebody like me?" he repeated. "What exactly is that?"

"Well…I never would have thought that you liked dudes. You were always with Taina. Always. And…just because I think somebody's attractive doesn't mean they necessarily 'get down' like that. I just liked you from afar."

"Well if you had liked me from a-close, we coulda been together way before now."

We laughed even more.

"You like me, Isaiah?" I asked.

"Hell yeah," he said. "I always liked you."

"But what about Taina?"

"We're taking a break, you know that. I know she is probably dating other people right now. I'm cool with that. I'm hoping she finds somebody else."

"But, what about before…when you were with her? When did you start liking dudes?"

"I always liked dudes. I'm no saint. In fact, I've been with way more dudes than girls. Even after I started dating Taina. Plenty of times. She's only the third girl I been with, you know. I got with her the summer before freshman year, when we were both on that summer program together. You know the one where they pick minority students to come take a class ahead of time. Well, we hooked up then. One thing led to another, and next thing you know we were serious. Adrian, I really did think that having a steady girlfriend would 'cure' me somehow. I didn't want to be this way.

"Taina is sorta pushy, but she's always been a good friend. She listens to me all the time and she is fun to be around. But she's bossy and she's clingy and…well, at the end of the day, she was never who I wanted to be with. I like being her friend, but I never felt like I had an easy out with her. It's not like I could tell her 'Hey, I am leaving you and your entire gender.' I mean…if I had met you before I met her…"

"Wow," I interrupted. "That's…whoa."

"Dude…I'm bi. And really, I don't even feel bi, I feel gay. I can have sex with a woman, but it's not the same as when I'm with a man. I been in the game for a minute now but I never found anybody that could make me stay on this side of the fence until…"

"Until…what?" I asked.

"Until I found out about you," he finished. He kissed me again, on my lips, my cheeks, my forehead, my ear.

"Adrian, I had no idea you even liked dudes until you told me."

"Not even a clue?" I asked.

"I mean…not really. I wanted you to like dudes, but I never thought you really would. Don't you remember that day last year that you got tipsy and couldn't get up from that bean bag chair? I pulled you up, real close to me. I did that to see how you might react. You didn't pull away, but still…I was scared. If I said anything to you, anything could happen. You might tell Nina, or Taina, or the whole damn world. I wasn't ready for all that. But this summer, I learned so much about you and who you really are. I started putting together all the pieces, and it all made sense. I acted so funny when you came out to me because…I just couldn't believe it. Everything I wanted… happened."

I hugged him close to me.

"Yeah. Me too." I whispered.

"You dated Savion, didn't you?" he asked.

"Yeah," I admitted. "For pretty much all of last year."

"You loved him, didn't you?"

"Yeah, I did. Very much."

"Do you miss him?"

"Sometimes."

"I can't say that I'm sorry y'all broke up. If you didn't, I might not have this chance."

I blushed.

"Well, that's in the past now," I said. "This…this is now." I cupped his face with my hands and kissed him on the lips. He let go of me and let me slide away. I kissed every single place on his face as he leaned back onto the bed. His hands searched my back, my ass, and my legs as we got comfortable in our horizontal position. Laying on him made a lot more sense – I could definitely breathe better without his weight on me. As I straddled him, I could feel his manhood become harder, even this soon after our initial romp.

"Isaiah?" I asked.

"Yo," he responded.

"How far have you gone?"

"Sexually?"

"Yeah."

"Pretty far."

"How far?"

"I dunno…I've hit it before. Never had my own ass tapped before, though."

"Why not?"

"Cuz…that look like it hurt."

I smiled. "Well it's not the greatest feeling in the world the first time. I don't do it all that often. But me and Savion did it sometimes."

"Do you like it?"

"It's okay," I said. "I can take or leave it. He never pressured me."

Isaiah turned me on my side and faced me. He leaned in, kissing me for the millionth time.

"I like you," he said. "I really do."

"I like you, too," I said. I wrapped my arms around him and rested my head on the pillow that we shared. I closed my eyes and felt him nibbling on my lips as I drifted off to sleep. All through the night, no matter what position I slept in, Isaiah was there, never letting me get more than an arms length away. It had been a while since I enjoyed such comfort and protection from anyone.

And he liked me.

I was awakened a few hours later by a warm, familiar feeling between my legs. I looked around me, but Isaiah wasn't next to me. I felt hands on my thighs, and suddenly I knew where he was.

"God…damn," I uttered. He was waking me up with a blow job. I felt his mouth move up and down on my shaft while all I could see was his massive body under the sheets, gyrating like a big, white monster attacking me. His mouth released its grasp on me and Isaiah emerged from the sheets with a Chesire grin.

"What'chu trying to do?" he asked. I smirked and got beneath the covers myself. The sun was already rising outside and gave the room just a touch of gray illumination. Although we nearly got entangled in the sheet, I finally had Isaiah where I wanted him: flat on his stomach. Snatching the sheet off the bed and throwing it to the side, I kissed his legs at the calves and inched my way up to the backs of his knees. I caressed his left thigh as I licked his right all the way to the curve in his ass.

He moaned softly. I grabbed each of his cheeks in my hands and massaged them. Isaiah was a large man as it was, but his ass was just perfect. It jutted out from his back like two hills on a country road.

I repeatedly kissed the place where his ass met his thighs, from the outside to the center. I spread his cheeks apart and buried my lips there, parting them, kissing Isaiah's center.

"Ah," he said. He writhed around in complete pleasure. I kissed him slowly, letting his cheeks envelop my face. He gyrated his hips up and down, slowly getting used to the feel of my lips.

Without warning, I plunged my tongue deep into him, past his expanding and contracting muscle.

"Shit!" he shouted, grabbing my wrist and holding it tight. "Oh shit, Adrian, damn!"

He was writhing with intense pleasure as I relentlessly attacked his ass with my tongue. He let go of my wrist and I spread his cheeks wide with my hands, licking him from his balls all the way up his crack. It was one big valley that I intended to explore every inch of. He muttered obscenities when he was able to say anything at all.

I loved the power I had. Reducing Isaiah to a quivering mass of flesh was beyond my wildest dreams. I still couldn't quite understand how I had gotten there.

"Okay, okay," he said, clenching his butt and flipping over. "I can't take anymore. His dick was rock hard and sticking straight up in the air. I straddled him, pressing his manhood down toward him with my crotch, and slowly moving my hips back and forth.

"What do you want me to do?" I asked. He silently reached for my penis and stroked it slowly.

"Oh shit," I said. "You're gonna make me come if you keep on doing that."

"That's what I want," he growled. I grinded my hips into his fist slowly and he grabbed my behind with his other hand to steady me. His hands were like magic. He knew exactly when to squeeze and release his fist – exactly in rhythm with my body. I still used my thighs to provide friction with his dick as I thrust.

We continued like that for a good ten minutes until my piece was slick with pre-come.

"Isaiah, I'm gonna come. Do you want me to come on you?"

"Yeah, baby," he said. "Come all over my chest. Come for me baby. Yeah, that's it."

He jacked my dick for about fifteen more strokes as I grinded into his hand hard. His other hand reached around my ass and tickled my anus with his fingertips. I was through. I climaxed, shooting warm, white semen on his chest, all the way up to his neck in long spurts. I grunted hard with each spurt until it was all out. Isaiah squeezed the last drop out and wiped his hand on his abdomen.

"Damn," he said. "That shit is tight." I kissed him on his lips and slid over next to him. He held me with one arm and fondled himself with his free hand, using some of my own come to lubricate himself. I watched with amazement as his dick glistened with my own juices and his own. I sucked his nipple while watching him bring himself to a climax. As he began to shoot his load, I lightly bit on his chest. His entire body seemed to spasm and jerk as he experienced his climax.

Minutes passed and we laid still. Finally, he sighed.

"Damn boy, I don't know what you're doing to me, but it's good."

I winked at him and stood up from the bed. I took him by the hand and he hesitantly stood up, not wanting to let our juices drip to the floor. I grabbed an old towel and gave him a cursory wipe down until we could make it to the bathroom. Once there, I turned the shower on and let the water run.

"Get in," I commanded.

Isaiah obeyed and stepped behind the shower curtain. While he began to get wet under the cascade, I stood in front of the mirror and began to brush my teeth.

As the steam began to cloud the mirror, I could still see Isaiah's silhouette through the translucent shower curtain. As soon as I was finished, I joined him in the shower stall.

His body was even more amazing when he was standing up. From his calves to his ass to his back and shoulders, he was well defined. I hugged him from behind and kissed him between the shoulder blades. He turned around with his soapy wash cloth and switched positions with me, so that I might feel the warm water. He scrubbed me down from my chest to my balls and hugged me close to him so he could scrub my back and my ass.

Soon, the soap and washcloth both hit the floor, and Isaiah and I were at it again. We had become rock hard once again and were kissing each other passionately in the water. Every moan and every smack of lips was echoed from the tile in the bathroom. His hands groped me everywhere and finally rested under my ass.

Since Isaiah was nearly a foot taller than me, it took some maneuvering to align our genitalia from a standing position, so he lifted me up off the shower floor. I wrapped my legs around his waist and held onto his neck with one arm, my other arm grabbing the showerhead for balance.

His head burrowed into my neck and his mouth sucked and bit my flesh. His hips crashed into mine with a fast rhythm. I moaned louder and louder, completely oblivious to the fact that possibly anyone in the hallway or adjoining room could hear me. Responding to my moans, Isaiah grunted louder, too. His rhythm reached a feverish pace until we both practically screamed.

"Fuck!" he cursed as he ground into me for the final time. I felt his warm semen splash onto my thighs and drip downward to the drain. He slowly let me go so I could stand upright and stop straining the showerhead. As I stood up straight, he kneeled underneath the shower, letting the water beat him in the face. He took my hard dick into his mouth without any aid of his hands, which he placed on my hips. I quickly thrust myself into his waiting mouth. He seemed to demand my thrusts with his body – I couldn't keep up with his mouth, which met the bottom of my shaft before I could even fulfill my thrusts. I moaned louder and thrust frantically until I could take no more.

"I'm gonna come, Isaiah," I said. I tried to push him away, but he refused. "I'm gonna come, man, I'm gonna…ahhh, shit!"

Isaiah had locked himself on my dick and wouldn't move. I climaxed deep into his mouth. With his eyes shut, he took every bit of me, never even allowing it to see the light of day. I was weak in the knees.

Isaiah finally released me from his mouth after I had gone soft. He stood up and kissed me repeatedly on the neck, grabbing the soap and washcloth and finishing his job of scrubbing me. I gladly returned the favor, soaping down every inch of him and allowing the water to rinse him dry.

We stumbled out of that bathroom weak and weary, but at least finally clean and dry. We collapsed onto Isaiah's bed and got under his comforter to stay warm. We stared at my bed -- the scene of the crime.

We looked at each other one last time and gave each other a deep kiss.

"Damn," Adrian said. "If I knew you had it like that…I wouldn't have waited this long."

"Well, I think this is a good way to make up for lost time."

"I'll say. I ain't never lettin' you go boy. Never."

We laughed together and finally fell asleep in each other's arms. When we awoke, we went out to brunch. Once refueled, we came back to our room and started the dance all over again.

November 10

"And finally, Brothers, I would like to give the floor to our new chapter advisor, Brother Michael Spector." Aaron introduced the tall, bald man to our chapter near the end of a regular chapter meeting.

Brother Spector uncrossed his legs and rose to his feet. He wore a gray pinstriped suit, accentuating his already above-average height. He was a slender, brown-skinned man. I couldn't tell how old he was – he could have been anywhere from 30 to 45.

"Greetings, Brothers of Sigma Chapter," he began. "As you have heard from your esteemed President, I am Brother Michael Spector and I have been chosen to become your chapter advisor for the remainder of the fraternal year. I was made in the Buffalo Alumni Chapter in 1989 and moved down to DC a few years later. I've been active with Washington Alumni."

The brothers in the room listened intently while shooting each other glances. He was grad-made. I still wasn't sure whether I should trust anybody over 30, much less someone who came into my fraternity through a grad chapter.

"I know that you lost your previous advisor rather abruptly and had to carry on your programs with little guidance so far this year, but I wanted to let you know that both me and Washington Alumni are here to support you in whatever your needs are," Brother Spector concluded.

"Thank you, Brother," Aaron said.

"And," Spector added, "I will be ensuring that Sigma Chapter adheres to our national rules and regulations regarding hazing and risk management. We would like to see Sigma Chapter exist in perpetuity on the Potomac and Rock Creek campuses."

Aaron shot Spector a dirty look for a split second, but quickly resumed his composure.

"Thank you," Aaron said flatly. There was an uneasy quiet about us as we assembled to sing our hymn. We had been working alone all year, speaking freely in our meetings and conducting our programs with no help from an advisor. Now there was a stranger in our midst who was assigned to us arbitrarily, probably to spy on us.

We were all sure to grip Spector after the meeting ended, but few stayed to make small talk. We had already made plans to scatter and reassemble at Ciprian's suite to take care of some off-the-record fraternal matters. I was among the first to leave, along with Ciprian.

"So what's been up, LB?" I asked as we left the academic building on Rock Creek's campus that we used for our meetings.

"Same old, same old," he replied. "Just trying to make sure these niggas don't spend everything in the chapter treasury. We're working with a little less than we expected since…well, since Jamal didn't come back and he never paid dues. But whatever. What about you? Stats class still kickin' your ass?"

"A little bit," I replied. "But it's all good."

We walked a snaky path down a hill toward Ciprian's suite. Like Calen and I, he had decided to share living quarters with his line brothers Peter and Mohammed, who we could hear talking well behind us in the distance. The buildings at Rock Creek were taller than at Potomac. They had mostly high-rises, while ours were a mixture of residence halls, garden-style apartments, and even a few townhouses.

We made our way into the building and within minutes, I was sitting on Ciprian's couch. It seemed like the whole living room was burgundy and gold – I guessed that's what happened when three neophytes lived in the same place. A Beta flag hung on the far wall of the living room. On the floor were three burgundy and gold cinder blocks, spray painted with line numbers. They were the burdens that we had to carry during the last week before our initiation. Stuffed lions lined an entire shelf on my line brothers' bookcase. Although the lion was an unofficial mascot of the fraternity, Sigma chapter didn't have any sort of particular attachment to them. Nevertheless, the women in our lives loved giving them to us as gifts, so we kept them. The one Nina had given me when I crossed was sitting on my desk next to the teddy bear Isaiah had given me.

"Adrian, I gotta ask you something," Ciprian said as he undid his necktie and slipped his shoes off.

"Yeah?" I asked.

"You know me, man. I'm never gonna hold back, especially not to frat. So…last month…did you and my spesh have an altercation?"

"Ciprian, I know you and Jamal are cool, that's why I never said anything. In fact, I haven't told anybody. But yeah, me and him had an altercation."

"I see," he said. "Why didn't you tell anyone?"

"Why should I? Jamal hates my guts. He always has. If I told the chapter, it would be a big deal. When he walked away I was hoping that would be the end of it."

"Well, you sure taught him a lesson, whatever happened."

"What do you mean?"

"I saw him that night. Face all puffy, lip busted, black eye. And his nose is broken. You fucked him up bad, but I don't think he'll be harassing you anymore."

"Oh, but I didn't-"

"Oh, but you did. For whatever reason, he just can't stand to see you in the chapter. I think you've handled it like a pro so far, but if he really came all the way down to Potomac just to fuck with you, he deserved having his ass beat."

"Wait. Ciprian, did he tell you what happened himself?"

"Naw, but I kinda put the pieces together myself. He was just kinda cussin' and mumbling under his breath. Talkin' about 'Fuck Beta.' That's how I knew I wouldn't really see him anymore. It sucks because he's my personal, but…if this is what keeps him from being a good Beta, I can't do much about it."

I couldn't believe Jamal hadn't said how things really went down that night. At least he was divorcing himself from Beta, which meant I would probably never see him except in passing.

"I still got your back, frat," he added. "You know I'm never gonna understand how you can turn down all the pussy in the world for some ragamuffin like Savion, but hey, if that's what floats your boat, so be it."

"You know I ain't with him anymore," I laughed.

"Well, whoever or whatever. It's not for me to understand. But, we brothers regardless."

"Thanks." I nodded and smirked. The suite doors flung open and soon the living room was crowded with the entire active chapter. The boys brought in chairs from the kitchen and we made a circle.

I sat in the middle of the couch. To my left was Ciprian, to my right was my apartment mate, Calen. Tommy, our chapter pledgemaster, took the big chair to the right of Calen. He was never what we might have considered slender (like me) or built (like Calen). He was just an average college senior, unable to shake those freshman fifteen. Tommy wasn't one of my favorite Brothers to pledge to, but he was a nice guy once you got to know him.

In the three kitchen chairs assembled on the living room carpet were Aaron, Mohammed, Peter, and Ed. We were a diverse bunch, indeed. There was no way you could stereotype a Beta.

"Aight, black people," Aaron said. "Fuck what you heard in the meeting, I am not feeling this advisor."

"Fuck naw," Tommy said. "At least with Brother Washington, we had somebody who was made in an undergrad chapter. He knew what the deal was. He knew we be making boys how they needed to be made, not how Nationals says."

"Word," Peter added. "I can't imagine being a Beta without all that extra shit we had to do."

"Well, you ain't never have to do it," Tommy said. "If you really wanted to just be paper, we couldn't have stopped you."

"Paper?" Mohammed echoed.

"Yeah," Ciprian said. "Paper is when you just pay your dues and go to the workshops. Then you get initiated. It's like you can either pledge for real or just go by the book and be a Beta on paper only."

"Not in your heart," I added.

"But…" Mohammed began, "We didn't have the choice."

"Of course not!" Aaron said. "We ain't letting no paper into Sigma Chapter, boy! You want Beta, you got to come in the same way everybody else did. No way over it, no way around it."

"Oh," Mohammed said. I knew something was churning in his mind as he processed everything. People gave him a lot less credit than he deserved. He wasn't a native English speaker, but that didn't mean he wasn't smart as a whip. He wanted Beta as badly as the rest of us, but he never did quite understand why we had to be abused to get it.

"That means we have got to be extra, extra careful," Tommy said. "We got this new nigga who has made it quite clear he's waiting for us to slip up."

"Looks that way," Peter said. "I am definitely trying to make sure these boys get everything we got."

"You can't *wait* to haze these boys up," Ciprian said.

We all laughed.

"No, seriously y'all," Tommy said. "We cannot afford to have Sigma snatched. If we get suspended this year…well, next year there will only be Ciprian, Calen, Adrian, and Mohammed. And y'all will be seniors. Imagine being a four person chapter trying to pledge two years worth of aspirants. And that's if we only got suspended for a year. We could get kicked off the yard for more than that. They are cracking down on the process hard."

"Yup," Aaron said. "So listen. Do not contact these boys. Let them contact you. Don't be making all sorts of extra, obvious contact in public. Don't let them drive you nowhere, don't be sending them on errands and quests. Let everything go through Tommy. He knows what he's doing."

"But like, what about Orlando?" Calen asked. "We live with him. How we gonna not talk to him."

"Well of course you can talk to Orlando," Tommy said. "I am talking about people we don't know yet. The closer we get to rush, more people are gonna be coming out of the woodwork expressing their interest. Just be discreet, just like you were when you were trying to get in. Let people come to you and you should be fine. Just don't let Spector find out."

"This is a joke," I said. "How is Spector not gonna know? Does he really expect us to take these boys to workshops once a week and then let them cross? I mean, think about all the joint sessions we have with all the other chapters. That's probably the best part of the process. Remember that first night at College Park? It was like fifty Brothers in that room. And I know some of them were grad."

"Believe it," Aaron said. "Some Brothers know and don't care. In fact, most Brothers are like that. But Brothers like Spector…man, you can't trust him. He walked up in our meeting talking about rules and regulations, like he expects us to fuck up. Like he just knows off the top we gonna try to kill a pledge."

"Let's be positive," Ciprian said. "This is not a bad thing. We just need to keep on our toes. We can't get in trouble if we're careful."

"You're right," Tommy said. "Okay, let's get down to business. Who do we want on this line?"

"Well, y'all know Orlando is interested," Calen said. "He's a good guy. He's been to the events and I've known him for two and a half years now through football."

"He's cool, for real," I added. "That guy on the track team at Potomac seems cool, too. He's been to a few events. What's his name… Rick. Yeah, Rick Brown."

Tommy took notes as we spoke.

"Angel Rosario," Ciprian chimed in. "Dominican dude at Rock Creek. Been to everything so far. I like him."

"Sure would be nice to have some Latinos in a Black and Latino frat," Ed said. "I also like that dude Alex at Potomac. Another Dominican…or Puerto Rican, I can't remember. He hasn't been to many events yet because he works a lot."

"I've met him before, though," Aaron said. "Cool dude, real smart. What about Dexter?"

Tommy rolled his eyes. "That nigga. His attitude. He's just too…I dunno. He think he's God's gift to the world."

"Yeah, kinda," Aaron said. "But he's interested. I'd like to see if he shows up to rush. See what he's made of."

By the time our meeting was over, we had a list of about fifteen men who we knew were interested in the fraternity. Since we had compared notes, we knew who to watch out for, who to observe on campus. It would be nice if all fifteen made it, but we knew that was unlikely. Some might decide it wasn't for them and for others, the timing wouldn't be right. There was also a chance that men might show up to rush who we hadn't even considered but wanted to give a chance to.

The good thing about our process was that it was fair. Pledges had time to show themselves to the chapter in good and bad times well before they would be initiated.

"You sure are quiet," I said to Mohammed as the meeting went from business to socializing.

"I've got nothing much to say," he said in his Algerian accent.

"You okay?" I asked.

"Will I ever be?" Mohammed asked.

"That's it," I said. "Come on, we need to talk."

I led Mohammed into one of the bedrooms and sat down on the bed. It had to be Ciprian's room – he was the only person I knew who could make his bed with hospital corners.

"What's wrong, Mo?" I asked. Mohammed sighed and rubbed his hand slowly over his short, curly hair.

"I'm not feeling this," he said.

"Why not?" I asked. He stared at me like I was stupid.

"Need I remind you of the paddling, fights, eggs, water balloons, onions, vinegar, vomiting, and mind games?" he said.

"I mean…I feel you, man. I just didn't know it was still bothering you."

"I can live with the fact that it happened to me," he said. "But how can I sit here and help plan the next round of abuse for the next batch? They lied to us, Adrian. They said we wouldn't be hazed."

"They had to lie, man."

"I know they did. But if I knew then what I know now…"

"Don't say it."

"You know it's true. I wouldn't have done it had I known."

I was crushed on the inside.

"Adrian, don't you understand? You and me are just alike. We were outsiders who came to this organization looking for brotherhood. And we found it alright. Had it beat into us. And now here we are, plotting against the next group of men who want to be part of us so badly."

"We can change things," I said.

"Who, us?" Mo asked. "Adrian, it's easy for you to say. You're the chapter's golden boy now. You fit right in, too. You know as well as I do that this chapter is not trying to hear about change, especially not in the process. And I think you like it that way."

"Damn, Mo," I said. "I thought we were cool?"

"It's not about being cool," he responded. "We're different."

"So what does this mean, you're leaving the chapter, too?" I asked.

"Absolutely not," he said. "I'll be here. But don't expect me to participate in pledging any new guys."

"They're gonna need you," I said.

He shrugged.

"The least we can do is to stick it out and make sure that things are better for the next line."

"But is that what you really want?"

"Of course I do," I said.

"I don't know Adrian. I think you'd sooner die than let anyone 'skate' into Sigma chapter."

"They're going to have to work hard, but no abuse, man. I promise you. We can do better."

"Then it's a promise," he said, stretching his hand out. "I'll stick around. I'll even come to some sessions. But you promise me not to get sucked in."

"Man, that's not even in my character," I said. I couldn't let my boy slip away from the chapter like that. He might never be comfortable with the process, but I could guarantee that someone would be looking to him for strength and wisdom.

"And yeah…we're still cool." Mohammed smiled.

"We just better be," I laughed.

August 6

"Are you getting hungry?" Isaiah asked me.

"A little bit," I replied. We had ventured out to Dupont Circle, a neighborhood in DC that was a smaller version of Greenwich Village. There were boutiques, bars, clubs, bookstores, and plenty of alternative lifestyles on parade. It was hot, but we had decided to get off-campus for a while and make our regular convenience store purchases from the CVS at Dupont Circle. We wandered up Connecticut Avenue, getting a kick out of the erotic boutiques and thumbing through magazines at the book stores.

That night days before…was amazing. Years of mutual attraction – and more – had exploded into an evening, then a week, of unusually intense lovemaking. I hated to admit it to myself, but even with penetration, sex with Savion was nothing like it was with Isaiah. I had never been with someone so muscular and masculine. I loved Savion, most definitely, but Isaiah was both powerful and tireless.

Even our conversations were deep. I was learning so much about him with every passing day. It was sometimes too much to process. He wasn't crowding me, but I was overwhelmed by his attention to me. He had total recall of every conversation we had ever had since meeting our Freshman year. Thoughts remained in his memory that the average person would have forgotten moments after they happened.

It was as if he waited all of his life to be with me. Yet the problem of Taina remained. He told me that he wasn't technically with her, but I was still troubled. How was I to know that I wasn't just a summer fling to him? I was scared to ask these questions. I wanted to just live in the moment and deal with the hard questions later. The summer would be over in a matter of weeks – no need to cause more stress than necessary.

We walked down Connecticut, satisfied that we had seen all the stores we wanted to, in search of dinner.

"Hey, look up there." Isaiah pointed to a sign hanging above a doorway sandwiched between a music store and a gay bookstore. Had we not been meandering about so leisurely, we would have missed the sign entirely: "Miss Ethel: Psychic, Palm and Tarot Readings."

Wearing a Chicago Bulls basketball jersey, matching baseball cap, and jean shorts, Isaiah stopped and folded his arms.

"Let's go up in there," he said. By his stance, I knew it was more of a demand than a suggestion.

"You want to see a psychic?" I asked.

"Yeah, it'll be fun," he said. He pushed the door open and grabbed my hand at the same time, pulling me in behind him. We found ourselves in a narrow stairwell leading to the second floor of the building. I followed close behind him, watching his strong legs support his ass as it bounced up the stairs.

At the top of the stairs was another door. Isaiah turned to me and smiled, ringing the small buzzer. I rested my hand on the small of his back as we waited for service.

The door creaked open, and we were greeted by a young dark-skinned girl with her hair braided tightly in cornrows. She wore purple shorts, a plain white t-shirt, and purple flip-flops. She couldn't have been older than nine or ten.

"Are you here for a reading?" she asked politely.

"Yes," Isaiah asked.

"Palm reading, tarot reading, or the works?" she asked.

"Umm, I don't know," Isaiah asked. "What comes with the works?"

"Aunt Ethel will tell you your past, present, and future, give you spiritual guidance, and you get a free incense holder."

"Wow, a free incense holder." The little girl glared at me and I quickly shut up.

"The works is forty-five dollars. Each," the girl said.

"We'll both take the works," Isaiah said.

"Isaiah!" I exclaimed, pulling him to the side. "Excuse us," I said to the girl. I took Isaiah by the elbow to the corner.

"Boy, you can't drop ninety bucks on a psychic!" I whispered sharply.

"Adrian, you know dropping ninety bucks ain't a problem for me," he said. "Come on, it'll be fun."

"Ninety dollars?" I said to no one in particular, as Isaiah had already made his way inside the door. I followed him, shutting the door behind me. The little girl asked us to have a seat on a couch that was a bit too low to the floor. The waiting area was tiny, nothing decorating it but the couch and a lamp.

"I'll be back in a few minutes," the girl said, disappearing behind a curtain connecting the waiting room to another room.

"I can't believe we're doing this," I said. He leaned in close to my ear.

"Don't you think it's about time you started believing the unbelievable?" He pecked me quickly on the cheek. I smiled at him.

"Aunt Ethel is ready," the girl said, holding back the curtain. We stood up and walked through. This room was large and comfortable. I quickly figured out that this whole area was a converted apartment space. Miss Ethel, or Aunt Ethel, was seated on a large white leather couch are the far side of the room. She looked out of the window, up Connecticut Avenue, as though she wasn't even interested in us. There were two plain chairs across from the couch and a coffee table in between.

"Welcome, gentlemen," she said. She was a dark skinned woman just like her niece. Her hair was hidden, wrapped underneath a white head wrap. She wore a plain white caftan, loose fitting and covering her body from neck to ankles.

"Hi," we said.

"Have a seat," she said, gesturing toward the two chairs. I looked around me and saw that there was little around me other than a few abstract paintings and tables adorned with candles. If she really wanted to, she could pack everything up in a suitcase and move her show anywhere.

"You're in transition," she said to me.

"Who, me?" I asked.

"You. You've been through a lot in the past year."

"Yeah," I said. "I guess so."

"I know so," she said. "Tea?" She motioned to her pitcher of iced tea on a table in the corner.

I looked at Isaiah and then answered for both of us.

"No thanks. So, um…what exactly are you going to tell us today?"

"Nothing you don't already know," she replied.

"And that's that 'the works' gets us…I see," I replied.

"Don't be so dismissive," Ethel purred. "After everything you've been through this past year, you could use some insight."

"You seem to know a lot about me, yet you don't even know my name. What's up with that, Ethel?"

"I don't need to know your name to know your story," she said.

"My story? Why don't you tell me my story, then?"

Ethel sat straight up on the couch and let me have it.

"You have a horrible relationship with your parents. You don't relate to your mother and barely know your father. You recently went on a quest of self-discovery. In the process you found a whole new family, but you lost a friend, someone you loved dearly. You will never get that relationship back, but you think of this person often. You ask yourself 'what if' on a regular basis, whether you would trade your family for true love."

"Oh," I said.

"Is any of this familiar?" she asked. I nodded. She continued.

"Fairly recently, you reconnected with your father, right? But your relationship with your mother is still strained. You need to go to her. You need to make things even in all aspects of your life. You have much unfinished business with both your parents and your brothers. You have pain in your life, but you can take care of it if you are determined to do so."

"What about…love?" I asked. "Will I ever…you know…be in love again?"

"Who's to say you aren't in love now?"

"Oh, I'm not…"

"You think you're not, but you're getting there," she said. I looked at Isaiah, who was stone-faced and attentive. "But there are a lot of other things on your plate that you need to take care of before you start worrying about love."

"Okay," I said, stunned.

"Don't worry. You will reconcile with your parents. Your bond with your brothers is strong. And you will find love."

"Thanks." I said. Ethel never once looked me deeply in the eyes. She wasn't some con artist like I thought she would be. In total control, she turned to Isaiah.

"But you, sir, need to get it together," she challenged.

"What?" he scoffed.

"You heard me. You are living two lives and you know it."

"Oh," Isaiah said. "Is that right?"

"You know it is. See, you have a pain that runs deep inside you. It comes all the way back in your childhood. You lost someone and you never found anybody else to fill that gap. You've lived your entire life trying to be the person you thought he'd want you to be. You're so ashamed of yourself that you live a lie."

"Okay," Isaiah said, slowly letting his eyes shut.

"I know you're in love," she continued. "But do you really think it's fair?"

"But I don't know what to do. I just don't know." he said softly.

"Yes you do," she said. "You know who you want, you know who you love. You know who is just a front. If you decide to keep living the lie, who knows what could happen? Maybe you'll live happily ever after. But I do know this: living the life you know you ought to will be a lot harder than living a lie. Are you brave enough to do that?"

Isaiah sat in silence.

"Follow your friend's lead," she said. "This young man does not have an easy life, but he handles his business. He knows what it's going to take for him to be happy. He lives one life now. He's learning to love himself. Do you love yourself?"

"Yeah, I love myself," Isaiah said.

"Then if you love yourself, and love who you think you love, then you know what to do." Ethel stood up and poured herself a glass of iced tea.

"Sure you don't want some?" she asked.

"No thanks," Isaiah said, clearly spooked.

"Now, I've run my mouth all this time," she said. "Is there anything you boys would like to know?"

Isaiah and I looked at each other.

"I think I've heard enough," Isaiah said as he reached into his pocket and produced a hundred-dollar bill. He threw it across the table and got up to leave. I stood up with him.

"You sure?" she asked.

"Yeah. Thanks." He turned around and proceeded out of the curtains to the waiting area.

"I have one last question," I asked Ethel in low tones. "I mean, you were right on target. But…I've been in love before, and I messed it up. I guess I wasn't ready for it. And my partner wasn't willing to tough it out with me. I just want to know…am I going to be hurt again? Like I was before?"

"Honey," Ethel began. "Love is like cutting a slice of ham. Turn the knife one way and it's like the meat falls right off the bone. Turn it the other way, there's gonna be resistance. You love him, don't you?"

"I don't know, we're just kickin' it," I said cautiously. "I never even thought I had a chance with him before a week ago."

"You know he's got issues. It's up to you. Yes, you have been hurt. But hurt is just resistance. You got this, baby. Cut that ham the right way!"

"Uh... okay. But does he love me?" I asked.

"Ask him," she said. "Besides, he's waiting for you now. Come back anytime, I'm not going anywhere."

"Thank you, Miss Ethel," I said. I hurried out of the room and Isaiah was already outside the door, going down the stairs.

"Yo, wait up!" I said. I hurried down the stairs and caught up with Isaiah outside in the August humidity.

"That was amazing!" I exclaimed. "She was definitely in my head."

"Fuck her," he said.

"Dude, what's the problem? You're the one who wanted to see her in the first place."

"Yeah, and I didn't know she was gonna tell me I was a fucked up individual. Can you believe that? Telling me I live two lives and shit."

"I don't think that's what she meant," I said.

"Fuck it, I don't want to talk about it," he said.

"No problem," I said. We walked in silence toward the park in the center of Dupont Circle. There was a fountain in the middle that was the focal point of the entire neighborhood. City traffic went around the perfect circle busily and the park itself was bustling with activity.

One whole quarter of the circle was filled with men playing chess under the setting sun. Men with men and women with women laid on blankets together, hands interlaced. Goth kids wearing all black in the summer sun. Everything was in motion. I walked up to the fountain and let its roar drown out all the noise of the city.

I turned around to face Isaiah.

"I'm not fucked up," he said, hands buried deep into his pockets.

"I know you're not," I said.

"You bring out a side of me that nobody else can."

He stopped.

"What is it?" I asked, selfishly waiting to hear more. He cupped my face with his hands and planted a long, wet kiss on me, right in the middle of Dupont Circle. His hands slid down my face and down over my chest. He hugged me tightly at and let go of my lips. The next thing I knew, I was being hoisted up into the air by his hug. I instinctually hugged back and allowed him to hold me up briefly.

"When I'm with you," he continued after letting me down, "I can be me. This is me. Kissing you in the middle of Dupont Circle, with all the other freaks…that's me."

"I like you," I said. "I like you a lot."

"Don't believe what she says, Adrian," Isaiah continued. "Don't believe that psychic. She's crazy."

"Come on, let's go get dinner," I said.

We decided to eat a sumptuous dinner at Hotel Rouge, which was very close to the circle. The restaurant was very modern, but elegant. The floors were made of black tile and the walls were painted a deep crimson. We sat in black wooden chairs with high backs. It was unlike any other place I had been before.

The three-course dinner was great. Isaiah and I constantly had great conversations. We weren't always intense. Sometimes, we talked about the random, everyday things that college men loved, whether it was music, tasteless jokes, television, or sports. There was never a dull moment. I had known him for so long as the big, silent man with so little to say. When it was just us, however, he always had something new and thoughtful to discuss. I loved it.

After dessert, he gave me a surprise.

"Guess what?" he asked.

"What?"

"I rented us a room here for the night."

"Are you serious?"

"Yup!"

"But we didn't pack anything…no clothes, no toothbrushes… no underwear…"

"I got you, boy. I already made us an overnight bag and sent it ahead of time. Our room's already ready."

"What? How'd you do that?"

"I have my ways," he said.

Sure enough, when we checked into the room, an overnight bag was already situated on the bed.

The room was luxurious. We had a huge king-sized bed with off-white linen. The headboard was made entirely of a crimson, fabric-covered cushion, from the floor to the ceiling. They called it Hotel Rouge for a reason: the entire room had deep shades of red everywhere, accented with splashes of white, brown, and gold. We had a huge flat screen television, as well. The window overlooked the busy street below as the sun just slipped under the horizon.

Isaiah slipped behind me and gave me a hug. I reached for his strong arms and leaned my head back into his chest.

"Let's talk," I said.

"Alright," he agreed. He let me go and sat down in the huge, throne-like chair next to the window. I sat on the bed next to the overnight bag.

"What are your plans for the fall?" I asked.

"I'm going back to school, of course," he said.

"Naw, that's not what I mean. See, I'm just really curious about your situation with-"

"Don't say her name," he said, rolling his eyes.

"Come on, Isaiah, you know I've got to. I need to know what the deal is with you and Taina."

"I told you…as far as she knows, we're on a break."

"And when you see her again, what's it going to be?"

"I don't know man. I'm just playing it by ear."

"Okay," I said. That wasn't what I needed to hear. I needed Isaiah to say that he loved me, that he needed me, and that he wanted to be with me forever and ever. But all I was hearing was that I was his "between."

"What's wrong?" he asked.

"Nothing," I said.

"Don't bullshit me. I said something that upset you." He rose and came to the bed. He kicked his shoes off and sat cross-legged next to me.

"What is it?" he asked.

"You know I can't compete with her," I said.

"I don't want you to compete with her. I want you to keep being you."

I looked sideways at him.

"I've never been 'the other man' before."

"And I don't want you to be," he said. "I'm not cheating on Taina. You're not breaking us up. It's not like that."

"But…you cheated on her before," I said. "You told me."

"Yeah, you're right," I said. "I have. I've been with dudes while I was with her."

"I don't know, Isaiah. I just feel weird. It's like one minute, I can be with you and not have a care in the world. But the next minute, I have a random memory of you and Taina. My whole time I've known you, you've always been with Taina. It's hard for me to kick it with you without feeling like I'm doing something illicit."

"Adrian, do you like me?"

"Of course I do. I've 'liked' you since I met you. Hell, you've done some things above and beyond my boyfriend ever did."

"Ex-boyfriend," Isaiah corrected.

"Yeah…ex-boyfriend. You know what I meant. Anyway…I like you. Yes, I like you a lot. So that's why I'm scared. I don't want to like you and then see you arm and arm with Taina. That's going to hurt."

"The reason I asked if you liked me if because if you do, have some faith in me. I don't know what I'm doing from one day to the next, much less what's going to go down in the fall. But I like you. I like being with you. I've never felt like this and I want to keep it up for as long as I can. Hell, you never know who I could see *you* with in the fall. How am I supposed to know Savion won't come back? He was your man. No matter what, he has a hold over your heart, and I can see it. Let's just live for the day. Not the past, not the future. If we just enjoy ourselves and do what comes naturally, everything is going to work itself out. Aight?"

He kissed me on my cheek.

"Aight?" he repeated.

"Yeah, I guess so," I said. "I just don't want to be hurt, Isaiah, you know that."

"And I'd never hurt you. If you don't know that, now you do. I, Isaiah Aiken, will never hurt you, Adrian Collins. Period."

"Since you put it that way…"

"Good," he said. We lay down together and watched a little television for a while. I kept the doubts in the back of my mind as Isaiah caressed my hands.

November 20

The weekend before Thanksgiving, I took a day-trip to Philadelphia to visit with my father. I needed the time away from campus. Finals were coming up soon and it seemed like I had less and less time to study. Those solid two hours on the train were just what I needed to focus on the assignments I had to complete by the end of the semester. My dad had purchased the tickets for me and arranged for me to meet him at the Marriott for lunch. He was at some sort of convention for his job.

I hadn't been to Philly since I was a pledge, so everything looked rather different in the daylight hours. The city was reminiscent of Washington, only bigger and older. The train station reminded me of those old-fashioned stations with all the open space under a large dome, and plenty of benches on which to sit. I found a taxi and was soon on my way to the hotel. We drove along the Schuylkill River and I was able to see much of the city. I think I could live there if I had to. It was a good mix of old and new, black and white.

My dad lived not far away in a town in New Jersey. He had taken up residence there soon after he left DC, rebuilding his life and his career as an investment banker. The man was paid well, even though I didn't quite understand what it was he did.

The Marriott was a beautiful gold and ivory palace in downtown Philly. I walked through the lobby, in awe of the crystal chandeliers and white tile floors. I was to meet my dad right in the lobby, so I wandered about until we found each other.

"Dad," I said. Every time I saw him, I was a little more at peace with our situation. At times, I couldn't believe that he was back in my life after so long. But seeing his face, a face that looked so much like mine, reminded me that we were of the same flesh and blood. He was my dad, and he was trying to do right by me.

"Son," he said, embracing me. "You look well."

"Thanks, Dad. It wasn't that long that you saw me last," I said.

"This is true," he said. "But it's still good to see you, every time I see you. Hungry?"

"No doubt," I said. "What have they got to eat in this joint?"

"Let's see…well, there's Allie's American Grille over there."

"Works for me," I said.

We walked about twenty feet away to a nice little restaurant in the hotel lobby. My dad was in full convention attire, with a plastic name tag hanging from his suit jacket.

"You don't have to wear that to eat, Dad."

"Oh," he laughed. "I guess this is kind of embarrassing, huh?"

I smiled softly. We were quickly seated in the restaurant and I took off my jacket. I had put on my Redskins jersey over a gray, hooded sweatshirt. Although not fraternity paraphernalia, my jersey was a gift from Steven, my Dean of Pledges and personal big brother. That burgundy and gold sure looked good to me.

We pondered the menus in silence. I decided that since I was hungry and my dad was paying, I'd go ahead and get a nice steak, some fries, and a large Coke.

"Before you ask," I blurted out, "School is going okay."

"Okay," he said. "You sure? I wasn't even planning on asking right away."

"Yeah," I said with a grin. "It's just that everybody asks me that, and I wanted to get it out of the way."

My father smiled in return. "You are really more similar to me than you know, boy. That's something I might have said at your age. I was always gettin' smart with your grandmother."

"Really?" I asked. I knew my grandmother had died about eight years ago and that my grandfather had passed when my father was a young man. My dad was an only child, so when his mother died, he truly was alone.

"Yeah, but we had a good relationship. She raised me right, I guess."

"How did she feel when you pledged?" I asked.

"Well, your grandmother was an AKA at Alpha Chapter."

"Grandma went to Howard?"

"Yes, she did. Anyway, she always thought I would be a Kappa or an Alpha…she never guessed I would pledge a 'new' fraternity. She was happy if I was happy, though."

"That's tight," I said. "Wow, grandma was an AKA. Was my grandfather Greek?"

"No, but he joined the lodge when he got older."

"Lodge?"

"He was a freemason," my father clarified. "All they did was get together and smoke cigars on the weekends though. At least, that's all I knew about as I was growing up."

"Interesting," I said as our food arrived. I noticed that my dad was wearing a fraternity ring that I hadn't seen him wearing before. It was a plain gold band with the letters inscribed in an oval.

"When'd you get that ring?" I asked.

"Oh, I ordered it on the internet a few weeks ago off the frat website. It's nice, ain't it?"

"Yeah, it's cool."

"You want one? I can order one for you when I get back to the office on Monday."

"Dad, stop, you can't keep giving me money and…merchandise all the time."

"But you're my son," he said with a slight pout.

"It's starting to…I don't know, it's like you're giving me shit to make up for…"

"Not being there for you. I knew you'd think that's what it was, but it's not."

"That's what it feels like. Like you're buying me off or something."

"Son, that's definitely not the case. Well, that's not all of it. Yes, I feel like shit for abandoning you and your mother. I always will. The way I see it, I missed twelve Christmases, twelve birthdays, twelve Easters…so yeah, I do feel like I need to make up for it. Can't I do nice things for you? Can't I make sure my son doesn't have to have a job while he's a college man? A fraternity man? You mother did an excellent job of raising you. I just want to make sure you have all the advantages I didn't when I was in college. And besides all that, son… business is booming. I have a great job, many wise investments, and plenty of disposable income. I am a bachelor in his fifties. Most men my age have a wife and several kids and debt. I've got none of that, except for one great son. So yes, I am going to keep spoiling you. You deserve it."

"Dad, I understand But you're spoiling me too much, man. I never had it this good before."

"And neither have I. So suck it up and take what I give you," he laughed.

"Okay, okay. But you gotta make me a promise," I said.

"Anything," he said.

"Just slow it down, Dad. I don't need money every time you see me. Sometimes I just want to hang out and get to know you. The time we get to have together is more valuable to me than anything else. Aight?"

"I understand, boy."

"Good," I said. "I also have a question…you've given me a lot over the past few months. And maybe this isn't my place…but… mom…"

"Your mother is taken care of," he said. "Don't worry about her. We've been talking and I made sure she got what she was owed."

"Oh. I didn't know."

"Some things are still grown folks' business," he said with a smirk.

"Ha ha," I said. "Sure. Well, that's my momma. You know I want to make sure she's okay."

"Understood. But enough about that," he said. "How is Sigma Chapter?"

I sighed.

"We're good. I had some issues with one of my prophytes, but he went inactive. Now the rest of us are holding it down well. We only have two older brothers in the chapter, but they are strong leaders."

"Your prophyte went inactive as an undergrad? That's crazy!"

"Dad, this dude was a little…off. Kind of violent…kind of abusive. Trust me when I tell you Sigma is better off without him."

"Man…that's sad. You say he was abusive?"

"Yeah. He and I never saw eye-to-eye."

"Things sure are different nowadays," my father said, his days as a charter brother of Delta chapter flashing before his eyes. "Man, I know our founders must hate what Beta has become. They actually made my line."

"Dad, the founders pledged you? Wow, that's crucial!"

"Well, we were Delta chapter! The frat was founded in 1970; we came along in Fall '73. A brother who transferred to U. Mass from Tufts got the ball rolling, but when the line was going, we got pledged by all the founders plus damn near every Beta who ever had been made at that point."

"What were they like?"

"Man, those were some cool cats! They were all in grad school and stuff by the time we came around, though. Let's see…we saw Lamont, Alvaro, and Jonathan the most since they were in grad school in Boston. Steven was in med school, so we didn't see him as much. And William was up at Cornell. He was a mean dude to pledge to, though. We saw him twice during our process and he was pure evil. Never once touched us though. He had really high standards and was just real bitchy when we weren't performing up to par."

"Big Brother Founder…shit, I mean Dr. William Lucas Wade? He was hard to pledge to?"

"Oh yeah, big time. So was his little friend, Ellis."

"Richard Ellis Dawkins?"

"Yeah…I take it you all learned about him."

"Yeah…first Beta to pass away."

"Sad story isn't it?" my father said. "Died of AIDS before we ever really knew what AIDS was."

"What? They told us he died of pneumonia," I said.

"What else did they tell you about him?" my dad asked.

I reached back into my memory to recount what I had learned about him as a pledge.

"He was a good friend to Dr. Wade and probably should have been one of the Founders, but he couldn't join the original group because he was President of the Black Student Union or something. He ended up pledging on the next line, though. He established a lot of undergraduate and graduate chapters, but never sought leadership positions in the fraternity. He wrote most of the frat's songs. Professionally, he was a teacher. And then he died in 1984. That's all I know."

"Interesting," my father said. "Did they tell you how close Ellis and William were?"

"I mean, I assumed they were best friends," I said.

"Yeah, they were," he said. "Well, I'm not one to speak ill of the dead, son. But rumor had it that Ellis was gay and that he died of AIDS. Such a shame, too. He was the hardest working man in Beta."

"Gay?" I asked, amazed.

"Yeah, as far as we knew. You could kind of just tell. But hey, we loved him just the same! He was still our brother."

"I'm just shocked," I said. "You mean, everyone knew but nobody cared?"

"Well this was decades ago, but yeah, as far as I can remember. See Adrian, Beta was always just different from the other frats. All the others had all these old school stereotypes. Beta was a collection of diverse men. We wanted something different. We were different. So how would it look if we didn't embrace our gay brothers as we embraced our straight ones?"

"And this was in the seventies," I said.

"Of course. We were progressive men, even back then."

"That's dope," I said. "It seems like we're not always that welcoming to each other."

"And that's what ticks me off," he said. "I recently got financial with Philadelphia Alumni, as a matter of fact, since it's the closest chapter to me. And shit has changed. The frat is so much bigger now. We don't all know each other. People don't speak like they should. Hell, I was made before everyone in this chapter, but when I walked into the room, only a couple rose to greet me."

"That's messed up," I said.

"Truly. Listen, tell me this," my dad asked. "What was pledging like for you?"

"Hard. But sometimes fun, now that I can look back on it," I said.

"Did you ever take wood?" he asked.

"Hell yeah, like it was going out of style." My father look displeased.

"You let them hit you?"

"Well, I never looked at it like them 'hitting' me. It was just understood that one of the consequences of not knowing your information would be some strokes from the paddle."

"Don't you know we never did that mess back in the day?"

"Never?"

"Never."

"Never ever?"

"Never! How can you inflict physical pain on someone you've selected to be part of your family? Those nights in college were long, hard, and cold. We had racist incidents on a regular basis at those schools. We needed a family to get us through college. Brothers who would be there for you when you needed it – and true community service. Not only was paddling not done to my line, we never even thought it would be appropriate to do to anyone else."

"That thought crossed our minds, dad, but we always thought that the adversity brought us together. Sure, taking wood didn't teach us anything significant, but I can't imagine being able to remember those key facts without the fear of that paddle. And I can't see my line being as tight as it is without that collective fear and pressure."

"I'm not saying the process needs to be a cakewalk. But the things they are doing now are crazy, and it's going to get us sued one of these days. You kids are going to hit the wrong boy and it's going to be all over. Don't you know all the major black fraternities have been hit with lawsuits of some kind? Don't you know the payouts have been in the millions?"

"Millions?"

"Yes! Judges aren't looking too favorably on young black men who like to bring gang mentality to college campuses."

"But dad, what are we supposed to do if we can't touch pledges? How do you think we could be this united as a frat without going through something physical?"

"How do you think the founders were made? How do you think I was made? We were given tasks. We had to write papers about black and Latino communities. In fact, I think we had to write a paper about each cardinal principle every week. There was a point system. If you didn't get the points, you didn't get in. We met once a week for like six weeks. Yes, we got lined up. Yes, there was social probation. Yes, we had to dress alike and live together all the time. Those things brought us together. The community service projects we did brought us together. When it was all over, the biggest lesson we learned was how to respect each other as though we were all blood."

"We respect each other, too," I interjected.

"I don't doubt that," he said. "I really don't. But I'm just disappointed that men today feel it's necessary to be abused to gain acceptance. I would think your mother, and everybody's mothers, would have taught them that."

"Dad, if I ever thought my life was in danger, I'd defend myself."

"Good."

"And anyway, I haven't even brought in a line myself, so who knows what it's going to be like from the other side."

"When are you guys going to have a line?"

"This spring. We have about 15 guys who are interested in some way. I doubt they all make it, but it will be nice to see the chapter grow."

"Just don't get too crazy with them, boy. Try to resist the urge to give them as much abuse as you got, and consider giving them some uplift."

"Don't worry dad, I'm not a hazer."

"Not saying you are. But just be careful. I don't want to have to bail you out of jail with my dues money for this here grad chapter."

"Dad, you got money for dues and bail for the whole region if we need it."

"See, there's that smart Collins mouth again." We laughed some more and the conversation shifted away from Beta and onto more benign topics like sports and the news. It was good to talk to my father like this, even if it was only for an hour or so during his convention.

"You dating anyone, boy?" he asked.

"Not really, dad," I said.

"What about that situation you were telling me about? Some sort of drama about you and two other people?"

"Oh, that," I said. "That's still…awkward. But, it's not really at the forefront. I'm just focused on me right now. School and Beta. That's about it."

"I hear you," my father said.

"How about you," I asked, switching the subject. "Are you dating anyone?"

"Nah, nobody special," he said. "I date, but I can't really find anyone who is just right, you know?"

"You still love mom, I can tell," I said. I don't know where I found the courage to talk with my father so openly, but as long as I was feeling it, I might as well ask the tough questions.

"Yeah, I do," he said wistfully. "But I'll never find a woman quite like her again. I date women, certainly. But at this age, I really don't think I ought to be married again."

"You never know, dad," I said. "You never know."

My father was a fun guy, a real man's man. Somehow, I related to him, even though I was still scared to tell the man that I was gay. We ate heartily.

Soon, however, he had to get back to his convention.

"You sure you don't need anything?" he asked.

"Not this time, dad. Lunch was great, and I really appreciate the train ticket to come up here."

"Any time, son, any time." We embraced in the lobby of the hotel as tourists and other convention goers passed us by on all sides. "What are you going to do for the rest of the day?"

"I don't know yet," I said. "It would be a shame to not see more of Philly before I leave."

"I agree! Enjoy yourself, son. Walk around a bit, see the city. It was good seeing you again."

"Same here dad. Take care."

I walked slowly out of the hotel and into the autumn air. Across the street from me was a Hard Rock Café. I arbitrarily decided to turn left and start walking down the street. The buildings in Philly were taller, more massive than the ones in DC.

After about ten minutes of walking, I found myself in an eclectic neighborhood with rainbow flags flying from every store window. Quite suddenly, it seemed as though every couple on the street was a same-sex pair.

"Well I'll be damned," I said aloud. I had unknowingly wandered into Philadelphia's version of Dupont Circle. I wondered if the neighborhood had a name or if it was just a part of downtown.

The neighborhood reminded me of the day Isaiah had kissed me in public, as though he had not a care in the world, and again just a few weeks ago in front of my apartment. I knew that he and I both had a burning desire to focus on the present, to live our lives the best way we knew how, to grow together without fear, and to think ahead to the future, whatever it might hold. I needed that man back in my life.

August 15

"I'm going to run to the Foot Locker, aight?" Isaiah asked.

"Cool," I said. "I'm going to sit on one of those benches in the circle."

We spent another warm day in Dupont Circle. It was quickly becoming our hang-out spot, since we never ran into anyone we knew and we both felt comfortable with the vibe. One might not expect two young black men to feel at ease in a mostly white and gay environment, but it worked for us. If we could attend Potomac and comprise about five percent of the population, wandering about a sea of gay men would probably be the only time we'd be in the majority.

Isaiah walked away from me and toward his beloved shoe store. I couldn't even begin to count how many pair of basketball shoes he had. Many were promotional gifts from shoe companies to the school, but he always absolutely had to have the latest "kicks" that were available.

I parked myself on a bench underneath a few trees and took the latest Vibe Magazine out of my shopping bag. In addition to some new jeans and t-shirts for the school year, I bought a few magazines like Vibe and The Source to pass the time. As I leafed through the magazine, a breeze blew through the circle and cooled me off.

Slowly, a figure walked past me. I might not have been aware of him if he hadn't sat next to me on the bench. I pretended not to notice him in hopes that he would leave me alone. I couldn't see his face, but I knew that someone who would sit next to me on a bench in Dupont Circle was most likely trying to pick me up.

"Nice lavaliere," he said.

"Thanks," I said, finally looking up. He was a handsome young man, very dark skinned with dark eyes, and a head shaved completely bald. His smirk was reminiscent of someone who might be just a tad too confident in himself. Yet, he was very attractive. Extremely so.

I noticed he was wearing a dime-sized Pharaoh's head on a chain around his own neck. If I had to take a guess, we had more in common than the bench that we shared.

"That's a nice piece you have, as well," I said.

"Thanks," he said. "It was a gift."

"Cool," I said, and got back to my magazine.

"So you're a Beta?" he asked, not skipping a beat.

"Yup," I said. "I just crossed this spring."

"Congratulations," he said. "I crossed Alpha three years ago at Harvard."

"Yeah, you look like an Alpha," I said.

"Thanks. The sex appeal and the intelligence gives me away every time. But then again, if we use those standards, then you could be an Alpha, too."

I looked at the dude with a smirk.

"Yeah, right."

"I'm just joking man, lighten up," he said.

"I know," I said. "You're not irritating me. Yet."

He laughed heartily.

"You're funny," he said. "My name's Eugene. Eugene Brady."

"Adrian Collins," I said, extending my hand.

"You go to school around here?" he asked.

"I'm a Junior at Potomac. You?"

"Grad student at Howard, School of Education."

"Sounds cool," I said, wiping the sweat from my face.

"How do you like Potomac?" he asked.

"I like it. The first year was tough, but I found my niche last year."

"I hear ya," he said. "Potomac's a really good school."

"Thanks. So is Harvard. Howard, too."

"Thanks. I really wanted to come to an HBCU to further my education. They say if you can make it at Howard, you can make it anywhere."

"So I hear. So, um…what brings you to Dupont Circle?"

"Just looking around," he said. "I hear it's an eclectic neighborhood."

"That it is," I said. "Very diverse."

"I'm noticing a lot of…alternative lifestyles."

"Yup, that's Dupont for you. They come in all types here."

"Is that why you hang out here?" he asked, gently sliding a few inches closer to me.

"Yeah," I said. "I'm comfortable here."

"Cool. So…you're in the family, right?"

"The family? Yeah. Yeah, I'm in the family."

"Cool. You're a handsome dude."

"Thanks, you're not too bad yourself. For an Alpha."

"Hey, watch it," he said with a smile.

"You ever go clubbing?" I asked.

"Not too much," he said. "But I like some of those joints down on Capitol Hill."

"I hear you," I said. "Yo…your brothers know about you?"

"Hell naw," he said. "What do they need to know all that for?"

"I dunno…just wondering."

"Do your bruhs know?"

"Yeah," I said.

"All of them?"

"Yeah."

"How did they take it?"

"It was a mixed reaction. Some were cool with it, some didn't care, some hate my guts. *C'est la vie.*"

"Damn, man. You're a better man than I. Why did you want to tell them in the first place?"

"It's a long story, man. Really long."

"I'd love to hear it sometime. Hey, are you doing anything tonight?"

"Well, I'm kind of hanging out with my friend tonight. But I mean hey, we could do coffee or something."

"That sounds great, man. Here, let me give you my number." He produced a pen from his pants pocket along with a piece of paper and started jotting down his number.

"Here. Make sure you use it."

"No doubt," I said, taking the scrap of paper.

"I hope we can hang out real soon," he added, letting his hand linger on mine as I took the scrap.

"Hello?" a deep, bellowing voice said behind me. Eugene and I turned around to see Isaiah towering over us. I stood up quickly, the phone number still in my hand.

"Isaiah!" I said happily. "This is Eugene, he's a grad student at Howard."

"Hey there," Eugene said, extending his hand. Isaiah looked Eugene up and down but kept his hands at his sides.

"'Sup?" he said in response. Eugene looked at his own outstretched hand and finally let it fall to his side.

"Didn't find what you were looking for?" I asked, noticing that Isaiah failed to return with any bags from Foot Locker.

"Nope. Ready to go?" he asked curtly, not even acknowledging Eugene.

"Well, yeah, I guess," I said. "Eugene, I'll get at you."

"Aight man, peace," he said. We shook hands and then hugged lightly. Eugene stole a quick, arrogant smirk at Isaiah and then walked away. I still held Eugene's number in my hand.

"Who the fuck was he?" Isaiah asked.

"Hold up, who the fuck you cussin' at?" I retorted.

"Shit, I turn my back for a second and you got some ink spot looking nigga giving you his number and shit."

"I know you are not talking about anybody's complexion, as white as you are."

"I ain't white, nigga."

"Come on, let's go," I said. We began to walk toward the bus stop, where we would wait for the bus taking us back to Potomac. I stuffed Eugene's number into my pocket.

Isaiah was fuming, but said nothing.

"Damn man," I said once we got to the bus stop. "Why are you so quiet?"

He glared at me and said nothing.

"Oh, so I get the silent treatment now because I made a new friend?"

"Whatever," he replied.

"Yeah, whatever." Soon, the bus had arrived and we began our quick trip back to Potomac. I sat down in the front of the bus and Isaiah walked past me to sit all the way in the back. Every time I turned around on the journey home, he was staring out the rear window, completely ignoring me.

The end of the line was our school. As soon as the bus came to a complete stop, Isaiah bounded off of the back and walked quickly across to the quad. By the time I had stepped off the bus and thanked the driver, Isaiah was already halfway across the quad, completely bypassing our dorm. I did not call out to him to ask where he was going. I simply walked to our building and walked up the stairs.

I entered our room and dropped my bags to the floor by my bed. I surveyed the room and briefly thought about all that had happened there over the whole summer. My friendship with Isaiah truly began in that room and over time blossomed into something else.

When Isaiah was with me, he was a different person than the man I had been acquainted with for two years. He was talkative, open, and he sure smiled a hell of a lot more. The Isaiah that I saw today… he was jealous, sulking, and downright mean. I needed to go to him, for I knew that what was brewing needed to be stopped, right then and there.

I found him in the very place he told me he would be when he wanted to be alone: the esplanade of the student center. I opened the heavy doors to see him surveying the campus, colored with the cool orange of the setting sun. He didn't move even though I knew he heard the creaking of the door. I walked to him and stood beside him, trying to see what he saw.

"You didn't have to disrespect me like that," he said, still staring into space.

"How did I disrespect you?" I asked.

"You got that guy's number," he said, still not looking at me.

"Isaiah, so what? It's just a number. I don't even know that guy. He's some Alpha…we were trading stories. That's it."

"You didn't have to talk to him, though."

"What's really going on, Isaiah? I mean, seriously. Look at me!" I said sternly. He finally faced me now that he knew I meant business.

"I really can't believe what I am hearing. Can you put yourself in my shoes for a minute?" I asked. "First of all, the minor issue is that a dude approached me, made conversation, and gave me his number. So fucking what? I didn't give him mine. But the bigger issue is that you act like I owe you something. I can't believe I cannot even fuckin' have a conversation in public with a dude before you come charging up to us like you're crazy, completely disrespect him, and then hurry me away. You're not my boyfriend and I don't appreciate you treating me like I'm your property."

"I didn't mean it, Adrian, not like how you're taking it. It's just…I kissed you in Dupont Circle, right in front of that fountain. You could see it from that same bench you were sitting in. I just felt like damn…I thought you'd appreciate what that spot means to us."

"Isaiah, I don't get you. You do all these things for me. You're romantic. You remember things that I wouldn't expect you to. You keep acting like you want us to go to another level. But you tell me to just play it cool, to take things one day at a time. How am I supposed to live like that?"

"I…I don't know man. I just know how I feel…" Isaiah tried to touch my arm, but I backed away. He was dejected.

"You just don't get it. This isn't going to be fixed by you just getting romantic with me."

"Don't you still like me, Adrian?" he asked.

"Of course I do! Isaiah, you know how I feel about you! I love every single minute that I spend with you. You have been my friend and so much more. But what you say and what you do don't add up."

"How so?" he asked.

"Taina…" I said.

"Fuck, why do you always have to bring her up?" he asked, walking away from me and further down the esplanade.

"Because you won't deal with her!" I walked quickly behind him, determined that he would hear what I had to say whether he liked it or not.

"Taina is a major part of your life and you haven't once made me any promises about what you're going to do about her when school starts. I know you still love her."

Isaiah paused and turned around.

"Why do you say that?" he asked. "I don't even know her anymore."

"Don't you mean she doesn't know you?"

"Yeah, whatever, you know what I mean. I don't feel the same way about her as I do for you. Believe that."

"I do believe it. But that doesn't mean I can keep on with you like this."

"What do you mean?"

"I mean that I cannot keep on being your 'other woman' while you're with her."

"But I am not with her! How many times do I keep telling you that we're taking a break right now?"

"Nigga, a break ain't the same as being broke up! Every time I sleep with you, I worry about whether you'll be back in her bed in September. You can't erase two years in one summer."

"What do you want from me then? Huh? What the hell is it that you want? I am doing my absolute best to treat you how you deserve to be treated. I give you all of me, Adrian. I take you out to eat, I give you nice things, I show you a good time. I treat you like…I treat you how I would treat anyone I'd want to be with. I've done everything right, haven't I?"

"What if I told you that I was still with Savion?" I said.

"What?!" Isaiah shouted. "You're still with that short Spanish nigga?"

"No, Isaiah, listen. Just imagine how you would feel if I told you that. If he and I were just taking a break for the summer, but in September we'd decide what we were going to do."

Isaiah was silent.

"Doesn't feel too good, does it? I care about you, and I would never put you in limbo like that." I stopped and gazed out into the landscape, waiting for a response from him.

"I…Adrian, I don't know. I just can't…"

"You can't what? You're scared, aren't you? Too damn scared to leave Taina's safety. Too scared to face Potomac University without a chick on your arm."

"Yes!" he shouted at me. "You don't have to be so fuckin' dramatic with it. You know I'm scared. You know Taina is all I know. You know that I'm not as strong as you are. You can live your life how you want, out in the open…I can't do that. Not yet, anyway."

"So basically, you're telling me this summer was just one big fuck party to you. You never had any intentions of leaving Taina, did you?"

"It's not like that at all. I…I feel so much for you, I can't even express it the way I want to."

"But you can't feel the same way for me as you do Taina. Because clearly, Taina is the one you want to be with."

"No, Adrian, that's not true."

"Then goddamn it, why don't you tell me what *is* true?"

"I love you."

In that moment, the world stopped. Isaiah looked into my eyes and kissed me softly on the lips.

"I love you," he repeated. I was too taken aback to respond. Instead, I hugged him tightly.

"We can't do this," I whispered.

"What?" he asked me.

"We can't do this," I repeated. "It's not fair to anyone. Not me, not you, not Taina."

"But I just said I…"

"I know what you said. And I believe that you mean it. But…I can't say that back to you yet."

"Fuck," Isaiah said, pushing me away.

"Don't walk away, please," I said.

"Fuck it, Adrian. I don't even care anymore."

"How can you say you love me then say you don't care?" I asked.

"Stop playing the fucking games, dude! Don't you realize you are the only man I've ever said those words to? The only one! How many ways can I say it before you start believing it?"

"But you are making me compete with Taina, don't you see how unfair that is? I can't compete with a woman. Never. Even if you do love me, I can't provide this safety net for you. Getting with me is a big old risk, no matter how you slice it. I don't think you're ready, and I for damn sure know I'm not ready."

"So you're saying you don't want to be with me at all?"

"I do want to be with you. I really do. I want to be able to move forward with you. But there's a lot of things that need to happen before I can. Listen, I am not as well put together as you think I am. I just got over just about nine months with Savion. And I did love him. And I probably still do. But I fucked up. And now we're apart because I fucked up. I don't plan on chasing after him. All I can do is learn from those lessons before I can move on with someone else. And trust me, I am still learning those lessons. The things I did caused him to walk away, and I don't want to repeat that."

"I am not him. I would never walk away from you."

"You say that, but you don't really know. You say that, and you have yet to promise me anything."

"So it all goes back to Taina, huh?"

"Partly, yes. Yes it does."

"If I break up with Taina, then what?"

"Then…you'll just be broken up with Taina."

"So shit, now I can't get any promises from you?"

"Isaiah…don't break up with Taina because I think you should. You need to search in yourself and decide what is truly going to be the best thing for you. As much as it hurts me, maybe you will end up deciding to stay with her. And maybe you won't. Who's to say? But you need to make this decision for yourself, and stick with it. I refuse to play some love triangle when school starts. I'm not going to be trading you off with her like a damn toy. If I am going to have you, I am not going to share you. Point blank, period. And don't you think that's the right thing to do?"

Isaiah was silent.

"You have to understand me. I have come too far to be involved in some Jerry Springer shit. We got to keep on getting better, not fucking up people's lives because we couldn't control ourselves or honor our loyalties to people we love or loved. You feel me? It's not fair for you to love two people and not pick one. It's not fair that Taina should have a boyfriend that can't be faithful. And it's not fair that I have to share you with a girl I can't compete with. She's a woman. I'm a man. Apples and oranges, baby."

"Adrian…I'm sorry I brought you into all this," Isaiah said. "It's just that…you were always like a dream to me. And once I had you, I thought I couldn't let you go. And I do love you, I really do. But I'm… scared at how deeply I do feel for you. I'm scared of what my life will be like if I do leave Taina. I am scared at how happy I am when I am just chillin' with you in Dupont Circle without giving a fuck about who sees me in public hugged up on you."

"I know, man, I know. It's not an easy life at all."

"So…what do you need from me? Tell me what I need to do for this to work."

I paused and thought for a few moments. In those few moments, the plan became crystal clear.

"I want to make a promise to you," I began, reaching for his hand. "A pact, I guess."

He outstretched his hand to me and I held onto it tightly.

"I want to promise you that from this point on, I will honor your relationship with Taina until you decide what your future with her will be. I will give you all the time you need to work things out however you feel they need to be worked out. And I will understand if you feel like things ultimately won't be able to move forward for us. But, I want you to promise me that you will also honor your relationship with her until you decide it's over, for real."

"So you're saying I can't be with you anymore?"

"Not until we are both ready to do this thing. No half-assing, no more remnants of Taina, no more guilt about Savion. We both have a lot we need to work on – this isn't just about you, it's about me, too."

"You're fine, Adrian," he said.

"No," I quickly retorted. "I'm really not. I have much work

that needs to be done before…before I can really love someone again. And that's only fair, right? I can't tell you I love you until I'm really able to say it, mean it, and live it. You deserve that."

"Are you going to see other people?" he asked.

"I don't know," I replied. "Isaiah, I want to be with you. That much I am sure about."

"I want to be with you, too," he said. "Adrian…I am going to do my best to make this work. I promise…I promise to do what it takes. And I won't try to get with you until we're both ready. It sucks, but…if it's what I gotta do, I'll do it."

I hugged him tightly. We had made some tough choices that night, but they had to be made. There was no way that I could let our relationship spiral out of control to the point where we were a couple without a commitment, or worse yet, Isaiah's male concubine. Yet, I was floored that he told me he loved me, and even more disappointed that I felt the same way, but hadn't the nerve to say so in the moment. Lord knows I loved the boy the moment I saw him, but between the two of us, somebody had to start thinking with our heads, and not our hearts.

We walked slowly back to our dorm room, where we slept in separate beds for the first time in weeks. In another week, the summer would end, and our love affair would truly be put to the test. Everything could have very well faded into the oblivion of summer love, those summer camp moments where everything is intensified because the moments are numbered and the passion ablaze in the summer heat. By the first day of classes, I could be just one of those things, one more person Isaiah had kicked it with in his life.

Or, Isaiah could really break up with Taina once and for all, just to be with me. Yeah, right. Those odds were slim to none. I had taken Isaiah to the edge of what a gay life was like, and he loved it. He felt as free as I did walking the streets of Dupont Circle, kissing me in the daylight hours, and taking me on dates, like a boyfriend might. But his fear was paralyzing, and I could not possibly function with Isaiah using Taina as a front while I become the mere "close friend" who always happened to be around.

That shit was for soap operas and talk shows. I had far more issues to deal with in my life. By summer's end, I had a strained relationship with my father, no relationship with my mother, and an uncertain future with my fraternity brothers. Far more work lied ahead for me in addition to working things out with a man that I loved.

On the day I moved out of the dorm room, Isaiah and I were somber. We knew we would see each other again in a matter of days, but there was no denying that the end of the summer brought an end to our romance. In silence, I packed my belongings, and Isaiah helped. It wasn't until I unpacked in my new apartment that I realized I had packed away his navy blue basketball shorts among my things. So much of my life was now intertwined with his and his with mine.

Hopefully, everything would work out for the best. Even if things didn't work out, I was no stranger to heartache, so I could rebound from anything under the son. That's why I was named "Lazarus" by my big brothers: I was never down for the count. Just when you think I am dead, I am reborn. The "me" that I was destined to become had only just begun to emerge.

December 1

"It's two in the morning, I can't do this anymore, boo-boo," Cat said. Almost all of my favorite people were gathered around my table in the student center, studying with me in earnest. We had a few more days left before the end of the semester, and we were all doing our best to make it count. Nina, Samirah, Cat, and Morris all joined me as we went that final mile.

Morris was struggling to keep his eyes open. Upon Cat's announcement that it was time to go, his eyes shot open and he pretended to take notes on his text. He was out of it, poor thing.

"Y'all leaving me?" I asked, feigning self-pity.

"Yeah, it's getting a little late," Samirah said. "Gotta get some rest."

"Morris, get up," Cat said, shaking Morris' shoulder once he had drifted off again.

"Huh?" he asked.

"Time to go, babe," she said.

"Oh," he replied. "Okay.

"I'm gonna stay here," Nina said.

"No doubt," I smiled. Morris, Cat, and Samirah quietly packed up their book bags. It may have been the lateness of the hour, but it seemed as though everything was happening in slow motion.

This was my crew. Sometimes I needed some objective minds to talk to. Sometimes I just needed a party buddy. And sometimes I just wanted to know that somebody not only sympathized, but understood what I went through. I thanked God that I had gone to that first Potomac Pride meeting and met Morris, Cat, and Samirah.

I hugged each of them tightly before they left, and so did Nina. She would always be my best friend and she knew it. I could never replace her. My friends were her friends, and through Cat and Samirah, she finally found some women that she could identify with. Nina loathed the superficiality of Potomac's women. To her, Cat and Samirah represented both quiet femininity and strong feminism.

I hugged Morris last and tightest.

"Take care," I said.

"You too," he replied. We hadn't said much since that night I called him. I suppose there was nothing much to say. We were friends, nothing more. And in time, all past indiscretions would be forgotten.

"Adrian, I really like them," Nina said once they were gone.

I smiled.

"I like them, too," I said fondly. "Hey, you want to take a break for a little while? We been studying forever."

"Works for me," Nina said while stretching her arms high above her head.

"I'll go get us some sodas," I said.

"Cherry Coke for me, please," she instructed.

I stood up, yawning, and walked away from the lounge in the student center. People nicknamed it the "airport lounge" because it was so big and filled with nothing but chairs, tables, and couches. It also had huge floor-to-ceiling windows that overlooked the campus, virtually the same scene that one could see from the roof of the building.

Of course, the nearest soda machine was empty. All the little orange lights were lit, so I walked down the hall toward the next closest one. As I entered the empty food court, which I had to walk through to reach the far side of the student center, I noticed a small, pale figure shuffling toward me. She looked pitiful, like she may have been a vagabond who found her way into the student center to find a place to sleep for the night. She grabbed herself as though she was shivering. Her long brown hair hung in stringy locks over her face. I was almost scared to walk past her, but when I got within ten feet, I was certain of who she was.

"Taina?" I asked. Her huge brown eyes looked up at me and her bottom lip began to quiver.

"Adrian?" she asked, sounding bewildered.

"What's wrong?" I asked. She took her hand and combed through her hair, fixing it behind her ear.

"Nothing," she said, her voice breaking. "Everything's okay!"

"Taina, are you sure?" I asked.

"Yeah, everything's fine. Except Isaiah never wants to see me again. Why is this happening to me, Adrian? I've done nothing but treat him like a king!"

Taina collapsed into my arms, sobbing and quickly getting my shirt wet with her tears.

"Shit," I said aloud. It must have finally happened.

"What's the matter, Taina?" I asked, slightly pushing her away from me so I could see her face.

"He told me tonight…that we should stop seeing each other."

"Let's sit down," I said while guiding her to a table in the quiet food court. "I thought you two had decided to just be friends."

"We were," she said. "That's all we were. But I know he wanted more, Adrian! How can you be with someone for two years and just give everything up because you want space? I gave him space. And I thought maybe once he saw what his life might be like without me, he'd come to his senses."

"I see…but I guess it didn't work out like that, did it?" I said.

"No," she said. "I feel so stupid. I feel like while I've been with him, this whole semester he's been seeing other people. Like, whoever he's with has seen me with him and been laughing at me. You know?"

"Wait, he told you he was dating somebody else?"

"Yeah," she said.

"Taina, I'm not trying to be insensitive, but please…start from the beginning. What happened tonight?"

"Okay…Adrian, I'm sorry, maybe I shouldn't even be telling you this. You're Isaiah's friend; I shouldn't try to talk about him to you."

"I understand. Hey, it's your decision. I won't tell him anything you tell me," I lied.

"Well…tonight, Isaiah and I went to the movies. And everything was cool. We went to Union Station like we always do. On the train ride back I tried to hold his hand. I've held his hand for two years and it's never been a big deal. But he snatched it away from me. So I asked him what the problem was. And he was like 'I don't need you to hold my hand' all nasty. So I asked him what his problem was, you know? And then he gave me the silent treatment. Then I stopped talking, too, and when we got back to campus, I told him I'd see him later. And he was like 'No.' And I asked him what he meant, and out of absolutely nowhere, he starts saying all of these mean things to me!"

"Like what?" I asked, riveted to her dramatic rendition of the events.

"He's all like 'Taina, I don't want to see you anymore. I don't think we're good for each other, and I tried to be your friend, but I can't.' So of course I'm shocked! So I asked him what happened to just being friends? And he's accusing me of wanting to be more than friends. I was like of course I want to be more than your friend; I was your girlfriend for two years."

"True," I said.

"Adrian, it was horrible. He accused me of being too needy of all things! He said I was needy, selfish, and never gave him any space to breathe. But that's all he ever wanted from me, Adrian! He never branched off to make any friends other than me until he met you. Every weekend it was me and him at the movies, me and him at the mall, me and him studying. And now all of a sudden he's the big, bad man who thinks he can be all independent."

"That's interesting," I said. "How did you respond to all that?"

"It didn't make any sense, Adrian. So I outright asked him if he was seeing someone else."

"What did he say?" I asked, holding my breath.

"He said no. But he met somebody over the summer that he had fallen for. And that he couldn't move on with this girl until he had officially ended things with me."

"Wow," I said. My heart stopped. "He met somebody this summer? Did he say who?"

"No," she replied. "He wouldn't tell me. And he even said 'Don't think about asking Adrian, because he doesn't know about her.'"

"Wow, I can't believe it." I really couldn't. Isaiah must have planned this out for a long time. He was able to break up with Taina, get her out of his life completely, and even divert attention away from me.

It was a sinister plan, but it was working.

"I just want to know who she is," Taina said. "I want to know what she's got that I don't."

"Taina, I don't know who it is. But you've got to know that's not even important. I'm sorry all of this happened to you, I really am."

"It's not your fault, Adrian," she said. "It's Isaiah and whatever little tramp he's fucking."

That one stung.

"Taina, I think maybe…maybe Isaiah wasn't the right one for you in the first place. You've been with him for a long time, but what do you have to show for it? Yes, you had good times. And you were good friends for a long time. But…people grow apart. And sometimes people can be assholes. Even the people you love. But when two people start growing in different directions, you've got to let them go. The way I see it, even through what you've told me yourself, is that Isaiah isn't really what you wanted."

"I mean, I love him, Adrian. Of course he's what I wanted."

"But you just said that he accused you of being all the things that he is…clingy, selfish. I mean think about the past two years…if Isaiah would treat you like this, is he really the ideal man for you?"

"People grow…people change…but they grow together, and change for the better."

"And sometimes they grow apart. Listen, Taina…I know you are upset, angry, sad…but I want you to know that you are a beautiful girl. Isaiah is my friend, and I can't speak for him, but I know that he did enjoy the time you two spent together. If he met someone over the summer and he's only just now got around to telling you how he feels now, then well…maybe it just goes to show that he loved you enough to try to work out his feelings for you. Know what I'm saying? If he was really feeling this other person this summer, he could have just kicked you to the curb off the top. But he stayed with you, even as a friend. I don't know what goes on through that boy's head, but I do have faith that he did what he felt was best for the both of you."

"We could have just…talked about it…tried to get to the bottom of everything," she said.

"I know. But we both know Isaiah's not always a man of many

words. Taina, do yourself a favor. Don't let him bring you down. You are worthy of excellent treatment by someone who can love you for who you are."

"You're right," she said. She looked up into my eyes, her own still filled with water. "Adrian, thank you. I really appreciate it. And I apologize if I've put you into an awkward situation by telling you all this. I just wish…I mean, I knew you were rubbing off on Isaiah in a positive way. I could tell by how he acted whenever he talked about you or got to be around you. I just wish you rubbed off on him a little more. I kinda think you wouldn't have handled things the same way if this was you and your…boyfriend, or something."

"Who knows? You'd be surprised at the drama I've had with men." We stood up and embraced. Although I tried to believe every word I was saying, I felt like the world's biggest con man by helping Taina to "get over" Isaiah. How could I honestly counsel her when I knew that I was the reason her man quit her?

She wrapped her arm around my waist as we walked back toward the lounge.

"Besides," I continued, "Don't you know how many dudes on campus would love the chance to finally date you, now that you're single, for real?"

She smiled.

"I think it will be a long time before I date anybody. I need some time to just think, you know?"

"I understand," I said. "I felt the same way after my last break-up. But you never know what's around the corner."

We rounded the bend to return to my table, where Nina was patiently waiting for me. She gave me a puzzled smile as she saw who was connected to me at the hip.

"Hey girl," Nina said.

"Hi, Nina!" Taina said, quickly fixing her hair a bit and standing up straight.

"How are you?" Nina asked.

"Oh, I'm fine!" Taina replied with a nervous smile. "I was a little down, but Adrian picked me right up!"

"Really," Nina said.

"Yup. Well, I guess I should go," Taina said. "I don't want to interrupt your studying."

"Taina," I began. "I…" I stopped. Nina looked at me with her lips pursed and one eyebrow raised.

"Yes?" Taina asked.

"I…I want you to know…that you're cool with me. Take care of yourself."

"Aww, thanks Adrian!" Taina gave me a huge hug that I didn't deserve.

"Take care," she said, walking away from us. After she was a safe distance away from us, Nina stepped right up and asked the question of the hour.

"What the fuck just happened?" she asked. "And where are the sodas?"

"Dammit, I forgot them," I said. "Nina, they broke up."

"What? Shut the hell up!" she said.

"I am not lying. He told her he didn't want to see her anymore, not even as friends."

"Chile, stop!" Nina said, flailing her arms about dramatically.

"I am just…blown…" I said softly.

"Baby, it is all over! Do you realize that? There is nothing standing in between you two now!"

"Wow…" I said. "I just can't believe he finally did it, you know?"

"Dude…you know what this means?" she asked.

"What?"

"You like…turned him out. That's kind of crucial."

"Naw, you know it's not even like that," I said.

"Okay, okay," she said. "But you have to admit, Adrian… Isaiah left her for you. He must really care for you to turn his back on everything he knows."

"I don't know what to say…"

"You don't have to say anything, boo. It's done. It's done!"

"I…I'm gonna get those sodas now." I quickly walked away, still in a daze from everything that had transpired. After months of longing, waiting, hoping, and praying, the moment I had been waiting for had finally happened. Isaiah had broken up with Taina and he was now single, free as a bird.

Now…now I was scared.

I walked through the empty food court for the second time that night and went back to the spot where Taina had told me everything that happened. It was surreal to me. A girl who I knew so little about had trusted me enough to tell me the details of her breakup.

Yet, I was the reason it happened.

How could I live with that?

I turned another corner to find that the area around the soda machine had been overrun with familiar faces, camped out on benches in the quiet hallway.

"Shit!" I heard someone whisper. As I came out of my daze, I noticed my housemate Orlando sitting with two other gentlemen I knew. Papers were scattered about between them and they hurried to hide them from me as I approached. I noticed the last paper they hid had my letters printed in bold letters: Beta Chi Phi.

"Hello, Orlando," I said. "And…Rick Brown…and Alex Valenzuela."

All three men stood up, said hello, and shook my hand. Instinctually, they lined up next to each other.

"So, if I was the chapter advisor, what would this look like?"

"Oh, we were just studying, Adrian. You know, what with finals coming up," Orlando said. He was as tall as Calen, but seemed to cower before me like a child.

"How many times do we have to tell you boys? Discretion is key!" I was highly annoyed. I had already had an emotionally charged evening and I was tired. Now I had to come across three aspirants of my chapter indiscreetly studying my history in public.

"We didn't realize anyone would be on this side of the student center this late, Adrian," Alex added.

"Yeah…we're sorry," Rick added.

"Sorry?" I repeated. "Gentlemen, I don't vote yes on 'sorry' men. You need to do better. The entire campus doesn't need to know who is trying to get down with Sigma chapter until the first day the pledges are revealed. And if you want to be in that number, I suggest you take your asses to my crib and study in the living room. Understood?"

"Yes, Adrian," Alex said. The gentlemen scampered around like roaches until they had gathered all their book bags. Soon, they had disappeared down the hall.

Damn aspirants. My line was much tighter than those guys.

December 5

The last day of classes wouldn't have come to an appropriate end without the Betas throwing the largest and best party of the semester. We rented the biggest room in the student center and hired one of the best DJs in the city for the event.

When the lights were out, everyone got their freak on with whatever and whoever was close by. It was a night where, under the cover of darkness, undergraduates could get away with nearly anything. It was a night of last-ditch efforts at a hook-up, whether it was someone to spend the night with or another free shot of alcohol. As usual, my partner in crime, Nina, was nearby, thrusting her body into mine in time with the pounding go-go music. A creation of my native District of Columbia, go-go was heavy on percussion and light on the melodies; repetitive call-and-response chants replaced traditional lyrics. Anytime go-go played, I was at home. Nina was damn near the only girl I would let get this close to me.

Though I still had a few sit-down finals, most of my research papers and take-home finals were already handed in and being graded. Of course, I had to have a bit of that Beta-ade in my system to help me celebrate the end of classes. Even though I had been a Brother for about eight months, I still wasn't quite sure exactly what was in Beta-ade. It was a blood red concoction meant to resemble the burgundy in our fraternity colors.

Nina and I danced in the center of the party, sweaty bodies slithering around us like a pit of snakes. Everyone and their grandmother had come out of the woodwork to relieve their stress that night. A strobe light served as the only illumination in the room besides the DJ's small light attached to his table.

She mouthed something to me in the darkness, but I couldn't understand her, so I closed my eyes and nodded my head as the beat continued to take over me.

I felt her grab my face and bring it toward her.

"I said...your nigga is up in here." She held my face and turned it around. Behind me, coming into the darkness from the hallway was

Isaiah, dressed in a crisp white t-shirt, white bandana, gold chain, and black jeans. I didn't catch his eye, so I turned back around.

"He look hot, don't he?" I said to Nina, grabbing her closer to me while dancing.

"Awww shit!" she exclaimed. I couldn't wait to see him again. Even though I knew for days that things were over between him and Taina, I was eager to hear what was on his mind. I had no idea what was going to be next between us, whether it was more time or time for a decision.

I was scared. My heart fluttered as it did when I simply had a crush on him. Those days were far in the past now, and the future was untold. I closed my eyes and let the beat take me again.

A warm hand grazed my shoulder and slid slowly down my arm. I opened my eyes to see Isaiah positioning himself behind my friend, still letting his hand linger on my forearm, coaxing out the goose bumps. I instinctually smiled at the sight of his pale skin in the darkness, illuminated by the strobe light. He smiled back, quickly licking his lips.

I tightened my grasp on Nina's waist and widened my stance so that she was practically sitting on my thigh. Using my arm as leverage, Isaiah danced behind Nina until he grinded into her. Although her face relayed feelings of surprise, she handled dancing with two men quite nicely, at least at the beginning.

I reached past Nina's waist and rested my hands on Isaiah's sides. I felt his hips grind into Nina over and over. I danced harder against Nina in response. He hands gripped both my arms and suddenly we were a sandwich of fully-clothed sex, writhing on the dance floor. It was as though we were making love to each other with Nina as our medium.

His hands slid up my arms and finally rested on my shoulders. His hips gyrated with as much ferocity as the first night I was with him. Beads of sweat broke out on his face and neck, giving him a ghostly glow in the darkness of the party. One of Nina's arms was wrapped around my waist, her other arm grabbed Isaiah's thigh.

We lasted in that position for about ten minutes, the duration of the go-go set. By the time it was over, Nina was drenched with sweat.

"Whew!" she exclaimed. "I'ma have to um…yeah. Let me go ahead and take a breather." She patted me on the shoulder and gave Isaiah a quick peck on the cheek before she disappeared into the crowd.

I stared at Isaiah long and hard, without moving. The rest of the party seemed to pulsate like an amoeba, but he and I just stood there, taking each other in.

"I want to tell you something," he said, leaning in close and letting his lips brush against my ear as he spoke.

"Alright," I said. He made his way to the door and past the admission table, where Calen and some of my other brothers lounged around.

"I'll be back," I told Calen quietly. He looked up at me from his chair, with one eyebrow raised. Although none of the other brothers paid much attention, Calen knew something was up.

"It's cool," I reassured him.

Isaiah was about ten paces ahead of me, checking behind himself every few paces to make sure I was following. I knew exactly where we were going as I had been there many times before: the roof of the student center.

He opened the creaky steel door and we walked up the drafty steps to the top. The second set of heavy doors was opened, and a rush of cold air greeted us. I immediately grabbed my own arms to stay warm. Isaiah seemed unaffected by the chill. He walked steadily to the edge of the esplanade, not stopping until he had assumed his favorite position overlooking the campus. The sky above twinkled with millions of stars; the buildings below, both near and far, seemed to be reflections of the night. I stood next to him taking in the cool night. It was a far different feeling than the last time we spent an evening on this roof.

"It's kinda cold out here," I said as I stood next to Isaiah. With the quiet agility of a cat, Isaiah quickly moved from beside me to behind me and wrapped his strong arms around mine. I leaned forward on the brick barrier and felt Isaiah's legs spread as he leaned on me for support and warmth. His fingers finally interwove with mine as our hands found each other.

"That better?" he asked. His lips tickled the side of my face.

"Yeah," I sighed. "I missed you so much."

"I missed you, too," he said. He softly kissed me on my cheek. The imprint of his lips remained like a hot brand against the chilly air.

"I saw Taina," I said. "She told me you broke up with her."

"Damn she got a big mouth. Yeah. It's over."

"She seemed pretty upset about it. I gave her some advice – told her to try to move on. It was weird."

"I can't believe she did that to you. Of all the friends she could talk to…man, I'm sorry she did that. You're my friend, not hers."

"It's okay," I reassured him. "I mean, it's not like she sought me out. She was upset and I happened to see her. It was awkward, yeah, but not painful. But tell me what really happened."

Isaiah loosened his grip on me and allowed me to face him. His strong arms were extensions of the barrier preventing me from falling up into the starry sky.

"Adrian…we gave each other space this semester…and…I can't tell you enough how much good that did me. Now, I ain't gonna lie. I was mad as shit when you first made me go through it. But after a while, I knew it was the right thing to do. Somehow, I just woke up. I realized that I wasn't the right man for Taina…and I just didn't love her the way she loved me. Not like a boyfriend should love his girl. And you know…I like dudes. That's not fair for her."

"Yeah…" I said.

"I didn't tell her I like dudes though, I guess you know that much. I thought she and I would be cool just as friends, like we decided earlier in the semester. But it was never just that for her. She always needed more from me, and I didn't want to give it to her. The last straw was when we went to the movies this week. She always tried to hold my hand when we were out, and I don't know, for some reason I always hated that. But I let her do it because it made her feel good. Well, this time, I kinda snatched my hand back. I had just had it, you know? Got tired of living the lie that we were ever going to get back together. And I told her that."

"Wow…just like that?"

"Yeah man. I tried to be as nice about it as I could, but she kept on egging me on. Playing the same old games. She wouldn't let me go. So, I had to force her hand. I had to let her know how I really felt… that I didn't want to be with her. At all. Ever. And then…it was over. I walked away. Then as I walked away, she asked me was there someone else. And I said there is, that I met the person over the summer. And I remember making up some bullshit on the spot about how you didn't know anything about it. I didn't want her in our business. Anyway, that was it."

"Are you okay?" I asked.

"Yeah. You didn't exactly tell me to break up with her, but if it weren't for you, I wouldn't know what I wanted to do with myself at all. I felt miserable, and now I don't. It's awesome."

"I'm glad everything is cool with you, Isaiah. That really makes me happy."

"I'm happy you're happy," he smiled back. "And guess what?"

"What?"

"I told my mom."

"Um…excuse me?"

"I told my mom…I told her everything about me."

"What!? You told her…"

"I told her that I'm gay."

"Oh my God," I said. "I need to…sit down."

He laughed and took me by the hand, leading me to the bench underneath the stars. I sat down, and he threw his leg over me to keep me warm, in addition to holding me in his arm.

"Your mom knows?" I repeated.

"Yeah man. I told her a few weeks ago."

"Shit. How did she take it? What did she do?"

"Well, my mom is…different. She's always been really cool, open-minded. But I still didn't know how she would take the news, you know? I was scared to death. I went home one Sunday afternoon, a few weeks ago and I told her that I didn't want to be with Taina anymore. She was surprised, but kinda glad – she always thought Taina was too prissy for me."

"A girly girl," I reiterated. "Yeah, I can see that. Nina would like your mom, I bet."

"Exactly. Well, she was pleased. Then, I told her I had found someone else. I said the person I met was a beautiful person, inside and out; that this person understood me like nobody else could. I told her that what I felt for this person was so deep that it scared me."

My eyes had been caught in his gaze until that moment. I looked downward.

"Look at me," he said. I looked back into his eyes upon his request. "I told her that I was in love with my friend. And his name is Adrian."

"And…and…what did she say?"

"She was shocked." Isaiah leaned down toward my face. "But that's to be expected."

He softly touched his lips to mine. We lingered on that moment forever. Everything I felt for Isaiah over the past few months all came flooding back. It was attraction, it was friendship, it was lust.

It was love.

We released each other from the grip of our lips and I let him continue.

"It was a heavy conversation. There were some tears. But at the end of the day, she told me she'd love me forever because she's my mom."

"That simple, huh?" I said.

"That simple," he repeated. "You taught me that."

"How so?" I asked.

"I know life hasn't always been easy for you, so I'm not trying to minimize your struggle. But…you make it seem so effortless. Baby, I've been in the game a while, but always on the down low, you know? I never thought I could be somebody who loves a man. But I see now that I can, and I do."

"You're right, it's not easy. This whole time you've been working things out in your life, I've been doing the same thing. I feel like shit is great with my dad when earlier this year, I thought maybe I'd never see him again. Me and my mom have an understanding, too. We can actually talk to each other like adults. And my frat…well, shit's never been better, you know? I feel like you let me have time to work things out in my life that were incomplete. You gave me the space I needed to make sure my own house was in order before I even think about making a commitment to you. Isaiah…I just…"

I stopped. I couldn't believe I was about to say it. My eyes misted over and a tear threatened to fall from my eye.

"What baby? Don't stop now, we've come too far to stop."

"Everything's working out the way it's supposed to," I said. "Everything. When I look at you, I see everything I could ask for. You're all man, but you're still sensitive. You know exactly what to say to me, any time of day or night. You've always got my back. And…I know you're not perfect, but I know you're somebody I can grow with. Isaiah…I love you."

Instantly, Isaiah squeezed his eyes shut and inhaled deeply. Once he opened them, I could see the tears glistening.

"That's all I've ever wanted to hear you say."

He scooped me up into his arms and lifted me straight off the ground as he hugged me, spinning me around. When he finally placed me back on the ground, I reached around his neck and kissed him. As my lips touched his, my body warmed from deep within my chest to my extremities. For the first time in ages, our mouths became a sweet arena for two dueling tongues. Isaiah's caress slowly found its way down my back until his hands rested on my buttocks. We kissed forever.

When I heard what sounded like the click of the steel door to the roof, I froze.

"Someone's here," I said.

"So what?" Isaiah asked, continuing his thorough lashing of my mouth with his tongue.

"Wait," I said. I broke free from his grasp and yelled into the dimness of the night.

"Who's there?" I called out. I saw nothing on the esplanade and heard nothing further.

"You're just trippin'," Isaiah said. "It's just us and the stars."

We kissed deeply once more.

"Yo, it's mad cold out here," he said. "Let's go back inside before you catch pneumonia, okay?"

"That sounds good. I gotta help shut down the party in a little while anyway."

"You be lovin' some Beta Chi Phi," Isaiah chuckled while reaching for my hand.

"Not as much as I love some other things," I said with a wink. We walked to the door, hand in hand, and pushed it open. We both looked back onto the esplanade one last time and then into each others eyes.

"I'm glad it turned out this way," he said.

"Me too," I replied.

December 24

My stomach was in knots at the prospect of Isaiah meeting my mother, and me meeting his. Of all times of year, of all holidays, and of all mothers, why now?

"You okay in there?" Isaiah asked me from the outside of my bathroom door. We were quite possibly the last two people left on campus. The basketball players stuck around since they had a home game on December 23. By the afternoon of the 24th, most had gone home. Isaiah and I prepared to go to my mom's house for Christmas Eve and Christmas morning, and then later travel to Baltimore to have Christmas dinner with his mom.

I was not ready. I had put off worrying about it until after my last final, but it seems like right after that moment, my stomach had been upset.

"I'm okay," I called back. I had downed about half a bottle of the pink stuff and I felt like I was finally ready to face the world. I opened the bathroom door to see Isaiah standing there with a look of utmost concern on his face.

"I'm okay, really." I smiled at him and the tenseness in his shoulders melted away. We had been inseparable since the night of the party; making up for a semester's worth of lost time and missed opportunities.

"You sure, baby? You seem like you been sick the past few days," he said.

"I'm still not used to you calling me baby. Seems like you started doing that no sooner than that night."

He smiled. "Naw, you always been my baby. That night just made it official." He pecked me quickly on the cheek.

"Now come on," he said. "The cab is on its way."

The streets of Washington were all but desolate. Isaiah sat close to me in the back seat as our bags rode comfortably in the trunk. I silently hoped he hadn't seen his Christmas gift before I'd packed it safely away. I already had some of his other gifts shipped to my mom's house. Once I calmed down some, this would be a Christmas to remember.

As if he read my thoughts, Isaiah slid his hand into my lap and grabbed onto my fingers. We stole a glance at each other and smiled. He was coming to my house. There was no turning back now.

"We're here," I said once we arrived. Isaiah smiled so wide, so bright, you would have thought I told him that Santa Claus was real after all and he owed him some back presents.

"Are you serious?" he said. "Damn, I can't believe it. I'm here at the place you grew up in."

I laughed and attempted to pay the cabby.

"I got it," Isaiah said. I had learned by now that when Isaiah said "I got it," he meant it. Without argument, I stepped out of the cab and waited for the driver to pop the trunk. Seeing my mom's house in the twilight somehow put me at ease, at least a little bit. It's not as though she didn't know Isaiah was coming to spend Christmas Eve with us. And she had met him once before, even though it was briefly. I guess I was just scared that she'd wonder who exactly Isaiah was to me. It was weird. I was ready to share this part of my life with Isaiah, but I wasn't quite ready to share the hidden part of my life with my mother or father.

Isaiah slung his tattered gym bag over his shoulder and followed me on the short path to the front door. As I approached, it flung open, revealing my mom in all her glory.

"Hi, son!" my mom beamed. It was probably the first time I had seen her smile so sincerely, so deeply, since the day I graduated from high school.

"Hey mom," I said. My mom was a beautiful woman. Her twists were tied into a ponytail, probably to keep them out of her face while she baked. She wore her apron over her old sweatpants and a U. Mass sweatshirt. She was definitely baking.

I reached my arms out toward her and we embraced. She smelled of sugar, butter, and a little bit of perfume.

"Mom, you remember Isaiah," I said, standing aside so my mother could see him well.

"Of course I do!" she said while extended her hand to him.

"It's nice to see you again, Ms. Collins," he said.

"Likewise," she said. "Now come on in out of this cold air. I was just finishing up a few things."

We made our way into the foyer and I saw the living room of our house. My mom had outdone herself: in the corner stood a real Christmas tree!

"Mom!" I exclaimed. "Since when do we do Christmas trees?"

"Well, I figured you were bringing a friend home this year, might as well decorate a little bit. I haven't quite finished with the decorations yet, though. You think you could help with that a little later?" she asked.

"Sure," I said, glancing at Isaiah. "It'll be fun."

Isaiah smiled.

"Hey, let me take your bag upstairs," I said, taking his gym bag from his shoulder.

"Thanks," he said.

"I put that other thing in your room," my mom said.

"Thanks, mom." I knew she was talking about the other part of Isaiah's gift that I had ordered.

"I'll be right back," I told Isaiah. I left him standing in the living room as my mom retreated to the kitchen. By the time I hit the top of the stairs, I could hear my mom calling for Isaiah from the kitchen. She'd probably found something for him to do in the kitchen to kill some time.

My room, with its door wide open, was immaculate. All of my "stuff" had traveled with me to college, so all that was really in my room was my old stereo, desk, posters on the wall, and a double bed. I still had some old awards from high school on the walls, and some pictures of friends I hadn't seen or spoken to in years. Those days were a lifetime behind me now.

After about ten minutes of fooling around with Isaiah's gifts and wrapping paper, I made my way back downstairs. I found my mom with Isaiah in the kitchen. He had his sleeves rolled up…baking?

"What's going on?" I asked. Isaiah and my mom looked up from the counter simultaneously.

"We're making cookies!" Isaiah said.

"Oh," I replied, surprised.

"Yeah, I was about to put some chocolate chip cookies in the oven and figured Isaiah might like to help roll the dough. Those big hands have got to be good for something in addition to basketball, right?" my mom said matter-of-factly.

Isaiah silently held up a ball of cookie dough between his thumb and index finger, smiling the whole time.

"Alright," I laughed. "Anything I can do?"

"No, I think we're good!" my mom asked. "Why don't you go ahead and watch some television in the den? You know we got digital cable now."

"Oh," I said. "Well, okay. I'll do that."

As I walked out of the kitchen, I realized that I had never helped my own mom in the kitchen before. And now that I wanted to, there was nothing for me to do! Go figure that my boyfriend would get in the kitchen before me.

I left the light off in the den and turned on the big screen television. Mom still had the big leather easy chair in the corner facing the screen. I knew my mom rarely used the room unless she was entertaining. Even in the darkness I could see that the room was a shrine to our family, with framed pictures of me at all stages of my growth, as well as pictures of family members near and far.

I was home. If I wasn't comfortable now, I'd never be comfortable. My stomach finally settled, and I fell asleep watching ESPN.

"Oh, here he is."

"Look at that. Leaned over in that chair just like his father used to. Sleeping like a baby."

"He wasn't feeling well earlier today."

"Stomach?"

"How did you know?"

"His stomach used to always get upset when he was younger. Happened when he had a lot on his mind or was stressed out."

"Yeah…that was probably it."

"I miss having him around…so you're very good friends, huh?"

"Yeah."

"Take care of my baby."

"…Ms. Collins?"

"I'm not blind, boy. I know my son. You don't have to say anything. Just take care of him."

"…I…I will."

My eyes fluttered open and I saw Isaiah sitting on the floor in between my legs. He rested his arms over my knees. I was surprised he hadn't woken me up when he sat down.

I yawned. He turned around and smiled at me.

"Hey, baby," he said.

"Hey," I said. "What time is it?"

"Like six thirty," he said. "Your mom said we could eat whenever. Food's on the stove."

"Cool," I said, reaching down to hug him from behind. "Where is she now?"

"Upstairs taking a nap. Hey, I thought it might be nice if we finished decorating the tree for her before she woke up."

"You're really trying to impress her," I said.

"Nah, not impress…but you know, she is the woman who made the man…" He kissed me on the lips, briefly letting his tongue slide in.

"Mmm," I said. "Hey…when I was sleeping, did you and her come in here?"

"Well, we were in the hallway for a minute or so, yeah. Why, did we wake you?"

"Naw," I said. "I just remembered…I thought I heard you two talking, but I didn't know if it was a dream. Did she say…"

"Don't worry about it, Adrian," Isaiah interrupted. "Everything's cool. For real."

"For real?" I repeated.

"Yeah…for real."

We decided to eat a quick dinner first, and then finish decorating the tree. All that was left to do was hang a few more ornaments and the star. Isaiah was the perfect height for that.

"It's perfect," my mom said as she emerged from the hallway. "Isaiah, plug in the lights so we can see how it looks."

Isaiah found the socket and plugged in the lights while my mom turned off the lamps in the living room. Although in essence it was just a tree with cheap garland, tinsel, and glass ornaments, there was something about the way the multicolored lights gave the room a soft glow…it took me back to the days when I was five or six and my whole family was together. It reminded me of the times when everything was right with the world and I had no worries. The lights slowly began their magical dance, flashing on and off, reflecting their light off of the silver tinsel and old ornaments. At the top of the tree was a lighted star. For all I knew it was from the seventies, as old as it looked, but it still blinked a steady pattern of white lights to top off the tree's beauty.

"It's nice, isn't it?" Isaiah asked. I nodded in agreement.

"Thanks guys," my mom said. "Now it feels like Christmas. Well, I'll be back late this evening, don't wait up for me!"

I faced my mom, who I just realized was wearing a nice blouse, slacks, makeup, and her trench coat.

"Where are you going?" I asked.

"I got a date!" she smiled.

"Well I'll be…"

"Oh don't worry, he's just a coworker. I'll be back later. Have fun!"

And like a cold winter breeze, she was gone.

"I can't believe she has a date!" I exclaimed, still frozen in the same spot. Isaiah laughed and moved toward me with his arms outstretched.

"It's all good. Mommy just wants her groove back, that's all," he said. We giggled as we held each other.

"Hey," I said. "I want to give you your present."

"Now?" he asked.

"Yeah, why not?" I said. "It's almost Christmas!"

We raced each other upstairs to my room to get our bags. We were like two little boys who were home alone. Isaiah was the first to reach his sports bag, while I had to get my carefully wrapped present from the closet. He sprinted out of my room and down the stairs.

By the time I met up with him, he had just finished throwing my gifts under the tree.

"You suck," I joked. "Hey, open mine first."

"Okay," he said. The package I had wrapped was large. I knew he would have no clue as to what was on the inside.

"This better not be socks," he said.

"Isn't that what you wanted?" I asked as he tore open the wrapping paper.

"Nigga, stop playin," he said. He finally tore the paper away and saw what I had gotten him.

"Dude…it's a new gym bag!" And was it ever. I had ordered Isaiah an extra large black leather duffle bag and had his initials, I.C.A. for Isaiah Christopher Aiken, embroidered on the side.

"This is beautiful," he said. "Damn, I guess I really needed a new one, huh?"

"Yeah, your old one is on life support, dawg," I said. "But yo, open up the bag."

"Okay," he said. He carefully unzipped the bag and reached inside. The first thing he pulled out was a bottle of cologne.

"Oh snap, baby…Issey Miyake. It's my favorite."

"I know," I said. "Keep going, there's one more present in there."

He reached in again. This time he pulled out an 8 by 10 inch picture frame, with a familiar image inside.

"Oh my god," he said. "Where did you get this picture?"

It was a framed action shot of Isaiah taken at the season opener.

He was on the offensive, palming the ball with his tongue slightly hanging out the side of his mouth. In his face was frozen all of the intensity that I was familiar with in him…his passionate lovemaking, his uncontrolled rage when protecting me, and his tearful anguish when we had to part. All of those emotions were focused in the game. That's what made him win games. The photo had been printed in the campus paper, but I had gotten the original print and framed it.

"I know folks," I said simply.

"Baby, this is great! You are really spoiling me this Christmas."

"You deserve it," I said, pecking him on the lips.

"I put yours under the tree," he smiled. I crawled over to the tree and saw two small packages and one long package, each individually wrapped.

"Which one should I open first?" I asked.

"Try the big one," he said. I picked it up and felt that it was sort of heavy and very hard. I ripped open the packaging and a wave of surprise and joy washed over me. Inside the paper I saw the familiar burgundy and gold colors of my fraternity and smelled freshly varnished wood.

"You made this?" I asked.

"Yup," he said. Isaiah had created from scratch a fraternity paddle. This had to have taken him weeks to do. On the front was a decal of my fraternity shield and three huge Greek letters, cut from another piece of wood and glued on the paddle. Underneath the letters was all of my pertinent fraternal information: Brother Adrian Collins, aka Lazarus, #4 – Sigma Chapter – Uprising. On the back, Isaiah had somehow glued a picture onto the paddle and then coated it with clear varnish. The picture was of me and my dad, from the step show I had performed in earlier that year.

"Wow! This is fuckin' awesome man! Thank you!"

"You're welcome, but keep going!"

I grabbed the other two gifts and tore the paper away from them. The second gift was a brand new MP3 player.

"I know you haven't had no music for a while now…figured I you could use this, you know?"

"It's great, Isaiah! I definitely need this. And now, what could this other package be?"

I carefully opened this one slowly, to build my own suspense. Inside, I found a small, leather journal.

"This is nice," I said.

"Open it," Isaiah requested. I turned open the journal to the inside cover and saw that it had been inscribed with a message from Isaiah.

"To Adrian," I read aloud. "I know you've always got a lot on your mind. This way, you can write it all down. From this point on, I'm going to show you that you made the right choice when you chose me. I loved you yesterday, I love you today, and I'll love you tomorrow. Isaiah Christopher Aiken."

I put the book down in my lap and saw Isaiah turning beet red with embarrassment.

"I just wanted to…let you know how I was feeling," he explained.

"You don't have to explain yourself," I said. "I love you, too. I loved you this summer, I loved you this fall, and I love you now. I'm glad I'm with you."

I reached out for his hand and he grabbed mine.

"Come here," I said. I cleared out all the presents from under the Christmas tree. "I want to show you what I used to do when I was a kid." I laid on my back and scooted myself under the tree.

"Come on," I said. "There's room."

Isaiah stretched himself out and slid next to me.

"What now?" he asked, looking me in the eyes.

"Look up," I said. We both slowly turned our heads up, gazing deep into the tree. It was like gazing into space. All of the lights, ornaments, tinsel, and garland blended into the tree and we became lost in the light fantastic for a few minutes. The tree even seemed to be slowly spinning, like we were inside a kaleidoscope.

"It's beautiful," Isaiah whispered.

"I knew you'd think so," I replied. I slid my hand into his and finally exhaled. As I turned to face Isaiah, I saw his eyes slowly close as he inhaled and exhaled in peace. It was all real.

Tomorrow we would go up to Baltimore to meet his mother and extended family. But tonight, we would just gaze into the Christmas tree from the bottom up. Tonight, we wouldn't even wonder how we made it from casual acquaintances to lovers. Tonight, we would not think of the second-guessing and doubts. There was no yesterday or tomorrow, only tonight.

And tonight…was ours.

Also by Rashid Darden

ISAIAH is head over heels in love with his boyfriend and isn't afraid to let the world know it. His unwavering love threatens his future as a professional basketball player. Though he is being forced to choose between the love of his life and his career, it appears that he could be making a decision which could irrevocably affect his future.

Meanwhile, ADRIAN has unfinished fraternity business. As a Big Brother for the first time, he has an obligation to uphold the chapter's sacred traditions, yet feels a responsibility to end the cycle of violence.

Friendships will dissolve. Rivals will return. Secrets buried in LAZARUS and maintained in COVENANT will finally explode.

EPIPHANY

Available Fall 2011
from Old Gold Soul

www.oldgoldsoul.com

A native of Washington, DC, Rashid Darden strives
to both entertain and inspire social change through his
writings. *Covenant* is his second novel.

Please visit

www.oldgoldsoul.com

to place additional orders.